LOST GIRL

Neverwood Chronicles
Book 1

D1560131

CHANDA HAHN

ISBN-10: 0996104860
ISBN-13: 97800996104869
LOST GIRL
Copyright © 2016 by Chanda Hahn

Cover design by Steve Hahn
Edited by Bethany Kaczmarek
Final editing by Kathryn DiBernardo
Beta Readers: Ben Hale, Kathryn Jacoby, Jenna Moore

This is a work of fiction. Names, characters, places and incidents are either the product of the author's imagination or are used fictitiously, and any resemblance to actual persons, living or dead, business establishments, events or locales is entirely coincidental.

www.chandahahn.com

Also by
CHANDA HAHN

The Neverwood Chronicles

LOST GIRL

LOST BOY (2017)

Underland Chronicles

UNDERLAND

UNDERLORD (2017)

Unfortunate Fairy Tale Series

UNENCHANTED

FAIREST

FABLE

REIGN

FOREVER

The Iron Butterfly Series

THE IRON BUTTERFLY

THE STEELE WOLF

THE SILVER SIREN

For those that follow
the second star on the right.

-1-

I T NEVER HAPPENED. *It was just a dream.*
The young girl ran her chilled fingers over the goose
bumps on her arms and rocked back and forth in the
dark oak chair, chanting the mantra over and over again
in her head.

It never happened.

Trying to make herself believe the hollow words.

It was just a dream.

Or at least to sound convincing enough to fool her
psychiatrist.

I made it all up.

She shuddered again as she heard the ancient heater on
the far wall kick on with a long rattle, followed by a
whoosh of steam. Maybe now the room would warm up
and she could stop shivering.

But it really didn't matter. She would still shake. The
cold did little to hide the nervous trembling that had
plagued her since she mysteriously showed up here a few
months ago.

The days, hours, weeks—they all ran together, creating a void that consumed her memories and numbed her to the world. All she knew was her next treatment, her next appointment, her next test. Sorting real memories from terrifying images and clinging to what remained of her true self—or what she guessed was herself—was becoming a challenge.

It never happened.

She bit the tip of her thumb to cause just enough pain to snap her out of that dark place, away from the horrible images she'd seen.

The shadows.

Don't go there. Concentrate on better things.

What did her doctor always say? That's right. Happy thoughts. She needed to focus on happy thoughts to chase away the darkness.

There weren't any mirrors in the hall, but she caught a glimpse of her reflection from the glass window of the nurses' station across the way. At first it startled her. She didn't recognize the scared young girl sitting curled in the chair, biting her thumb. Dark rings showed under her eyes, and her dull blonde hair fell past her shoulders, begging for a trim. Her freckles seemed stark against her pale skin. Had she always looked so young and scared? Had she lost weight?

Pop! She accidentally bit too hard and cracked the nail on her thumb.

Stop that! You have to get yourself together. Be calm. Be confident. Be normal.

Normal. Such an odd concept. A state she would never

experience as long as she kept ranting about things no one else could see. She glanced down the hall and noticed the armed guard sitting on the other side of the fire door.

The office door swung open, and the psychiatrist's black heels clicked on the tile as she stopped by her chair. When the doctor turned the full force of her dark brown eyes her way, the girl shivered.

A loose black bun rested at the nape of the woman's neck, and her white physician's coat hung open, revealing a somber black pantsuit. The doctor's silver-painted finger beckoned her into the office, and the girl followed, taking a seat in the chair facing the desk. The building smelled sterile, except for this room, where the scent of fresh roses filled the air. It was hard to miss the pale pink buds in the vase on the filing cabinet. A gift from a suitor perhaps, or maybe the doctor's way of bringing something living into a very dead environment?

The the gold-lettered nameplate on the desk read *Dr. S. Mee.*

Dr. Mee walked around slowly, pulling open a manila file folder and splaying it across her desk. She pushed *record* on a small digital tape recorder and set it down. Elbows on the file, the woman clasped her hands in front of her face and looked across at her.

"Subject number 1-04," Dr. Mee started.

The girl shook her head, refusing to acknowledge her assigned number. Her doctor's lips pinched together before she smiled softly. "Okay, but only in here. This is between us, all right?"

The child nodded, confident she could keep a secret.

Dr. Mee's eyes squinted ever so slightly as she read the folder. "So, my darling Wendy. Do you still see shadows fly into your room at night?" She chuckled slightly in a disbelieving tone, "and do they promise to whisk you away from Neverland?"

"No," Wendy lied, and a small tremor began in her hand. She tucked the hand under her thigh. Maybe the doctor wouldn't notice.

"I see," Dr. Mee intoned, dragging the last word out. "That's a bit disappointing." She pursed her lips and made a clicking noise with her tongue. "So you don't see shadows?"

"No," Wendy recited, trying to smother her nervousness.

Her doctor lifted a piece of paper and read something that was written across the bottom. "That's not what the night nurse is saying here. At two a.m. you were screaming and pounding on the doors because there was a shadow in your room. Is this true?" She looked across the table.

Wendy shrugged. "I don't remember saying that."

"You know, Wendy, I only want what's best for you. If you don't tell me the truth, I am unable to help you. What about other side effects...anything at all from the treatments you've been given? Do you feel stronger, can you jump higher...anything at all?"

Wendy shook her head. Silent tears trickled shamefully down her cheek.

"Wendy, the corporation wants results, and so far we've seen very little—especially from you." Dr. Mee said.

"You're special. I've known that since the moment you came to my facility. You were chosen to be a part of something that will one day help a lot of people. Unfortunately, I don't see how hallucinating shadows will help anyone. It's not what they're looking for. I think you're going to do extraordinary things someday." She closed her folder. "It just won't be today."

She took her glasses off to rub her hand over her tired face. "I just wish we had something more to show for our efforts." Dr. Mee looked over at the calendar and sighed. "We're running out of time," she said to no one in particular.

Wendy held her breath. She knew she and the other kids were undergoing special treatments, getting tested for something, but she wasn't sure what. Every few weeks, a group of soldiers would come to the facility and whisk the special kids away. The ones whose results were promising. Her best friend had been taken a few weeks ago, and she'd been so alone without him. She couldn't have imagined how lonely the place would be without his mischievous smile and wild tales.

A rumor circulated among the other kids that they were taken someplace special, given new families. Wendy wasn't sure what she believed.

Here, at least she was given meals and a bed. And what if the kids were right? What if those who showed progress were given to new families, were given a home? Maybe she shouldn't hide anymore, maybe she should tell the truth to Dr. Mee about what else was happening to her. The doctor probably knew more than she was letting

5

on anyway. Then maybe Wendy would be selected like the others, and she could find her friend.

But as soon as the thought crossed her mind, fear loomed up and overwhelmed her with doubt.

Did the government even know this facility existed? She bet not. The only people who ever came in and out of here were the staff and the soldiers who wore the badge bearing a red skull. Was the chance of a better future—a home—worth facing the cruel gossip from the other kids?

Dr. Mee gazed down at her hands. "I like you, Wendy, and I really want to help you, but I don't think you're ready yet for the next step in the program. What you have is a gift. You can see things no one else can. Unfortunately, that's not something they consider useful. They will probably label your results a failure."

Wendy's mouth opened, and Dr. Mee raised her eyebrow and cut her off. "You're not hiding it well enough, and since you're so adamant about lying about your gift, you'll have to continue pretending for a bit longer."

Wendy blinked. She wasn't surprised when Dr. Mee called her out on her lie; she wasn't good at it. But was confused about why she suddenly encouraged it.

"If anyone, kids and staff included, ask about what you can do—lie. Can you do this for me?"

Wendy couldn't contain the trembling, but she nodded slowly.

"Good girl, Wendy. You haven't told anyone else about the shadows?"

"No ma'am."

"Keep it that way. The less they know the better," Dr.

6

Mee said. "I don't think it will hurt them if we delay reporting your results for a little longer. Maybe something will change in the next few days." She studied Wendy with a pensive stare. "But that's all I can give you. A few days—maximum—because *I* know Wendy. And if *I* know…they'll soon know. Understood?"

"Yes, ma'am."

"Good. You can go back to your room."

Wendy pushed out the chair to stand and hesitated. Now that she'd started thinking about leaving this place, she couldn't stop. "Dr. Mee, when do you think I can go home?" Her voice sounded smaller than her ten years.

"Home? Why, Wendy, you are home."

-2-

WENDY PADDED BACK TOWARD her room but paused when she came to the main gathering hall. Pale yellow couches and sterile tables furnished the space. Metal bars secured the windows lining the far wall. On a sunny day, she could look out and see the dark woods surrounding the facility. The front of the room overlooked the cliff and the calm cerulean waters of the ocean.

Boys and girls ages six to twelve lounged about the main room, but Wendy knew there were kids even younger in a hidden away nursery. Every once in a while she'd see a nurse carrying a crying infant.

The room felt different. There were glances, stares, and more agitation than normal. That's when she noticed who was causing the disturbance. Everyone had taken notice of the boy in an armchair in the corner of the room. About thirteen years old, he had auburn hair and the greenest eyes.

Some were upset, but Wendy's heart sang with excitement—he was back.

The boy.

That's what she always called him, since they were forbidden to call each other by their given names. If they were caught using them, they'd end up in the containment room with no food for a day. Within the facility they were nothing more than numbers, statistics on paper instead of actual living beings.

She hated using their subject numbers, so in her mind she gave each of them their own unique nickname. She had thought the boy was gone for good since he was taken away a few weeks ago. She knew it was because he'd showed positive results to the treatments. Why was he back? What had gone wrong? He should have been taken out of this place and—if the rumors were true—given a home.

Wendy went and sat in the yellow armchair across from him and tucked her knees up to her chest, wrapping her arms around them. She held still and studied him. The boy scrutinized her as well, but his eyes seemed a bit wild. Like a scared rabbit. When their eyes met, he turned away and began to mutter to himself.

Oh great, she thought. He didn't remember her. Being with Boy was the only thing that gave Wendy happy thoughts. She didn't shake when he was around. And that made her want to stick by him until he remembered her. He looked over at her and she smiled wanly.

"Hey, Boy," she said. "I'm glad you're back. I was getting lonely."

He rocked back and forth and looked away from her. Was he ashamed? Too embarrassed to talk to her? Determined, she stood and walked over to the bookshelf filled with timeworn books and board games and searched until she found their favorite game.

She brought the game back and set it on a coffee table. Wendy kneeled down, lifted off the battered lid, its corners held together by yellowed tape, and began to pull out the familiar game board and cards. She knew the boy watched her, but he stayed silent. Wendy barely knew the fundamentals of Monopoly and really hated the game. It was too long and involved for her liking. But it was a game they had played before, had spent hours playing, quietly whispering to each other and going around the board and passing go and collecting two hundred dollars.

The boy loved games, any kind of games, and the crazier the rules, the better. Most of the time they just made up their own rules.

They'd made extravagant future plans together, wasting ages playing games and dreaming: If it were real money, they would spend it on frivolous things like gallons of mint chip ice cream or swimming pools filled with macaroni and cheese. They laughed together for hours, and sometimes when they'd get really serious, they'd begin to talk of a future outside of Neverland. She'd open up a bookstore, and he'd become a teacher. But when she looked at the boy in front of her, he wasn't the same person.

Her boy had been the epitome of joy, laughter, and youth. This boy displayed none of those attributes. She just had to bring it back, help him remember.

She nudged the coffee table closer to the boy's chair and set up the board.

Wendy hummed softly and continued stacking the cards. The chatter of the other kids turned to white noise around them. The boy closed his eyes and listened to her sing. He seemed to relax. She liked taking her time.

After a few minutes, he leaned forward and helped her set up the bank. Then it was time to play. All of the main tokens had disappeared over time, and only one piece remained—the thimble. It was impossible to play with only one piece.

Wendy offered the boy the thimble. "Looks like we're down to one token."

"That's never stopped us before, Girl." He smiled at her, his eyes dancing as a dimple appeared on his cheek.

She breathed a sigh of relief at her nickname.

He reached into his pocket, and placed an acorn on the board. "You go first."

"How long has that been in your pocket?" Wendy chastised. She tossed him a stern look.

The boy blushed and answered, "You really don't want to know."

Wendy stifled a giggle, and they began to play, just like old times.

A skinny boy with dark hair, glasses, and a slight limp came quietly and sat next to them, observing. He had a critical eye and frequently told them, "You're playing it wrong."

"No, we're not," Wendy finally answered.

"You're not following the rules of the game." He got out the tattered rules and read them aloud.

"Games are meant to be fun. This one just happens to

have too many rules for my liking." Boy said. He looked up at Wendy and winked, making her heart flutter. She tucked that away for the next time she needed a happy thought.

Whenever one of them had to pay taxes, they'd put it in the middle of the board and—if someone rolled snake eyes—they'd dive in and whoever snagged the most money kept it. It usually amounted to knocking the board over and wrestling for the money.

A few other kids came to watch—most gathered to observe the boy. He was entertaining to watch and he played to the crowd. Taking the acorn, he would make it disappear, only to reappear near a dark-haired boy with a serious expression and somber gray eyes, who Wendy called Gray.

Gray kept himself aloof from the other kids. He always watched and never really joined in any of the conversations. When Boy made the acorn appear out of Gray's ear, Gray swatted his hand away and told him to grow up.

Boy laughed at Gray. "Never.

Gray occasionally rolled his eyes when Boy wasn't looking.

Wendy grinned because her Boy was truly back. He launched into an outrageous story of a beautiful mermaid that lived near an island they all lived on, and Wendy liked it. Neverland didn't seem so scary when he was around. She hoped he never left her alone again.

Wendy lay on the floor next to the coffee table and placed her hands behind her head. She studied the ceiling tiles and listened to Boy talk. His story became grim, with talk of kids being captured by Indians and imprisoned. Before she knew it, her thoughts had wandered back to that dark place she tried so hard to avoid.

Doctor Mee said they were here because of a trait they each possessed—a certain auto immune disease, and they were being treated with injections.

It actually seemed that they wanted the kids to be different. They praised the ones who could do things that weren't part of normal human abilities. Some of the kids reacted negatively to the treatment—the ones who withdrew inside their heads.

Wendy didn't know what they hoped for her. She'd had a negative reaction to the treatment and gotten really sick, and afterwards she began to see shadows in her peripheral vision. No one else could see them, not even Boy.

A rattling noise made her open her eyes to see that she was still lying on the floor. For a moment she had forgotten where she was. The air conditioning vent in the ceiling sputtered and clanged as cold air blasted down on her. She briefly smelled the salty ocean air. Wendy turned her head to the side and a single tear of disappointment slid down her cheek. She didn't want to see things or be considered crazy. She wanted the shadows gone for good.

Boy still sat in the chair. He seemed to be having a disagreement with Gray. A staff nurse came and announced that it was time for dinner. Wendy stood and followed the other kids as they filed down a long hall to the opened doors. The staff blocked every exit except for the one leading to the cafeteria.

When the double doors opened, her mouth watered at the sweet and spicy aroma from the kitchen. She paused and spoke aloud to Boy and Gray.

Neither heard her. Boy had his feet planted, his hands on his hips. Gray scowled and, using only his thumb, cracked the knuckles on his right hand.

"There's cinnamon rolls tonight." She spoke enticingly and tugged on Boy's sleeve.

By now the room was empty except for Boy and Gray, they still hadn't budged. She turned to go back but was cut off by more kids lining up. They would only have an hour after dinner before they would be escorted back to their rooms for the night.

She stood in line behind 1-84, a girl with an attitude who ran with a rough crowd. Wendy took the red plastic tray and waited without making eye contact with the girl. Others had learned to keep their distance. In front of 1-84 stood a brown-haired boy, about seven, with a teddy bear stuffed under his arm. He had come the same time as Wendy had. He never spoke to any of the kids or staff, but frequently sat by himself and whispered into the stuffed bear's ear. That's how he earned his unfortunate nickname—Teddy. He always stared directly at Wendy, but he'd never speak.

Wendy picked up her tray, which consisted of a bowl of thick red chili, a warm cinnamon roll, green beans, and a pint of milk. She took her food and sat at a round table in the corner of the room. Keeping her back to the brick wall, she ate alone. She preferred the corner table because it gave her a sense of security when she didn't have Boy watching her back. No one could sneak up behind her or steal her food.

Gray came in by himself. She tried to keep an eye out for Boy, but little Teddy drew her attention again.

He sat at a nearby table, propped the bear into a sitting position, and picked up his spoon to eat. One of the more aggressive kids came by and knocked over the bear, taunting Teddy. The boy panicked and quickly righted the bear, but when he turned back, his tray lacked his bowl of chili and cinnamon roll.

Teddy looked at his small portion of green beans, and his shoulders shook as he tried to hold back tears. Wendy watched the young boy. Her fingers curled around her fork, her knuckles turning white. She glanced toward the kitchen staff to see if they had noticed what was happening. They didn't do anything about it. As long as the kids weren't downright fighting, bullying was tolerated—even encouraged.

She leaned forward and watched as the bigger kid held the bowl of chili up in the air like a prized trophy, the cinnamon roll clenched between his teeth. Another kid walked behind with Teddy's milk.

The cooks didn't even bat an eye. They were, in fact, tearing down the trays and hauling the food away. They busied themselves filling a cart with more trays of food for those who were confined to their rooms. Wendy knew they kept the "dangerous" kids on a lower level—behind more locked doors and in padded rooms.

No, not rooms. Cells.

It was the threat of being taken to basement level two

that kept the bullying in check. But she believed that bullying of any kind should never be tolerated.

Teddy's lip quivered and his hand reached for his fork. He stabbed a green bean, brought it up to his mouth, and chewed slowly. In two bites, his small portion of vegetables had disappeared.

Come on, Teddy. Say something. Do something. She tried to mentally encourage him to act, to not let himself become the victim.

Teddy continued to sit and stare at his empty plate. His shoulders shook and the dull murmur of the crowd rose.

Disgusted and furious at the bullies, Wendy was even more upset at Teddy for not standing up for himself. She had only eaten half of her chili, but she'd lost her appetite. She stood and pushed her chair screeching across the floor, drawing attention. Wendy picked up her unopened pint of milk and her cinnamon roll, walked over to Teddy's table, and placed both on his tray. She saw his wide eyes turn glassy as he tried to blink back tears. He looked at the food in front of him and then back at her.

She jumped up and sat on top of the table. "Eat," she commanded. Wendy glared at anyone who looked their way.

Her body language was clear. Don't mess with her. She was his protector. Wendy proceeded to watch over Teddy as he ate her roll and downed the milk greedily. When 1-84 stared at her, Wendy gave her an ugly glare and crossed her arms threateningly.

Gray had watched the whole exchange. He picked up

his tray and moved to sit next them, as if there was a silent line drawn in the cafeteria and he had chosen a side. Wendy gave him a curious smile as he took over glaring at the group of bullies that stole Teddy's food.

"Just because you can't talk, or don't, or choose not to, that doesn't mean you can't defend yourself," Wendy whispered.

"It's true." Gray leaned over and spoke softly. "Rule one: Everyone is the enemy. Even me...even her." He gestured to both of them.

Teddy swallowed a mouthful of cinnamon roll and turned his soft brown eyes to her. They flared with anger.

"Relax. We know how to handle ourselves." Wendy winked.

Gray held up two fingers. "Rule two: Remember rule one." Gray picked up his discarded fork and held it in front of Wendy, tines facing up. "This is eating position."

He waited to be sure Teddy was paying close attention. "And when they come near you, flip it like this." With a quick flip of the fork and his arm, the tines pointed down, and he brought the fork across Wendy's chest in an aggressive stance. "Normally, it's what you'd do with a knife, but since we aren't given any, the fork will do."

Teddy's eyes widened in fear, but Gray smiled encouragingly. "Relax, kid. I've never had to stab anyone with a fork. Just the action alone will make them back off. But you have to toughen up here, be an army of one if you have to. There's no room for weakness." He gently placed the fork down on his tray. With a respectful nod to Wendy, he walked out of the room.

When Teddy was done eating, Wendy gave his shoulder a gentle squeeze, and he started to shake. Was he crying? He turned and wrapped his arms around her neck.

"Hey, chill." She awkwardly extracted herself from his grasp. "It was nothing. No big deal. Just some notes for next time, okay?" Uncomfortable with his display of affection, she stood and heard his choked sob. She turned back.

He looked up at her, eyes full of accusation and anger, lips pinched in a tight line. He grabbed the bear and began to whisper to it again. Maybe it would be better if she distanced herself from Teddy, let him fight his own battles from now on. She put the dirty tray on the rack and headed out.

Wendy passed back through the main room on her way down the hall to her own room, and noticed that Boy was gone. Strange. She hadn't seen him come into the dining hall to eat, so he must have gone back to his room. She was about to leave when she noticed the game board.

Even from a distance, she could see that another piece had disappeared from the board. Her thimble.

-3-

SHE BOLTED UPRIGHT. Her body was coated in a sheen of sweat, and she shook uncontrollably again. She skated her gaze around her small, white room. She was alone. Something scratched at her window, and she cried out in terror, pulling the blanket over her head as she continued to shiver.

"It's not real," she spoke aloud to no one. "It didn't happen." She lifted the corner of her blanket and peeked into her room. It had a sink with no mirror, a chair, her bed, a nightstand, and a small bathroom area that held the toilet.

The wind howled angrily, and the scratching noise came from the window again. Feeling a little bolder, she sat up, tossed her blanket to the side and stood up to peer out the window. Sure enough, the wind was only causing a tree branch to scratch against the pane. She released the breath she was holding and crawled back into her bed.

The moonlight filtered in along the far wall, and the clouds passing in front of it caused shadow-fingers to stretch and reach across it.

"No!" Wendy cried out again. She reached for the

small lamp next to the bed and turned it on, making the shadows disappear. "The shadows cannot harm me. The shadows cannot harm me."

Once her room was bathed in light, her unease started to dissipate. She pulled the covers back over her and felt a tear of unease slide down her face. It was natural for a ten-year-old to be afraid of the dark and of the shadows.

Wasn't it?

She had just fallen back into a restless sleep when a knock on her door made her jump up again. It was one of the night staff doing her rounds.

"It's past eleven. You know the rules. Lights out." The nurse spoke softly through the glass panel in the door. Wendy was locked in. She couldn't leave until morning.

"Please, don't make me," Wendy whispered through the blankets, but the nurse didn't hear.

"Turn off the lights," the nurse said, a little firmer.

Wendy's hand snaked out from under the blanket. She clicked the lamp off and yanked her hand back under the covers, as if the darkness would bite it off. She didn't breathe, didn't move, just heard the soft steps of the nurse's feet move on down the hall.

She was getting hot from breathing under the blanket, but she wasn't about to poke her head out. The scratching noise at the window came again, followed by a soft click of the window's lock turning.

"The shadows aren't real. It's all in my head."

Then came the sound of the window sliding open.

She closed her eyes and held her breath. If she didn't see it, it didn't exist.

It wasn't here.

It wasn't in her room.

The temperature dropped, and now she was shaking not only from fear but also from chills that sneaked between the covers and touched her skin.

"Go away," she whispered.

This wasn't happening. Not again. How did the shadow keep finding her here? She thought she'd banished them from her mind.

Wendy whispered frantically. "Go away, leave here."

The heavy bolt slid as her door was unlocked, and the door creaked open.

The shadow was leaving her room. Where was it going? Why did it open her door? She flipped back the comforter just enough to see the shadow slip out of her room and into the empty hallway.

Wendy leapt from her bed and scrambled to the open door to look down the darkened hallway. Her heart thudded loudly, the rushing of its frantic beat in her ears.

Where had the shadow gone? The hall was void of movement. The nurse had already made her rounds and retired back to her station.

Wendy thought she'd seen a slight movement down the hall to her left, so she followed, taking soft steps and peering into each room, looking for darkness. The first two rooms in the girls' wing showed the inhabitants blissfully sleeping.

She paused when she peered into Lily's room. Her dark hair fell around her caramel skin, and she was snuggled into bed, the blanket pulled up to her chin.

Wendy checked every room, and there were no shadows. She turned and was about to head back to her room when she saw the shadow pass through the double doors and head toward the boys' wing.

Wendy felt like she was sleepwalking as she followed the shadow through an unlocked door and down another hall. Where were the guards? How come so many doors were unlocked? She looked into the glass doors as she wandered through the boys' hall.

Teddy tossed and turned, his mouth open in a silent scream. Night terrors?

Had to be. He was experiencing night terrors like she did. One of the most unholy experiences ever.

The staff told her she had an "episode."

Now, here she was seeing one in front of her, and she was helpless to do anything. She tapped on the glass, but Teddy didn't hear her. She tried calling his name. "Teddy. Wake up."

Nothing.

Wendy looked up in the corner of the hallway directly at the blinking security camera. Any minute, they would notice her in the hallway and force her back to her room.

"It's okay. Think happy thoughts." She spoke Dr. Mee's mantra through the pane.

Suddenly, the distressed movements stopped.

He sat straight up in bed and stared at her.

His pupils were dilated.

And he started to scream. Loudly.

Wendy jumped back in alarm and scrambled into an empty room, just as nurses came in to try to subdue Teddy. He continued to scream, and Wendy tried to put her hands over her ears to block out his cries. She heard scuffling as two nurses wheeled him, strapped to his bed, out of the room and toward the elevator.

Teddy gave up and the screaming quieted. His body went limp, but he still clutched the bear under his arm. When the doors opened and they rolled the bed in, his hand twitched and the bear fell to the floor. He cried out in distress, but no one saw, and the elevator doors closed.

Wendy came out of the empty room and picked up his tattered toy, gently pressing it to her chest. She started to follow Teddy.

A door opened at the other end of the long hallway, drawing her attention back to the other problem. The shadow. Chills ran up her arms as it glided behind Boy, his hair tousled from sleep, almost as if it were herding him. He ambled toward the emergency exit stairwell on the other end of the hall, still in his pajamas.

The shadow paused, flittered a few feet behind Boy, beckoning for her to follow it.

She had let herself get distracted, and now the boy was too far away. She took off running after the shadow, dropping the bear on the floor. Boy was about to push on the emergency door, and Wendy prepared herself for the loud alarm that would go off when the handle was pressed.

But it didn't.

What was happening?

She was closing the distance, but she didn't know if she could catch up to the boy or the shadow. The pale yellow light of the stairwell lamps illuminated the darkened hallway when the door opened. The shadow started to lose focus, but it was bright enough that she could still see it.

Something about the shadow slowed her for a moment.

It had a human form. The realization that it wasn't in the shape of some monster made her pump her legs even harder. The heavy metal door swung closed as the shadow and Boy moved away. She wasn't going to make it, but she pushed herself even harder.

The door picked up speed. Wendy dove forward and shoved her hand between the frame and door before it closed. She yelled out in pain as it crushed her hand but quickly stifled her cries. Pushing the door open, she entered the stairwell. The door thudded shut behind her.

She leaned over the railing but only saw more darkened stairs downward. She looked up and spotted the striped sleeve of Boy's pajamas as his hand brushed the railing.

Wendy charged after them. "Hey. Stop!" She had no clue why, but she couldn't seem to close the distance between them. They were ascending the stairs at inhuman speed, while Wendy pursued them at barefoot-girl speed.

Up and up she followed, looking at each of the floor signs as she ran past.

5th.

6th.

They were running out of floors. She paused and leaned back over the railing to look down. Had she missed them? Did they exit onto another floor? She hadn't heard any of the exit doors open, and she had been listening for just that sound.

She kept going up until she saw the sign that said ROOF.

Wendy noticed the rusted metal door swinging slowly outward. She ran out into the night, and her feet burned on the gravel-covered roof. Searching past the large air conditioning units, she spotted them on the other side of the large satellite dish.

The shadow was floating in the air as Boy stood on the edge of the roof, looking pensive. She had never been on the roof, and now that she was there, it terrified her. The rushing ocean water thundered below, the briny smell of the water hung in the air.

"What are you doing?"

"You shouldn't be here." He turned to study her, confusion shrouding his face. He had something in his hands, something he kept twisting and turning.

"Can you see it?" Wendy pointed at the dark being floating just behind him. She could have sworn she saw the shadow use its hands to make a face and waggle ghostly fingers at her.

Boy turned to look where she had pointed, but the shadow had dissipated.

"The shadow, can you see it?"

He shook his head no.

"We can't stay here," he yelled into the darkness, the wind whipping his voice away.

Wendy took a few tentative steps in his direction. She

tried to speak softly, in a motherly tone. "No, we can't. Come down off the ledge, and we can go back inside. It's dangerous here."

He shook his head. "It's dangerous inside, too. They lied to us. They've been lying the whole time. There's no family waiting with open arms for us if we excel. Just more tests, more experiments, and another prison. We have to escape."

"But we're on an island. There's nowhere to go," Wendy called out, fear bubbling within her.

He looked over his shoulder at her and smiled wryly, even as his green eyes pleaded with her. "An island won't stop me. It won't stop us. We'll leave here and do all of the things we planned. We'll buy all the ice cream and build the largest tree house. I can take us away from here."

The shadow continued to float behind him. It flew closer and pulled on his pajama top. She wasn't sure if the shadow was trying to steady him or push him over.

"Get away from him!" She shouted and rushed forward as the boy began to topple, but he regained his balance, his arms spread to his sides.

The shadow flew at her. She screamed and ducked.

"Don't you see it?" Wendy pointed at the being now flying around her, taunting her. She ducked as the shadow flew her way. Boy was oblivious to her hallucinations.

"I lied to them. Failed my tests, so they sent me back. I did everything I could to be sent back here to get you. But I can do it. I'll show them." He spoke angrily into the wind.

"Do what?" she asked fearfully.

He fidgeted with the object in his hand, and she saw it was her silver thimble. He tucked it into his pajama pocket and smiled confidently at her.

"Fly."

The roof door slammed open, and she heard the sound of rushing feet behind her. She knew what that meant. They'd be caught and taken to a containment unit.

"Come with me?" he begged. He held his hand out to her, waiting for her to take it. His smile promised safety, security, and adventure. "I won't let you fall."

"But...I can't fly." Her hand brushed across his palm, and it started to tremble as her fear quickly took over.

"No, you're wrong." His voice became distant as he looked at the soldiers rushing toward them. He grabbed her hand and tried to pull her with him. "We can. If you just belie—"

Strong arms wrapped around Wendy's waist and yanked her from his grip. He tried to grab for her, to yank her from her attacker's arms, but he lost his balance.

He slipped, his arms pin wheeling as he fell backwards off the ledge of the roof and plummeted toward the rocks below.

-4-

H ER BREATH CAUGHT IN her throat, and time
seemed to freeze, but those three seconds caught
up with the present, and her scream echoed into
the night.

She attempted to fight off her attacker, but he pushed
her to the ground. The gravel scratched against her cheek
and cut off her vision. Someone's hand shoved her head
down, and a knee pressed into her back.

"Let me go!" Wendy struggled to move.

Black army boots crunched on the rooftop in front of
her and stopped at the ledge. At the edge of her vision she
saw soldiers with black uniforms, black bandanas, and a
red skull and crossbones patch on their arm.

"Nooo," she breathed out, feeling herself go faint as
she struggled to keep her footing. This couldn't be happening. The Red Skulls were here.

Dr. Mee said they would be back any day. Wendy just
hadn't expected them to show up within hours of her
meeting. When the Red Skulls came, fear and intimidation
followed. They weren't your daily variety hospital guards.
They were the boogeymen, mentioned on whispered

breaths in the facility. They had beaten a kid when he had refused to go with them for the next treatment.

When Red Skulls arrived, it meant there'd be new faces to get to know—and a few less familiar ones walking around.

"Did he fall?" From the man's gruff tone of voice and posture, she assumed he was the one in charge. The skull patch on his uniform had a second set of crossbones beneath it, suggesting a higher rank. The soldier with the rifle strapped across his back leaned over the roof's edge and looked down. He nodded in affirmation.

"Scour the rocks below, find his body," the leader ordered.

Tears filled her eyes and Wendy trembled, her breathing ragged.

"Let her go, Hook. I'll take her." A gentle hand helped her up. "Hold it together, Wendy." The voice was deep, soft, and familiar. "Now would be a good time to keep your wits about you." She tried to turn her face to see him, but he pressed her even tighter against his chest. All she saw was his gray hair, but she recognized him—one of the lead doctors who came in and examined them from time to time. He was kind, sweet, and smelled faintly of spices. And he knew all the children by their real names, not their subject numbers.

He was the only father figure she could remember—Dr. Barrie.

He pressed a cold injector gun to her throat, and she felt a prick and heard a release of air.

The captain of the Red Skulls came over, grabbed her

chin, and shined a flashlight in her eyes. "Was she one of the ones we came for?" His face was angular, unshaven, and his nose was slightly crooked.

Wendy stared at the captain in terror, his face swimming in and out of focus. And then everything went black.

"I don't think you want her. Her results have been lackluster," Dr. Barrie said as he handed off the unconscious girl to a waiting tech. He turned to stare down his arch nemesis, Captain Hook of the Red Skulls, Neverland's private mercenary army. Dr. Barrie knew better than to duel with a man lacking a moral compass.

Captain Hook sneered. "All the results have been less than appealing. This whole program has been an utter failure. We've wasted millions on this, and our corporate sponsors have had enough. The few successes we've had have been minor."

The captain's gravelly voice raked across Dr. Barrie's nerves. The man needed to be challenged. "Sir, we need more time. The PX-1 will develop as the kids age. It's why we chose kids this young—their bodies can adapt to the treatments easier than an adult."

"It's Captain Hook to you, Dr. Barrie, and it's not fast enough. We have an enemy closing in on our ranks. We need our own weapons. We don't have time to waste. Especially, the years it may take to change their DNA. We need it to work faster."

"I can't give you microwaved results. The kids' minds will burn out. And we already know it doesn't work on adults."

"Then start over. Get rid of these PX-1 rejects. If we want D.U.S.T. to work, I need faster, stronger kids. You said the PX-2 was almost ready."

"Yes, it is, but it hasn't been tested yet. Let us place these kids back into the foster system." A chill ran over his body from the cold glare Captain Hook leveled at him.

"Not an option," Hook ordered. "They belong to Neverland, to the D.U.S.T. Program. We can't let anyone else get their hands on them or learn what we're doing here. We want no proof of this failure."

"This is ridiculous," Dr. Barrie said. "I never agreed to mass homicide. I will not take this program any farther."

"Unfortunately, Dr. Barrie, this is above your pay grade now. My orders come from someone higher than you, and they want their army."

"I'll shut down the lab. Send all of my technicians home," Dr. Barrie roared like a lion.

Captain Hook pulled his GLOCK and pressed the cold gun barrel under the doctor's chin. "You do, and I'll send you home the fast way. What do you think? Is your soul prepared? Are you going to go up," he pointed with his chin before looking down toward the rocks below. "Or down? Your entire staff—they choose to work for me or die. What say you? I could just have them walk off the edge of the roof instead, meet their maker at the bottom of the rocks, and wash out to sea."

"You...you pirate," Dr. Barrie spat out.

The captain laughed. "I don't need to be on a ship to start a mutiny. Maybe you need more incentive. You're going to get me results ...or I'm going to go say hello to your daughter, Isabelle. She's the right age to be the first volunteer for the PX-2 trials."

Bile filled the doctor's mouth. "No, please... I'll do what you say," Dr. Barrie murmured.

"That's a good follower. Neverland needs you, the Company needs you, I need you. And they demand results."

Dr. Barrie swallowed nervously and wet his lips before answering, "I'll get you your results."

The captain smiled, revealing uneven teeth. "That's what I like to hear."

-5-

DR. BARRIE TOOK THE young girl back from the waiting technician. He was physically carrying her body weight and mentally shouldering the responsibility and lives of every child in Neverland. She looked to be coming in and out of consciousness—he hoped she stayed out.

He slowed when he came to a locked door, and one of his techs entered in the code. The door buzzed and unlocked. They entered a monitored hallway, security cameras focusing on them. The tech held the door open as Dr. Barrie carried Wendy inside and gently placed her on the stiff white sheets of a hospital bed in the medical wing.

He placed his warm hand over hers. "You should have jumped with the boy. Your fate would have been much better than what you'll encounter here." He looked up at the mirror and studied his face under the halogen light, taking in his white lab jacket and silver bifocals.

He turned away, ran his hands through his prematurely gray hair, and sighed. "This is a mistake. I've taken it too far. It must be stopped...but how?" He paced back and forth in the room, shoulders slumped and his lips pressed into a thin line.

The door opened and Dr. Mee entered. She looked disheveled, as if she'd awakened last minute. Without seeing him, she rushed to the girl in the bed. "Wendy? Not you. I had such high hopes for you."

"She's alive," Dr. Barrie said softly. "She's unharmed."

"Doctor?" She stared at him in disbelief. "What's going on? I wasn't expecting you here for another week." Dr. Mee hesitated and tried to smooth her loose curls.

"I've been hearing rumors about Hook—what he was doing to the kids who advanced to Stage 2. Have you heard?"

She shook her head.

"They want us to start over," he whispered, his voice hoarse. He sat on the edge of the hospital bed next to Wendy and placed his head in his hands. "And they want us to make them disappear."

Dr. Mee fisted her hands, her petite brows furrowed. "They're just children."

"It's either that, or they'll kill us and do the same to our families."

Her cheeks flushed with anger. "Hook already took everything from me."

A regret-filled sigh escaped. He'd never meant to put anyone at risk, not Dr. Mee and especially not the children.

"They may be our orders, but I don't like them." Her gaze fell on Wendy. "I can't do this job anymore. No more death."

And that's when he realized. He couldn't do the job either.

He stood and checked the hallway before he stepped closer. "Dr. Mee, this has gone on long enough. We have to act quickly. Get the kids out of here…tonight."

Her eyes glistened with pride and tears. "Tell me what you need me to do."

-6-

WENDY ROLLED OVER AS she slept. Something tickled her nose, a harsh smell that reminded her of camping.

Smoke! Not just smoke! Fire!

A blaring alarm pierced the air, making her clasp her hands over her ears.

Wendy jumped up disoriented and pounded on the door. Another buzz and click sounded as her door automatically unlocked. She rushed out into the smoke-filled hallway and got lost among the uniforms of soldiers running to investigate.

She frantically made her way down the hall to the girls' wing. Her heart plummeted when she saw the double doors secured with a chain. Girls crowded on the opposite side of the door, banging on the window. Lily was near the front. All the girls screamed at her, trapped in the hall.

"Help us!" Lily shouted, her hand snaking through the opening to grab Wendy's nightgown.

Wendy shook the door and the heavy chain rattled against the handle. "I can't! The door is chained. We have to find a different way out." A few, clearly not in their right minds, stood idly in the middle of the halls, not moving. Just standing and staring.

A door opened behind them, and Red Skulls came in with guns. Immediate fear flooded her. The soldiers weren't there to help them. "The whole wing is compromised. We have to clear it. Follow us, girls." They directed the mob of girls down a hallway.

"Noo!" Wendy tried to reach through and pull on Lily's arm, as if she could forcefully squeeze her through the six-inch opening between the chains.

A Red Skull grabbed the girl from behind and dragged her away kicking and screaming. Her little hand gripped Wendy's nightgown so hard, it ripped. The thickening smoke made breathing difficult, and she couldn't focus. She had to find a way out. The Red Skulls were herding the girls down the halls to the farthest west wing, an area the children were forbidden to enter.

She ran into the common area and even more smoke filled the air—but not the same as the smoke from before. This bitter smoke stung her eyes, making her cry.

Tear gas?

Wendy's mouth started to burn as hacking coughs wracked her lungs. She pulled her shirt up over her mouth. The closer she came to the exit, the thicker the smoke grew. She could feel the heat on her bare arms.

Shouldn't the sprinklers have kicked on? Why weren't there any water sprinklers? A sinking feeling came over her. They didn't want any. This was a horrid facility, not government run. If they wanted to dispose of the place—

and fast—this is how they'd do it.

With fire.

She passed a few frantic nurses in the corridor, but they were all running *away* from the closest exit, and she wasn't sure why. She released a breath, covered her nose and mouth with her sleeve, and saw movement as a yellow siren light begin to flash on the other side of secured door. It was a large fire door dropping from the ceiling, about to close her in.

Wendy looked over her shoulder and saw another one coming down behind her.

She was out of time. Trapped between two closing fire doors.

Trembling, Wendy spun to gauge the possibility of making it back the way she came before the door closed. She was about to give up when a dark body ran and slid in her direction under the fire door—just before it slammed into the ground.

Gray. He rolled to his feet and continued running toward Wendy.

"Move!"

She moved to the side. On his way by, Gray grabbed her hand and pulled her after him. This fire door was lowering more slowly, but she still didn't think they'd make it. Wendy slowed her steps, fear making her freeze.

But he tugged her hand, wouldn't let her stop.

At the door, she froze anyway. There was only a two-foot gap.

"I can't. I can't do it," Wendy screamed.

"Do you want to die?" Gray shouted.

"No."

"Then roll." He grabbed her by the neck, forced her to her knees, and shoved Wendy under the fire door. And she rolled. It wasn't the most graceful attempt, because she landed on her fist and knocked her head into the lowering wall. But she continued to roll, scared that if she stopped, she'd be crushed to death.

She stopped and glanced over just as Gray tried to squeeze through the twelve-inch gap. He didn't have room to roll, so he lay on his back and slid under, his face turned to the side. Both fear and determination were evident in his eyes as the wall started to pin his chest down.

He cried out, pushing with his feet and scrambling backwards. He pulled his foot out just as…*thud.* The door closed.

Gray dropped his head to the floor and lay there for a few seconds. But he quickly regained his composure and was up on his feet. Grabbing Wendy's hand, he led her out the main doors and into the night through the forests.

"This way," he called and ran ahead of her.

"How do you know where to go?"

Gray wouldn't meet her eyes, but kept escorting her through the woods until they were joined by others in lab coats who were also ushering kids into the night. Wendy recognized Dr. Barrie, whose flashlight moved to blind them for a second before he directed the light back down to the earth. A look of relief crossed his face. As he ran, the glow of the inferno from the building illuminated Dr. Barrie from behind.

The mixture of the damp earthy forest and the acrid

smoke lingered in the air, making Wendy's stomach roll.

Movement sounded from behind them, and Dr. Barrie turned with his flashlight on a group of scared kids and a tech who held up his hand to shield his eyes from the light.

"How many?" Dr. Barrie yelled to a young technician who met up with him, leading kids hand-in-hand through the dark.

"Not enough." The technician said, his eyes blood shot. Black soot covered his jacket. "They knew. They cut off the group escaping through the west tunnel. They" his voice dropped to a whisper "didn't make it."

"What about the lab?" Dr. Barrie asked.

"Destroyed. We erased the computer data and burned all our research."

He hadn't done enough. Each breath became harder to draw as guilt assailed him. So much lost, but at least they were able to save the kids. "Have you seen Dr. Mee? What about the girls? She was going to get the girls."

"Here," Dr. Mee called out of the darkness. She ran toward them carrying a wrapped bundle. Her feet were bare and cut up, her heels abandoned somewhere in the forest behind her.

Dr. Barrie looked behind her and waited. "Any more, Dr. Mee?" The fire glowed red above the tree line. He hoped that the fire would destroy Neverland, that no one else would ever trespass or learn of the sins they'd committed there.

The glow made Dr. Mee's tears glisten in the dark as they washed streaks through the soot that spattered her tan face. "No, I tried to get to the girls in time, but I didn't make it. The Red Skulls had already taken them and cleared the floor."

An intense throbbing filled his chest and he gasped in agony. He reached into his pocket and pulled out a bottle of his pills, barely able to shake two into his palm. They hurt as he swallowed them, and he waited for the pain to subside, but a pill couldn't quell the guilt. And he didn't have enough to last him more than a few months once he made it safely home.

"I was able to grab this little fellow," Dr. Mee said. "He was the only one in the nursery. The others were gone. I don't know how this little one got passed up." She pulled back the blanket and showed Dr. Barrie the infant, who started to cry when his face was exposed to the cold air.

Dr. Barrie considered the number of kids surrounding him—so many less than he had hoped. He looked back at the burning building and he fell to his knees, overcome with guilt. "We failed. We didn't save them." He pitched forward, his hands burrowing into the dirt.

"Shh, you saved *them*." Dr. Mee turned and gestured to the group of children, standing scared and huddled together for warmth.

"God will never forgive me," he cried out. He pulled himself up and turned to wrap his arms around the nearest boys. "I promise you, I will take care of you forever. I'll build a haven for you where you'll be safe, where you

41

will be accepted…as God is my witness."

"Mr. Barrie?" One of the technicians came up with his flashlight. "We need to get to the boat. We need to get the children to safety before the Red Skulls find us."

"Yes, yes you're right." He gestured for the boys and Wendy to follow. "Come, children. Quickly, to the boat."

Wendy's lungs burned. She kept coughing and trying to catch her breath as they ran barefoot into the night, heading toward the shoreline. They were trying to be quiet as they ran, but she heard crying and whimpering from the boys as she followed the glimpses of white and blue pajamas in the darkness. She lost Gray as they were running, and she couldn't see Teddy no matter how hard she searched.

She tried to focus on following the others, but then she heard something crashing through the darkness behind her. Fear of the unknown caused her to look over her shoulder, and she tripped. Wendy let out a terrified scream as she slid down an embankment.

"Over here, I heard something." A male voice called out from above.

The Red Skulls!

She pressed her body against the hill and hid under the

fronds of an overhanging bush. A flashlight beam passed over the exact spot she had vacated seconds before. Her hands flew to her mouth and tried to stifle her frantic breaths.

The loud crashing continued, but was moving farther away. Then she heard a shout in the distance as the Red Skulls spotted and began to pursue the others. She leapt up and tried to run after her group, but now she was behind the Red Skulls. There were no paths to follow. Just forest and the sound of the ocean.

She jogged as quietly as she could and tried to head toward the shore. The ground under her feet became softer. She must be getting close to the beach, just a little farther. Then six shots echoed in the night, her heart thudded in dread with every single one. Her legs pumped harder as she tried to catch up to the others. Hoping that she wouldn't be too late.

One second she was surrounded by trees, the next Wendy stumbled onto the beach and the ocean loomed before her.

Farther ahead, she saw a yacht moored to a dock and Wendy didn't stop running until her feet thudded on the wood. She slowed when she recognized Dr. Barrie standing at the edge of the dock, looking into the water. He tucked something into the back of his pants and leaned down to toss the lines to cast off. Dr. Barrie's shirt was ripped, like he had been in a struggle.

"The Red Skulls are here!" Wendy tried to warn him.

"I know." He turned his head toward the edge of the dock. "More will come."

A large objected floated in the water, catching her eye. It bobbed once, then twice, before sinking into the dark depths of the water—a body. She looked behind her and spotted a second Red Skull unmoving in the sand; he looked like he was sleeping, except for the splash of red across his chest.

So much death.

"Isabelle, tell them to start the engine," Dr. Barrie yelled to a young girl who peeked out of the bridge. He turned, and she saw the handle of a pistol in his waistband. Wendy's heart stuttered, but she willed it to slow. To trust. Dr. Barrie was on their side—one of the good guys, one of the guys risking everything. The engine turned over, and the white yacht pulled away from shore, picking up speed. The children stood at the stern by the rails and watched the beach light up with flashlights followed by a spattering of gunshots from the shore. Some ricocheted off the boat.

Wendy screamed and took cover. Another engine roared nearby, and she realized where the other Red Skulls had gone. A military speedboat raced down the coastline toward them.

"Jax!" Dr. Barrie yelled toward Gray, who was shivering in the night.

"Yes sir," he said, looking up at Dr. Barrie with wide alarm-filled eyes.

"I need you, son." He touched Gray gently on the arm. "I know what you can do. I've seen your reports. Can you do it again...once more...for me?"

Jax shook his head in defiance, and Dr. Barrie's face

crumbled. "I know. It's not fair of me to ask, but if you don't, we're going to die...all of us."

Jax looked back at the speedboat now gaining on their slower moving yacht, doubt evident in his face.

"No, Barrie," Dr. Mee called when she overheard what he was trying to do. She still held the baby close to her chest. "Not fear. That one is motivated by anger."

"But he can do it?" He looked at Dr. Mee with hope in his eyes. "He's done it?"

She nodded her head. "He's done it once...and only once."

"Okay, son, do this for me tonight, and I swear I'll never ask you to use your gift again." Jax hesitated. "They're not going to take us prisoner, Jax. We're disposable to them. You're the only one who can stop them now. If you don't, everyone on this boat will die."

Jax looked over Dr. Barrie's shoulder. As the boat pulled up beside them, the soldiers turned their guns on the yacht and opened fire.

Ping. Ping. The bullets hit railings and the sides—some found their marks, and voices screamed in pain.

"Quick! In here!" The same young girl with white-blonde hair came down a ladder and opened the door to the main living deck. She gestured for the boys to take cover inside.

"Isabelle, stay inside!" Dr. Barrie shouted.

There was a mad rush as the boys ran and pushed to avoid being hit by the bullets. The yacht bounced as it tried to fight the waves, to evade the attack of the Red Skulls. Wendy darted across the deck, but the yacht turned and her feet slipped from beneath her. She slipped under the guard rail just as the boat tipped on a tall wave, and she slid over the edge, just barely clawing and catching the rail post. She screamed and clung for her life.

"I got you." A boy rushed forward and grabbed ahold of her arm, struggling to pull her back onto the rocking ship.

"Don't let go!" Bright green eyes—was she hallucinating again?

"Boy!"

He grunted as he held tight, trying to lift her dead weight.

The Red Skulls fired, another stream of bullets sprayed the boat.

The boy cried out as one hit him square in the chest, and a splattering of blood hit Wendy's cheek. His grip loosened just as her own gave out, and she screamed in terror as she fell below the crashing waves of the relentless ocean.

Dr. Barrie and Jax spun at the scream, in time to see Peter hit by the bullets, to know someone fell into the ocean. One glance at Jax's determined face told Dr. Barrie what was coming.

46

Jax stood, hands clenched at his sides and shaking with rage. A primal roar tore from his mouth, all of his anger focused on the Red Skulls' boat. His right hand came up, glowing red with power.

The boat exploded outward, and flaming pieces of wreckage rained down around them. Even though Peter was bleeding, he tried to go over the rail and dive into the water after whoever had fallen in.

Isabelle ran onto the deck as Dr. Barrie shouted after her, grabbed the boy around the waist, and pulled him back over the rail.

"NOOO!" Peter screamed when he couldn't go after her.

"Stop! You're wounded." Isabelle yelled.

Dr. Barrie joined her, but it took every ounce of strength they had to drag him back onto the deck and over to the galley. He pulled a kitchen towel off the counter and placed it against Peter's chest.

"It's suicide to go back out there," Isabelle said.

"I can still save her. Let me go!" The boy pushed her away and tried to fight.

"It's too late. We can't go back." One of the male nurses came to her rescue with a first aid kit from the head.

"No," he rasped out between clenched teeth as he fought for his own life. "I can save—"

A voice cried out from the water.

Dr. Barrie rushed to the railing and looked over, Jax still standing there in furious silence. A head bobbed from the side as a Red Skull began to climb aboard, his hand pointing a gun right into his face. Barrie heard the gun cock. He swallowed his fear and stared down the barrel of the gun.

The Red Skull never had a chance to pull the trigger. He erupted into a ball of flames and fell backward into the turbulent waves.

Dr. Barrie released his breath and felt his heart collapse with guilt and gratitude as he looked over at the young boy, who'd just ruthlessly murdered to save him. Jax wouldn't look at him, instead choosing to watch the burning boat slowly sink into the water. Dr. Barrie knew it wouldn't be the end.

He and his crew would be hunted for the rest of his life.

Neverland would never let them escape. His gaze turned back to the island—then toward Jax.

"Jax, dear boy." He held his arm open to the young boy who was staring at the devastation he caused. "One more time. We can never let what happened on Neverland be duplicated. Can you do it again?" He pointed to the facility. To Neverland. The fire might not reach the lower levels, and they needed everything erased.

Jax's face was streaked with tears, but he didn't need more urging. He closed his eyes, his hand reached toward the facility. The entire brick building exploded outward, the sky so bright with flames that it looked like morning.

"Goodbye, Neverland." Dr. Barrie spoke quietly. "You promised dreams, but you only brought us nightmares." He gave Jax's shoulder a slight squeeze and offered the boy words of affirmation. "You did good, son.

You did good."

Jax looked up at him, horrified. "I'm not your son." He shrugged Dr. Barrie's arm off and stormed into the cabin.

"Sir, the yacht's navigation system is down. I don't know where to go," one of his newer lab technicians whispered in his ear. "How do you own a five million dollar yacht without navigation?"

"It's a requirement of working here. No one is allowed to know where Neverland is, not even us." Dr. Barrie admitted.

"How do we get back to land?" He looked absolutely bewildered. He had come to the island like the rest of them, blindfolded.

Dr. Barrie grabbed his shoulder and pointed into the night sky. "Do you see that bright star there?"

"Yes?"

"Count over two. You see? Follow the second on the right, and sail straight on till morning. " He patted the technician's shoulder encouragingly.

"I've never sailed by the stars before." The man looked unsure.

"That's the problem with your generation. Let me tell you, boy. You'll have quite the story...if we live to tell anyone about it."

His young technician smiled worriedly and headed back to the engine room.

Dr. Barrie turned back to assess his circumstances—the boat filled with boys, his daughter Isabelle tending to Peter, who was covered in blood, his face a mask of agony.

Peter hadn't left the island. He must have stayed close by for a reason.

They were helpless unless they could get to the mainland, to a real hospital. Dr. Mee, who seemed very calm and collected amidst the chaos, was holding the young baby while sitting next to Jax, trying to comfort him.

Jax—the utter destruction he'd caused—all because Dr. Barrie had asked it of him. He'd just made the twelve-year-old a murderer. He only hoped he hadn't permanently scarred the boy, who was even now beginning to retreat behind a stone-faced mask of indifference. A ploy, a trick to protect himself from what he had just done.

The baby in Dr. Mee's arms made a slight cry.

A second later the baby disappeared with a flash of light and reappeared in Jax's lap. Jax's face went white with shock, and he almost dropped the baby, but caught him at the last minute. He held the small infant in his arms, looking very uncomfortable, but the baby just cooed and laughed, putting his chubby little fist into Jax's face. Jax tried to hold back the chuckle and looked around to see if anyone had noticed his slip.

"Well," Dr. Barrie thought to himself. "Maybe there's hope after all." He looked around for the young girl, surprised that he couldn't find her.

"Where's the girl? She was just here."

Peter's eyes were red rimmed, and he grimaced in pain, mumbling the words over and over. "Lost...I lost her...Lost girl." His head fell back against Isabelle's shoulder and he passed out.

Water.
Cold.
Blackness.
Sand.
Air.
Life.

Wendy coughed, her lungs expelling black water. She rolled over and found herself on a rocky coastline, shivering, freezing, and covered in seaweed. Seagulls called to each other, and one picked at something in Wendy's hair before flying away. Her eyes stung from the salt, and it was easier to keep them closed.

"George, there's something over here," a woman's distressed voice called. It sounded sweet and loving, and it was drawing nearer.

"Stay back, Mary," a man's voice warned. "Oh, Lord, it's a child." A warm hand touched her throat, then her wrist. "Call 911. She's still alive."

Wendy cracked her eye open—just a slit.

"George, hand me your sweater." Mary commanded the boy next to her. "We've got to get her warm. You too, John."

Wendy felt something soft wrap around her freezing body as the commanding woman's voice comforted her. "I've got you darling, I've got you. I'm not letting you go. I promise." For the first time in forever...she felt safe.

-7-

PRESENT DAY

SHE AWOKE WITH A gasp, her heart thudding, the blood beating in her own ears like the school's drum line. Coated in sweat, she laid her head back down on her pillow and tried to remember her dream, but it was already fading into nothingness. No matter how hard she tried, she couldn't recall even the faintest of details.

Just fire and water.

Nights were the worst. Especially those moments where she was almost-asleep-but-not-quite-awake, where she could get lost in the nether region of her dreams. There in that abyss, she was suddenly limitless—unafraid, unstoppable, all-powerful like a super hero—in a world without the constraints of time or space. Until the nightmares started about a fire, shadows, and water.

Thud! Something hit her window frame and shattered her reverie. Wendy was once again a mere seventeen-year-old, scared and vulnerable. Coldness permeated her semi-dark room, sending goose bumps across her arms and perpetuating the feeling that she was being watched...hunted.

Wendy sat frozen in her own bed and stared in terror at the shadow moving on the wall. She berated herself for leaving the curtains open and leapt toward the window to close them. Her heart beat loudly in her chest as she scanned her room for movement.

Nothing.

She heard a soft clicking noise and a ringing. Gathering her courage, she pulled open one white curtain—just an inch—and looked outside to see what the noise was. The front yard was empty. Just as quickly, she let the curtain fall back in place, the clinking of the metal rings against the rod making her already frayed nerves worse.

The medicine she'd been on hadn't been working as well as she'd hoped. She took the orange bottle labeled Clozapine from her dresser drawer and shook the white pill into her palm. Something her doctor had prescribed to help with her "momentary spells," as her adoptive mother called them.

No. She didn't want this. She put the pill back in the container and shut it back in her drawer.

Mary and George Owen, with their young son John, had found her washed up on a beach, half-dead and with no recollection of where she'd been or what had happened to her. She knew only her name. That family didn't give up on her: they paid for her hospital care, and when no one came forward to claim her, they fostered her until they were able to officially adopt her. That had been a blissful seven years ago, and other than the vivid nightmares and the occasional hallucinations, she had been able to lead a normal teenage life.

Too wired to sleep, she left her room and tiptoed down the hall to check on her sixteen-year-old brother. John was splayed across his bed, one foot sticking out from the covers and dangling off the mattress. Undisturbed, he slept. Not plagued by her malady or fears.

Out of habit, she crossed his bedroom and closed his blue curtains, cutting off the moonlight. The rest of the house was next. She checked all the doors and locks before heading back to her room.

Not once did she hear the ringing again, but the beeping was another matter. She tried to follow the sound, but it seemed to be coming from outside the house. Her mouth was dry with fear.

It was probably only a handheld video game that John had left on, and the battery was slowly dying.

Dressed only in her long nightshirt and shorts, she went to the back kitchen door, where the sound seemed to get progressively faster the closer she got to the door. The thud-thud-thud of her heartbeat kept pace with the beep-beep-beep of the noise. Slowly—painfully slowly—she unlocked the deadbolt and pressed her ear to the door.

The noise was just on the other side of the door.

She tried to peek out the kitchen curtain, but she didn't see anything.

"Okay, Wendy, you can do this. Don't be a scaredy-cat," she whispered. "Be brave for once in your life." Her shivering hand slowly turned the handle. She threw open the kitchen door to confront...silence.

The cool September breeze blew at her nightshirt, and she stepped barefoot out onto the patio. Her fenced-in yard was empty.

A large shadow flew overhead.

She spun back to the safety of her house, terror consuming her. Wendy slammed the kitchen door and threw the deadbolt, trying to control her trembling legs and runaway heart. It took a few moments before she was able to gather her strength and convince herself that she was once again imagining things.

Wendy hurried back to her room and slid under the now cold sheets. She pulled the comforter up over her head and tried to lull herself back to sleep. It was no use. She knew she'd lay awake all night again, and would probably do horribly at school tomorrow.

She was the only teenager she knew of who was still scared of shadows.

"You're the worst, Peter," Tink chastised. "You almost blew our cover." She took off the specter goggles and let them dangle from her neck. "Then we'd be back to square one—having to wait for them to show up again and lead us to a morphling."

"I had to. The shadow was at the window." Peter ran his hands through his auburn hair. "They don't usually act this way. Usually they just watch. It was going to go into her room." He looked back at the two-story brick house and studied it for movement. He was worried about the girl who'd come out into the night seemingly unafraid, and then run scared at the sight of a shadow. If only she knew.

She was right to be scared. She was probably their target. He needed to get to her before something worse did.

He walked his blonde sidekick down the road to her parked scooter. He kicked a rock out of the way and watched as it skipped across the paved road and landed harmlessly in a neighbor's empty yard.

"But you didn't know it was going to do anything," Tink challenged. "You didn't have to go shooting off and throw a rock at her window."

"They're bad news. You know that where the shadow appears, trouble follows. Your shadow box went crazy at her house. It's a dead zone. The shadows are gathering here, and they'll be back."

"We don't know that a morphling will come, though. They've been unpredictable of late, and I've been sitting out here in the cold all night. I'm calling this a false alarm." Tink closed the antenna on her mechanical box, turned the power off, and stowed it in her bag.

"If it's not a dead zone, why do the shadows keep gathering?

Tink shrugged her shoulders noncommittally and flipped the cover of her crossover bag closed. "Glitch."

"You're saying your machine—that *you* built—is faulty?" He crossed his arms to look down at her. Tink was his best friend, a little hotheaded at times and extremely protective, but she was also a bona fide tech genius. There was no way she'd admit that it erred.

"Maybe." She sniffed, as she got on her scooter and turned it on, cutting him off when he was about to press again.

"I just can't shake the feeling—"

"Fine," Tink interrupted. "I'll have some of the boys put on watcher detail for both of them. But I think we should let this one go. They have a family, so for now, they're protected. And being here is a waste of our time. We're sent to help those that can't protect themselves. Remember that, Peter."

He hated that she was right. Tink didn't look back as she drove off into the night. Peter turned, conflicted, to stare at the white house. Something big was coming—he could sense it. And there was this feeling in the pit of his stomach that told him, no matter how prepared he was, it wouldn't be enough.

-8-

ONE WEEK LATER

"TV ROTS YOUR BRAIN," Wendy called out as she jumped over the back of the gray microfiber sofa and ripped the DVR remote control from John's hands.

"Too late," he muttered, tapping his head. "It's all mush." Wendy held the remote way up in the air and quickly changed the channel to a teen drama with vampires. John made a gagging sound, and she grinned before clicking again. A crime investigator show. "Here!" she chimed.

John shook his head. "No way. Why do you torture yourself? This stuff gives you nightmares." Although he was younger, John was taller and had a longer reach and could have reclaimed the remote at any time.

Wendy scrolled through the channels. She finally stopped on the cartoon channel. A rainbow of colors and happy, sappy animals danced across the screen.

"Now, here's a show that will give you nightmares."

John grabbed the throw pillow and shoved it into Wendy's smirking face.

"Hey—mmmph!" She pulled the pillow down. "If you want to change the channel, that's fine." She got up and tossed the remote across the room to land on her mom's overstuffed chair. "You want it. Go get it."

"Noo!" he groaned.

Wendy grinned. She just doomed him to watch cartoons, because reaching the remote would mean getting up and walking across the room, and John was not motivated enough to do that.

John sighed and buried himself lower into the couch, getting even more comfortable. "I'm not moving," he said firmly.

"Fine," Wendy taunted. "Die here with the happy, sappy animals singing your funeral dirge.

Wendy walked over to the heavily draped window and threw it open. Light poured in and fell across his eyes. John hissed at her. Wendy threw her head back and laughed. "I can change it back to the vampire show."

"DON'T you dare!"

"R.I.P. John Owens. He died from sunlight and dumb cartoons."

"Put it on my tombstone," he said smartly.

"Hey, do you have any plans for tomorrow. We can go to the mall?"

"Do we have too?" John mumbled. "Anything but the mall."

"What about the movies?"

He paused for a second. "Okay, how about Death Escort 2?"

Wendy's brow arched, but he gave her the biggest wide-eyed look of innocence. She sighed and gave in. "I guess...but don't tell Mom."

"Not that new horror one," Mary called from the kitchen.

"Geez, that woman's got ears like a bat," John complained.

"I heard that!" Their mom came into the living room, hands on her hips. Mary's honey-brown hair was pulled back away from her face, her lips pressed firmly together. Her friendly eyes were staring them down, making them squirm.

"Yes, and those bat-ears are dialed up to ten right now," Wendy whispered.

John left, shooting Wendy an apologetic look. He mouthed the words "like a bat" again.

She started to giggle but held it in.

"Wendy, you've been through a lot, and you know our stance on scary movies."

"But I like scary movies," Wendy added. "And we don't know if they really have anything to do with my nightmares."

Her mom sighed and joined her on the couch. "That's really not the issue, dear. Though we have talked with John about it, and we mean it when we say no. But listen. I refilled your prescription and noticed you haven't been taking it for a while. You don't want to relapse and have to go back to that clinic do you?"

"I don't like the way the medicine makes me feel." She shrugged. "When I'm on it, I see puffy clouds and rainbow kittens."

"Well, isn't that nice?" her mother asked.

"Yeah, kittens that shoot laser beams out of their eyes and destroy earth as we know it."

"You do have quite the imagination." She gave Wendy a stern gaze. "But you still need to take your meds."

"No, I don't." Wendy tried to stare her down. Which was dumb. Anyone knows staring into the eyes of a predatory animal is really, really dumb.

Mary's eyes lit up in challenge, and Wendy could see that she was enjoying this. "Wendy, you are still our daughter, and you live under our roof, which means you obey our rules. You've missed out on a lot in life, and we care deeply for you—you're growing up so fast."

"I can be childish...see?" Wendy made a goofy face and swung one of the readily available throw pillows at her mother. It brushed the side of her head, making her red curls fly up in a comical way.

"Wendy!" Her mother shrieked.

The laughter died on Wendy's lips at her furious tone.

Mary stood and towered over her.

She was about to apologize, but her mom held up a finger to silence her. Wendy swallowed.

"That, young lady, was not nice," she chastised, just before swinging the pillow she'd expertly tucked behind her back at Wendy's face.

Wendy squealed as it whacked her on the side of the head.

"Next time, improve your aim," her mom said. The onslaught became a full-fledged war.

Wendy fell from her chair and grabbed the nearest pillow. They fired the pillows back and forth.

"Hey, what's going on?" her father yelled before entering the living room. Wendy and her mom both tossed their pillows and knocked him in the face.

They laughed at his shocked expression and waited for his response.

"Oh, I see how it is. Carry on." He slowly backed out of the room the way he came, his hands clasped behind him as he tried to keep a straight face.

Wendy and her mom collapsed on the floor in a fit of giggles amongst all of the pillows. There were probably fifteen pillows, and they had knocked over the lamp and a few picture frames, but nothing was really damaged.

"You know you really do have way too many of these." Wendy held up a small blue pillow with cute buttons sewn on the front.

"Oh, I know. I hate them," her mom answered. She positioned one of the pillows under her head and gazed up at the ceiling as they settled in to talk.

"Then why don't you get rid of a few—like this ugly one?" Wendy lifted a weird tan pillow with a cross-stitched peacock on it.

Her mom groaned and took the pillow from her. "I can't, because your father hates throw pillows on couches. He said *that* one was actually the ugliest pillow he'd ever seen. We'd just gotten in an argument a few minutes before, and I decided—then and there—that I must own said pillow as a way to stick it to him."

Wendy looked around at all of the horrid pillows in their living room, and it dawned on her. "So every pillow represents an argument between you and dad?"

"Yep," she giggled. "The bigger the argument, the uglier the pillow I buy. When he wants to find a place on the couch, he has to pile the pillows up or move them to the floor. It's my silent retribution...and I love every minute of it."

Wendy snorted. "I didn't know. It's kind of genius."

"Of course it is, because I'm your mother."

"I heard that," George crowed. They glanced up from where they lay sprawled across the floor. Her dad stood over them with a fully loaded Nerf gun. "Revenge is sweet, ladies!" he taunted.

He fired on his wife. She squealed, and the pillow fight began again. John came down the stairs to investigate. Dad pulled another Nerf gun from his back and tossed it to John. "Let's even the odds, shall we, son?"

John grinned, pumped the Nerf gun, and took aim. Wendy looked up just in time for the foam bullet to nail her in the eye.

-9-

S HE APPLIED A LITTLE more concealer under her eye and turned from the hall mirror. "How do I look?" Wendy twirled in front of John, who barely looked up from his video game. His mood had turned sullen as soon as he hit her in the eye, ending their game rather abruptly. He had tossed the Nerf gun onto the couch and stormed off to the family room to lose himself in his game. Was it guilt? Or was something else bothering him? Her parents had let him go, just nodding to one another. Her dad tousled her hair before he went into the kitchen with her mom. Wendy had changed and performed magic with makeup up in her room.

"Can't even tell my eye is swollen," Wendy called out and waited for a response. "Well, at least it stopped watering. But you don't see anything, right?"

"You did a good job hiding your face, Sis," he grumbled, before munching a chip and wiping away the leftover Dorito crumbs across the front of his shirt.

Wendy frowned at the jab her way. It didn't matter. She knew she looked good in her blue and white cheer uniform. She grabbed her silver pom-poms, shoving them into her bag by the front door. "John, you can skip any Friday night football game but this one. It's the biggest game of the season—against the Falcons. It's social suicide if you don't go. And change your shirt," she added, pointing at his Dorito-stained tee.

John repositioned his thick black glasses on the bridge of his nose and groaned. "As soon as we take the enemy base."

Wendy leaned down to tighten her laces on her white shoes and glanced up at him. "And how many hours does it take to do that?" He'd spend all weekend playing online with his buddies if it wasn't for her. It was her job to get him out in the world, to connect with real, live people, not voices that spoke through his Bluetooth headphones.

"Ah…go in…Slightly, surround him…on my command. Fire now!"

"John!" Wendy spoke his name a little louder.

"Oh, yeah…um, three hours?" He looked up and ran his hand through his strawberry blond mop of hair.

He'd never make it. She marched over to John, grabbed his headphones, and spoke into the mic, looking at the screen and reading her brother's handle.

"Sorry, boys. You're going to have to do this without Lt. J Dog." Wendy almost laughed out loud. "He's got a social function to attend tonight." She watched as the characters across the multi-section screen stopped moving.

"Hey, J Dog! Is that a girl?" a male voice came out, sounding nervous.

One voice had a distinct echo as it spoke. "I bet it's your mom."

John looked horrified. He snatched the headset back and spoke into it angrily. "No, Ditto, that's not my mom. It's my older sister."

"Is she hot?" The same echo voice asked.

"Can she play?" a different voice interjected.

"She can be on my team." One after another of John's troop rallied and called out for him to get her to play. Just then, the screen went red as the opposing team ambushed them and blew them up. John gave Wendy a disgusted look and shook his head. "Now look what you've done. You caused anarchy among the troops, and the enemy killed us.

"Yeah, not really sorry, baby bro! You can't miss tonight. All of your nerd friends will forgive you."

"That's not the point," he grumbled, putting away his controllers. "I'm the leader. Good leaders lead their armies, not let them get distracted by girls." He pointed at her. "They couldn't even see you, and they got distracted."

Wendy flashed her brother a grin. She looked in the mirror at her own strawberry blonde ponytail and straightened her blue bow. Her green eyes sparkled with mischief, and her light pink lip gloss made her look extra impish. The excitement of tonight's game and the fact that Jeremy might ask her out made her cheeks extra flushed.

"Here, Loser, the consolation prize, since I wrecked your game." Wendy tossed her brother the keys to her Prius. "You can drive."

John caught the keys midair. "Fine, I'll be sure to put a big scratch in it, Stinkenator."

"You do and you die, Spongebob Nerdpants," she tossed out.

Their mom walked into the room. "Both of you nerd herders better get going or you'll be late."

John laughed and kissed their mom on the cheek before he grabbed a jacket and headed toward Wendy's car.

Wendy grabbed her forgotten pom-pom bag and dashed out the front door to meet him. She had the top off the Prius—it was a warm fall evening, so the wind wouldn't bother either of them.

She climbed in, tossed her bag into the back, and clicked her seatbelt. John gave her a slightly irritated look. He turned the radio up and drove to the football game.

"After the game, meet me by the bleachers. We'll grab some ice cream with the girls," she said. Wendy frowned when John didn't immediately respond to getting ice cream with the cheer team. He should have, that was every boy's dream.

"What's your problem, John? You've been acting weird lately and only hanging out with your video game friends. I'm concerned. You need a social life outside of the living room."

He snapped back, "You're concerned for *me*? Wendy, you're the one with the problems."

"What do you mean?" she asked, her voice gaining an edge.

He gave her a sideways glance before looking back at the road. His shoulders tensed. "Your night terrors have gotten worse."

"What?"

He shrugged. "It's fine. I can sleep through almost anything, although it's upset Mom and Dad. They're scared you'll relapse, Wendy. They don't know what to do. I overheard them talking about another trial clinic."

Wendy was glad she wasn't driving, because her body went weak and tears formed at the overwhelming fear. "I'm not going back to that place, John, or any other clinic. Never again." She touched the back of her neck. All hospitals and clinics had the same effect on her. She'd go into hysterics and start hyperventilating, and—of course—to circumvent these fears, she had to go to more clinics for tests.

A stupid, vicious cycle.

She looked over at John and he nodded. "I didn't agree with them about sending you there, and I'm glad you're back. But you gotta know...they know. They're just trying to do what they think is best for you." His hands squeezed the wheel of the Prius. "Are you taking your meds to help?"

"No," she answered, waiting for his reprimand.

"Good. I'm not sure you needed them. I think this is something you have to work out for yourself, not try and suppress."

Her fingernails dug little nail impressions into the leather of the door handle. She was planning on going to the university next fall and escape everything. She loved her family and hated what she'd put them through. Wendy liked when everything was perfect and planned out, and now it was about to be ripped from her again.

She tried to change the subject, but John still wasn't in the mood. Something was definitely wrong, and it made her nervous. They pulled up and she hopped out of the car and ran to the field to warm up with the rest of her squad. Her best friend and captain Brittney gave her a cold stare as she walked up.

"Hey," Wendy said, out of breath.

"Hey." Brittney turned away.

Wendy's mood darkened at her best friend's chilled response. What was wrong with everyone today? Was it her? Had she done something wrong?

One of the newer cheerleaders came over and asked Wendy for help on a few dance moves, so she tried to push her worries aside. Tonight she needed to keep a smile on her face no matter how she felt inside.

The opposing team kicked off, and it began. The Timber Valley High School band played the school anthem and the crowd went wild. The game was intense. The Eagles were down at halftime, 14-7, and it looked like no matter how hard the boys played they would lose to their rival.

The cheerleaders turned toward the fans to get them pumped up when the school song played, but Wendy felt uncomfortable—like she was being watched again. Which was dumb considering she was jumping and screaming in front of hundreds of people. Of course she was being watched.

But that nagging feeling wouldn't go away.

Wendy scanned the crowd and noticed an older teen leaning on the railing by the stairs, eyeing her. He looked a little old to be a student, with unkempt reddish-brown hair that screamed to have a girl's hands run through it. He had a pensive look, brows furrowed, his hands clasped over the railing, but he was looking in her direction. He couldn't have worn more nondescript clothes. There wasn't a single label or design that could identify him as more than a passerby.

She made herself look somewhere else for a few minutes, but when she turned back, he was still standing there staring at her.

Wendy swallowed and smiled at the crowd, waving her poms in the air as she tried to watch him out of the side of her eye. He hadn't moved. They turned back to face the field, and Wendy could feel two holes burning into her back.

She glanced back over her shoulder again, and the mysterious watcher had moved. Now he was standing in front of the stairs on the other side of the fence. They locked eyes, his arms crossed over his chest and his face still frozen in a serious expression.

Wendy inhaled when the corner of his mouth crooked up in a smile and he nodded his head in acknowledgement to her. He was definitely watching her.

She didn't nod back but quickly turned away, ignoring him as she focused on the field. Still, she couldn't help but sneak a peek to see if he was still there. More importantly, was he still watching her?

"What's your problem?" Brittney hissed.

"Someone's staring at me. He's kind of creeping me out."

"Who?" Her friend turned to scan the crowd.

Wendy turned over her shoulder and tried to point him out to her friend but the spot he'd been standing in for the last quarter was empty. "He's not there…" Wendy trailed off and tried to find him among the milling fans.

"Maybe you imagined him." Brittney said sarcastically and flipped her ponytail over her shoulder. "Like you imagine everything else."

"No, I'm sure I didn…" Wendy trailed off but stopped in shock. She had shared her darkest struggle with Brittney, and now it was coming back to bite her.

She tried to ignore the sting and blink away the tears, and that's when she noticed something dark moving under the stands—opaque but ethereal. Her blood ran cold and her hands turned to ice.

No, not now. Wendy considered her options and tried to follow the thing she saw as it moved through the darkness.

She was terrified. Unexplainable shadows that flew through the night always seemed to be watching her, just on the periphery of her vision. Sometimes if she looked a certain way, they'd disappear completely.

Wendy's neck continued to turn as she watched the shadow move. She no longer cared about the game or its outcome. Something was wrong. This shadow was different. It wasn't like the ones she had seen before. It was bigger, darker, and it seemed more solid.

She should ignore it, return to focusing on her team and the game and pretend that she couldn't see the illusion, but something in her told her she needed to follow it.

"Pay attention, Wendy," Brittney chastised.

Wendy shook her head. "I'm sorry. Something's come up, I've got to go."

Brittney gave Wendy a panicked look and spoke through a fake smile. "You can't just leave with minutes left in the game. If you have to go to the restroom, you need to hold it."

Her attitude set Wendy off. "Oh, get over yourself, Brittney. I don't need to ask your permission to leave."

Brittney's eyes flared. "No, but we're the captains, and we set an example. How's it going to look if you take off before the end?"

"It's going to look like something came up, and I had to deal with it," Wendy snapped back. Tossing her poms to the side of the bench, she took off running for the field's exit gate. She didn't care what people thought; she needed to know once and for all if she was crazy.

She stepped under the bleachers and heard the roar of the fans above her as the other team fumbled. Screams and foot stomping ensued, and popcorn rained down on her. She ignored it and kept moving, stepping around garbage and bypassing numerous couples caught up in swapping gum.

She came to the edge of the bleachers and saw a smaller shadow, which seemed to be waiting for her.

Wendy slowed and crept to the corner of the school. She peeked around and spotted a lone teenage boy sneaking off to smoke a cigarette.

The shadow had a slightly human form. Its arm stretched and pointed toward the boy before disappearing. She rolled her eyes in disgust at what she began to chalk up to another one of her imaginary episodes. She was about to leave when she noticed a terrifying lizard-like monster crawling down from the side of the building. It was the largest creature she'd ever seen, but misshapen, its muscles bunched as if it were about to pounce.

It leapt onto the boy's back with a screech.

The terrified kid dropped his cigarette and grabbed at the air, choking and trying to scream—but all could hear was the beast's otherworldly cry. Never had her hallucinations seemed so real. And they'd definitely never had a physical effect on someone else.

"Stop!" Wendy shouted as she ran around the corner. She didn't know what possessed her to try and attack the beast, but she did. "Leave him alone."

She grabbed a rock and threw it at the monster's leathery back.

It turned, its eyes glowing in the night, and she stared at it. The monster's long snout opened and wailed in fury at her. Giant wings unfurled from its back, and it grabbed the boy by the shoulders and started to haul him up into the air and away from her.

"No, you don't!" Wendy jumped and caught the boy's pant leg and tried to pull him down.

"Don't let go of me!" the kid screamed. He looked up, terrified at the thing holding onto him. "What is it? What's got me?"

Wendy gritted her teeth and dug her heels into the ground, but it wasn't enough. Her feet were losing purchase, and they were being lifted as the beast furiously pumped its wings.

"Help," Wendy cried out. "Someone help."

Something or someone came crashing down from above. She saw a bright flash of light and heard a loud screech of pain. The boy and Wendy fell and landed on the grass in a tangle of limbs.

"Ouch! Get off me!" she cried as the scared teen flailed and punched at her. He was in flight mode, and she was taking the brunt of his attempt at getting away. She took an elbow to the cheek and saw stars.

"Get off her," a gruff voice threatened. One second the boy was there, then he went flying backward. She thought for sure it was the beast pulling him away again, but instead it was the guy from earlier. The creepy stalker with the melt-your-heart good-looking auburn hair.

He had the kid by the back of his jacket and shook him violently before tossing him to the ground.

Wendy scooted away from him, but he didn't notice. His eyes kept scanning the sky. "Who are you?" Wendy asked. "What do you want?"

"Now's not the best time for introductions," he laughed wryly. "It shifted back into the shadows. I don't know where it went." As he turned in a circle, something glinted in his hand. Was that a knife?

That was it, she wasn't going to stay and thank the guy. As she spun to bolt out of there, Wendy saw more movement behind her, so she ran in the opposite direction. The smoker-kid decided she had the right idea and took off running behind her.

Wendy heard the sound of someone cussing and feet rushing after them. She turned left and cut between the athletic building and the back of the lunchroom building, running as hard as she could toward the parking lot.

"Stop!" Stalker guy yelled behind her. "It's a trap."

Wendy skidded to a halt when an immense shadow emerged from a manhole in front of her. It didn't look like the smaller ones; this looked like the thing she'd seen under the bleacher. It morphed shapes! One second it was a giant shadow, the next an arachnid with legs flailing.

Wendy screamed.

The kid next to her said, "What?"

She threw up her arms to protect her face. Something grabbed her from behind—the flying dragon monster—and lifted her into the air just as the other monster lunged for her. *Two. There were two of the shadow beasts!*

The smoker kid gazed up at her, stunned. "Look, she's flying!"

The spider monster came up behind him and shot webbing at him, wrapping him in a filmy white cocoon. Wendy cringed. He'd just cried out and then nothing. The huge monster disappeared back into the manhole, and the dragon whisked Wendy across the parking lot.

"Nooo!" she twisted to see the beast that was carrying her. Glowing white eyes leaned toward her. Wendy scanned the parking lot and spotted a black Hummer rush toward them and come to a squealing stop. Soldiers in black uniforms with red skull patches on the arms piled out, brandishing rope.

A manhole near the Hummer pushed up from the ground. Rotating, it slid to the side, revealing a dark black hole. The spider beast squeezed its hairy body through, dragging the boy wrapped in the webbing after it.

The soldiers ambushed the shadow monster and it's prey by shooting the beast with a taser. Wendy heard a loud wail of pain from the beast, and it flopped over, it's legs contracting. They grabbed the convulsing monster and pried the boy from its grip.

Wendy thought they were helping, until the boy tried to wiggle free and the soldiers injected him in the neck. He went limp and they loaded him in the SUV.

The shadow monster carrying her quickly veered away from the Hummer and the painful cries of its companion. Wendy kicked and reached up in an attempt to scratch her captor.

A bright bolt of light emanating from the ground rushed her way, and Wendy felt the heat of it brush her cheek. And then she was falling thirty feet toward the cement.

Once again, a body broke her fall—the stalker's. Air rushed out of her lungs, and he fell to his knees under her weight. They rolled across the concrete parking lot, his back taking the brunt of the damage as he slammed into a tire of a pickup truck.

"Hey, you." His breath brushed across her cheek as he spoke. "Having fun yet?"

"It's a blast," she snapped and stared up into his green eyes, as deep as a forest. He saved her life again. Who was he? Her gaze came to rest on his lips. Why was she focused on his mouth?

"Then our next date will be even better...I promise." He looked down at her lips as well.

Her cheeks suddenly felt hot. "Better be."

He started to swim before her eyes, and the world became dizzy. She heard his worried intake of breath and heard him dial his phone. "Tink, I need backup. I got Red Skulls cutting me off—and a morphling."

Wendy heard the sound of bells and chimes, and then the strange boy scooped her up again. Her body hurt all over as her savior started to run, jarring her repeatedly. She forced her eyes open and saw his worried profile, just as the pounding of feet on pavement stopped. Her head fell back over his arm, and she watched the ground become distant.

Wendy hallucinated that she was flying.

-10-

"WHAT ARE WE GOING TO do with her, Peter?" Jax hissed as he paced back and forth on the tiled floor. "We just kidnapped a girl."

They had gotten the girl to a secure location, or as secure as an empty classroom could get, and she was currently passed out across a teacher's desk. Peter was glad Jax had been able to launch a light bomb and distract the Red Skulls long enough for him to escape with the blonde cheerleader. He'd been glad to see her—watch her around her friends—but she shouldn't have interfered with the morphling. She messed everything up and put herself on their radar.

Jax paced like a caged animal, and he kept glancing Peter's way. Peter knew that his second-in-command was good at taking orders, but he also knew Jax's temper would frequently get the better of him and he'd disappear for days to cool off. Tonight, in the heat of a moment like this, he needed Jax to have a clear head.

"We tie her up." Tink slid from the top of a desk onto the floor.

"We can't hold her against her will. Besides—because of her—we lost the morphlings," Jax said.

"Not exactly," Peter argued. "She actually got to the morphling before both of you. If I hadn't been there, they would both have been taken."

Tink walked over and looked at Wendy's unconscious body on the desk. "It doesn't make sense. How did she find the morphlings so fast? What's so special about her?" She tilted her head to the side and flicked the girl's cheek to see if she'd respond. She looked over at Peter, who stood by the classroom window and stared out into the darkness.

"She can see them." Peter ran his hand through his brown hair. "She can see the shadows, and she followed one to the boy. It was like it led her there. She didn't even hesitate when she attacked the morphling with a rock."

Tink looked up in shock. "Holy mother of *&%!" Her mouth moved, but all sound was covered by a loud ringing bell. "Those things are scary. She took it on without a brace?"

"That's so immature." Jax wrinkled his nose in distaste. "Control your mouth."

"You're immature." Tink stuck her tongue out.

Peter rubbed his hand on his chin, ignoring the squabbling between his best friends. "They've been getting more aggressive. They're not leaving much time in between attacks. And then the shadows' odd behavior toward the girl."

"They don't do that—ever. They watch. What's going on, Peter?" Tink asked.

"I don't know. We're going to have to double our watches and just try and stay one step ahead of them. But that leaves us with a problem: her."

"I volunteer to get rope and heavy rocks," Tink answered, raising her hand.

Peter shook his head and looked over at Jax, who was now studying the girl more closely. "She can't go home, it's not safe. Maybe one of the safe houses until we know what to do with her?" Jax offered.

"Finally a plan that makes sense." Peter let out some of the tension he had been holding.

"My plan made sense," Tink pouted.

Peter picked up his cell phone, hit speed dial, and waited for the voice.

"Hello?"

"Hey, we're going to be delayed getting back."

Wendy slowly came to. Hushed voices spoke nearby. She didn't know where she was or if she could trust the people who had her, so she pretended to still be unconscious.

A girl's voice came close, and then she felt a light flick on her cheek. It shocked her, and it took all of her control not to jump up and smack the ignorant girl. Listening in to what her saviors were discussing did not leave her a whole lot of hope. It sounded like they were going to try to keep her from going home.

Well, that wasn't going to happen. She needed to get home and away from these freaks.

"She's out cold, and bike or scooter won't do. We're going to need a car, Jax."

"I'm on it," he answered. "Do you want fast? I saw a nice Mustang in the parking lot."

"Nothing conspicuous."

"Minivan it is," Jax sighed before opening the door and heading to hotwire a car.

"Tink, I'm going to scan the area and look for more morphlings. We don't want any more surprises tonight. Wait here."

"But Pete—" She tried to argue, but he held out his hand to her.

"Wait. Here, give me your shadow box."

Tink pinched her lips and pulled out her mechanical box. She pulled up the antenna and handed it over.

"Jax will be back shortly, and when he is, load up the girl and get her to the safe house on Maple. I'll follow shortly behind." Peter looked back at her. "Thank you, Tink."

-11-

WENDY HEARD A DOOR open and close, and she assumed she was left with the girl they called Tink. The girl paced back and forth in the classroom and paused near Wendy's head, letting out a loud sigh. Her cell phone beeped, and she stepped out into the hall to speak.

Wendy immediately opened her eyes and studied her surroundings. The Science lab. She could only see the back of the girl's white-blonde hair through the pane of glass. She preferred to see the actual faces of the people who took her. Names weren't enough—Pete, Jax, and Tink.

Being careful not to make too much noise, she slid off the desk and crawled along the floor. They probably didn't know that this classroom actually connected to the next one through a door that looked like a coat closet. At one time it had been a bathroom and the two classes shared it, but that was eons ago. Now, only the sink and storage boxes remained.

Wendy tried the handle and suppressed a sigh of relief when it opened. She slipped into the room and closed the door after herself, locking it behind her. She made a careful path through the dark to the other side of the room, unlocked the door, and entered Mrs. Tillman's math classroom.

Most students didn't even know the old section of the school still had connecting doors. The newer wing was top of the line and very modern, but Wendy loved the architecture and hidden cubbies of the old wing, and now she was extremely grateful for them. Mrs. Tillman's room was the end classroom, so her door opened into a different hallway.

She opened the door and could hear the girl still speaking on the phone in the adjacent hall. Wendy slipped carefully away and entered the gym. Then she ran—across the basketball court, out past the lockers, and into the night.

The football game was over, and crowds of unrecognizable faces floated before her as she searched for her brother.

Her friends had already left, so Wendy ran to the parking lot. A stabbing pain pierced her vision, throbbed in her head. Where was John? She went back to the bleachers and blinked a few times. Her brother stood by her cheer bag, his hands in his pockets as he scanned the field of players and the surrounding crowd looking for her.

"John," Wendy cried. She almost collapsed when she got to him.

"Wendy, what happened?" He took hold of her elbows to support her.

"Home, get me home!" She knew she babbled on and on as her brother drove her home. She remembered vividly talking about the shadows and monsters coming for her. She cried, she shivered, and when her brother tried to touch her shoulder, she shrieked.

She closed her eyes to shut out the night—and she saw fire. Darkness and fire.

His foot hit the gas, and he drove like a madman up to their front door.

"Mom, Dad!" John left the car running in the driveway. He helped her down and hauled her inside.

His mom opened the door, and her face went pale at the sight of Wendy. "Is it happening again?"

John nodded as he pulled Wendy into the living room. She was scratched up, bruised across her arms, and it looked like she had a bit of a black eye. Mom gave Dad a searching look before going over to the nightstand and pulling out a white pamphlet with a crown and heart logo. She opened it, searching for a number.

John recognized the pamphlet, and knew his parents where sending her away. His heart dropped. His parents planned to betray not only Wendy, but him.

"Hello, um yes. I think it's time. Yes. You were right. It happened again. Just like you said it would. Tomorrow.

Yes, that will be fine. We'll be here...m-hm yes, she's okay." When she hung up the phone, Mom was in tears.

Dad gave her a quick squeeze around the shoulders. "You did the right thing, dear. They'll help Wendy. We can't anymore."

John ground his teeth angrily as he studied his sister. He disagreed. Sure, he didn't know how to help her, but he didn't believe sending her away was the solution either. He stormed up to his room and slammed the door, sending the pictures in the hallway swinging. He clicked on the Xbox and started playing. Soon his buddies logged on, and he relayed all his woes.

They helped him come up with a plan.

-12-

WENDY'S BEDROOM DOOR creaked open, and a tall figure came in. He loomed over her form on the bed, pressing his hand to her mouth. Her sleepy awareness turned into alertness as her eyes flew open and she tried to scream.

John flipped her lamp on. "Shh, it's me."

She squinted in pain and asked, "John, what's going on?"

He motioned for her to be quiet. At her dresser, he started to pull out clothes and shove them in her backpack. He paused when he got to her underwear drawer and looked over at her for help.

"Get out of there!" Wendy hissed. John rushed to her side and turned the light back off.

"Listen, Sis. You can't stay here."

"What do you mean? You'd better be joking."

He shook his head, his eyes wide in panic. "They're coming for you tomorrow morning. Mom made the phone call tonight."

Wendy sat up and clasped her brother's hands in fear. "I'm not going back. I swear I'm not insane. I'd rather die than go back."

"I won't let you, Wendy. Which is why you're running away...tonight."

Wendy didn't need any encouragement; she knew that—of the two of them—she was the one to make hasty and rash decisions, never John. He always thought everything through, and if he believed her only option was to run away, she wouldn't argue. She dressed quickly and took over the clothes packing.

"No, you can't take anything that's personal, and keep things tidy in your drawer. You can't make it look like you ran away on purpose. Keep them guessing. Which is why I packed my extra toothbrush, my outer jacket."

"Your jacket is too big," Wendy said as she reached for her sneakers.

"Here's all the cash I have on hand." He shoved the money into her hands, and Wendy tucked it into her pocket. "And you have to leave your phone."

"What? But how will I contact you?" Wendy had everything she needed in John's black backpack. She looked around her room. She really wanted to take a few photos or mementos, but she didn't have time. And he was right. She couldn't make it look like she planned this.

"You're heading here." John handed her a piece of paper. "Some of my gamer friends are going to meet you at the Pizza Parlor and help you. They'll keep in touch for you."

"You're kidding me. You're trusting my life to people you haven't even met in person? Don't tell me it's the crew I so easily distracted and got you all killed."

"Hey, that was a game. This is real life. I trust them, Wendy."

"Why can't I take the Prius?"

"GPS tracking—the police will find you in no time." He grabbed the bag out of Wendy's hands and stood beside her bedroom door, listening before opening it and going downstairs.

"You've really thought of everything haven't you, John?" Wendy's voice dropped as she reached up to give him a hug. His strong arms wrapped around her, and when they parted, both had tears in their eyes.

"No, if I'd thought of everything, I would have found a way to protect you." He looked down at his shoes.

"You did, you are." Wendy let the tears flow freely. They heard footsteps upstairs, and they both froze. A few seconds later, the toilet flushed and water ran. The steps retreated back toward her parents' bedroom.

They both stood staring at the ceiling, waiting for more sounds. Whoever it was might peek in to check on her.

After five minutes, they still hadn't, though. "I think it's time to go," Wendy whispered.

John nodded. "Be safe, Sis." He opened the door for her, and Wendy slipped into the night.

She turned at the end of their backyard and waved.

John held up his hand, fingers parted in the middle in tribute to one of his favorite shows. Live long and prosper.

Wendy whispered back. "I sure hope so."

She headed into the darkness, fear her only companion.

Wendy entered the dim parking lot of the Pizza Parlor. The glow of the red neon sign cast it's hue on the puddle she stepped through. Her fingers were chilled and she blew on them, then rubbed them together for warmth. The twenty-four-hour restaurant was the go-to place for famous deep dish pepperoni. College kids often congregated there for a late night food fix.

She stayed on the outskirts of the parking lot and stared at the people coming and going, studying them, trying to spot the contact person her brother had set up. She eyed the crumpled up piece of paper in her hand with the time written: 2 a.m. She had gotten here early. Her nerves had made her run faster than she ever thought possible.

She hated running.

It was fine, though. She needed time to scope out the place. A tan minivan pulled slowly into the parking lot and parked by the front door. Wendy ducked behind a silver SUV and watched as the side door opened and a blonde jumped out.

"Gah, I'm starving. I'm ordering a pizza to go," she said.

The dark-haired driver didn't react. He shoved his hands into his leather jacket and leaned against the van. "We can't stay here long."

The girl grabbed his jacket and yanked him toward the restaurant. "Come on Jax, I need you to pay."

They looked like they could be the group she was meeting. Wendy was about to step out from the darkness when the third person hopped out of the passenger-side door and slammed it. He ran his hands through his auburn hair.

No! It couldn't be. What were the chances? Stalker boy was here. She checked her watch and glanced back at the restaurant. The boy with the auburn hair leaned against the wall by the front door.

"Do you want anything Peter?" The girl asked.

"No Tink. I'm fine," he said.

Tink. Peter. Jax.

What were the chances that she'd hear those names twice in one night?

Saviors or kidnappers. She wasn't sure how to label them, but they were here in person. There was no way she could enter the restaurant now. She'd have to wait them out before she could look for John's gamer friends.

Tired of standing in one spot, she stepped over the curb. Her shoe accidentally kicked a rock and it scattered across the parking lot.

He moved away from the wall and looked in her direction. "Hello?" his voice drifted across the lot.

Wendy held her breath and peeked out from behind the car. He might be staring in her direction, but it didn't look like he could see her. His head kept panning back and forth, eyes squinting.

A shadow separated itself from beneath a nearby car and moved across the lot, drawing her attention. Her heartbeat drummed so loudly she couldn't sort out whether it was caused by another car pulling out of a spot or something else.

She didn't know what to believe anymore. She was wound tighter than any spring, and her muscles were stiffening from holding still for so long.

The shadow whipped out from behind a car and flew across the parking lot right toward her. *Eep!* She glanced toward the restaurant, and the boy was gone.

No way she would wait. This was no hallucination. She sprinted into the darkness. Away from the safety of the lit parking lot, away from the haven her brother's gamer friends offered, and away from the dangerous stranger.

-13-

SHE'D MADE A MISTAKE. She had to go back home. Being alone all night, sitting on a park bench freezing, was not her idea of the free-moving life of a runaway. It was nothing like the movies. At first light, she had made her way back to her neighborhood, and was about to turn onto her street when she saw the white medical van with a rose and heart logo parked in her driveway.

"No, not them!" Wendy whispered. Her mouth went dry and her skin prickled in fear. It was the psychiatric clinic for teens she was sent to last summer, when her nightmares and visions were becoming uncontrollable.

Wonderland.

The front door of her house opened, and she ducked behind the neighbor's hedges as the medical personnel stepped back onto the front stoop.

Mary stood at the door, rubbing her arms and crying. "I don't know where she is. How could she have run away?

"Are you sure she didn't know we were coming?" The female medic asked.

Mary and George gave each other a searching look. "No, we don't think she did, but maybe..." George's voice trailed off and he looked inside.

Wendy observed a curtain move upstairs as John looked out the bedroom window and watched the exchange on the front porch.

"But you helped her last summer. I thought for sure that she'd understand that this was for the best," Mary said.

"Well we did suggest that her time be extended," the medic responded firmly. "She could have really used a few more months at our facility, we could have tapped in, studied her psyche more, and found the source of her problems." She flipped closed the file. "We have here that you signed her out before her study was finished."

"Well that was because she only needed help keeping the nightmares away, we didn't need a full evaluation. And the medicine you gave us seemed to work. We felt that she could recover better surrounded by friends and family."

"Obviously, you changed your mind," the male medic said. "Otherwise you wouldn't have called us back. I do hope that you will consider admitting Wendy for the full course of our program when she comes home. We promise we can make the nightmares and visions stop for good, if you would let our staff and caregivers at Wonderland have full control."

Mary nodded slowly. She turned to cry into George's shoulder.

"We will consider your advice." George said, rubbing Mary's back.

"Well, hindsight is twenty-twenty," the female answered. She held out a white business card. "If you need to reach us again."

George nodded. "We have your card." His voice was firm.

The psychiatric clinic personnel climbed into the white van.

Wendy's stomach churned as she listened to everything that had transpired.

The van's engine roared to life and pulled out of her driveway. She ducked behind the bushes again as the van passed by her.

Her hands were shaking. Her heart was pounding in her chest.

She couldn't go back home.

John was right. Her parents thought they were helping and trying to do what was best. They wouldn't believe her if she told them the things she saw there.

Her heart broke when her parents turned and closed the front door. When the van turned the corner and drove out of site, she stood up. She pulled up her jacket hood to cover her blonde hair and walked at a brisk pace away from home. She steeled her heart, put on imaginary armor, and mentally said her goodbye to her family.

Wendy was sure—she'd never get to walk through the front doors of her home again. Not just any home. The only home she remembered.

-14-

WENDY STARED AT THE bookstore with the brightly painted red door. Situated in the downtown area, the new and used book shop occupied the first two stories of the red brick building. The other four floors were being rented out as apartments. A small plastic *Open* sign hung in the window next to a display table full of children's fairytale books.

The last few days had been a daze. She couldn't bring herself to leave the area, leave her family. But she was running out of money and needed to find a way to keep going. She couldn't afford any more cheap hotels. The headaches hadn't eased up, but she'd suffer through them any day if it meant she wouldn't go back to the clinic.

She stood with the newspaper ad in her hand and scrutinized it one more time.

P/T Help Wanted
Bernard Books
1412 Main St.
Apply in person between 2-4pm.

Wendy looked over her shoulder at the stone clock tower in the park. 1:50. Well, it was always better to arrive early to an open interview. Most of the full-time jobs had been filled months ago, and this was the only part-time job even remotely interesting.

Wendy opened the front door, and bells, attached to a leather strap, jingled softly above her head. She closed her eyes, took a deep breath, and sighed happily. There was no greater smell than that of books...and the older the books the better the smell. Other people might cringe at the slightly musty odor and the dust, but not her. It filled her with a sense of belonging. Wendy knew she was home.

Then she opened her eyes and noticed the number of people already there. At least three other people stood waiting or asking the man at the checkout desk questions about the job. The door jangled again, and two more girls entered and walked up to the desk—one with red hair so bright it obviously came from a box, the other with a loose brown braid. "We're here for the job interview," they said almost in unison.

The clerk wearing his black apron with a giant Saint Bernard logo on the front held up his hands and said. "Okay, okay. Quiet down, everyone." The man scratched his head. "Well, a lot more of you showed up for the job than I originally expected. I'm happy that so many of you are interested."

Wendy heard the dark-haired girl comment under her breath to her friend. "Yeah, so excited that all of the good jobs in this pathetic town were already taken."

The redhead nodded in agreement. "It also smells funny in here."

"I'm Mr. Bernard, the owner," the man continued, oblivious to the girls' snide remarks. He looked to be in his late fifties, with peppered gray and white hair and a thick mustache that lined his small upper lip. It was obvious that large crowds made him uncomfortable, and he wasn't sure what to do with the group of slightly desperate potential employees.

"Ah, I know." He clapped his hands together and his face beamed. "If you brought a résumé, put it here, and I'll start with those and interview you each one by one.

Wendy's stomach dropped as four in the room surged forward to put their résumés on the counter. She didn't think she'd needed one for a part-time job.

Mr. Bernard looked over the rest of the waiting group, and he reached underneath the counter and pulled out a pad of tear off employee applications. "The rest of you, take a moment and fill this out, please."

The pad went around the room. As soon as people got their forms, they retreated to a chair or a table and began working on the form.

Wendy tore off the white paper and took an empty seat next to the two girls who had come in after her. She watched as they pulled pens out of their purses and started filling in blanks. Name, address, education. Their heads bobbed, and they giggled and talked softly between them.

"Do you think he would hire us both?" the girl with dyed red hair asked her friend.

Wendy picked up a discarded golf pencil from a bin by the register and began to fill out the form.

First Name: Wendy

Last Name:

She stopped and felt that familiar plummeting in her stomach. This was never going to work. They'd find out who she was for sure if she wrote in her real name. Her breathing had quickened, and her grip on the pencil intensified until she snapped the tip and left a small rip in the application.

The two female heads at the end of the table turned to look at her, and Wendy mumbled an apology.

Last name. Okay, if she couldn't write Owens, she'd have to make one up. Her eyes scanned the bookstore, and her eyes came to rest on the small plug-in teapot and the green box of Darjeeling next to it.

Wendy Green? No. Darling—her mom always called her that anyway. So it wasn't a total lie.

Her hand automatically entered in Darling as her last name.

When it came to her current address, she stopped again. She didn't know how to proceed. She moved down to her education, hesitated, and finally wrote in a rival school, not Timber Valley.

Wendy heard the frenzied scratching of the girls' pens on paper, and her heart stuttered. There was no way she would get the job. She needed to stop fooling herself. But just to give herself something to do, for home address, she wrote Kinderly Park.

Mr. Bernard picked up the first application that was turned in and called the person over to a side table for a small one-on-one interview. Heat rushed to her cheeks. She folded the application in half twice, stuffed it into her brother's green jacket, and walked to the back of the store, hoping for a quiet place to wait until nightfall. This was stupid. How could she have thought she'd get a job with no address?

Wendy wasn't surprised when she found herself in the children's section surrounded by kiddie tables, large stuffed animals, bean bags, a small puppet theater, a reading stage with a curtain, and a large rocking chair.

Overwhelmed and exhausted, she sat in the blue bean-bag chair and folded her hands across her chest.

A soft huff to her left made her start. What she had originally thought was a large stuffed animal was actually a real life St. Bernard lounging across the stairs. The dog noticed Wendy and made another huffing noise before it crawled forward and placed its large square head on her lap, begging for attention.

"Oh, what a sweetie," Wendy cooed softly as she began to rub the dog gently behind the ears. The dog butted its head against her hand when she stopped her scratching. "Yes, I see that you're a bit spoiled, too."

This time when Wendy stopped scratching the dog, it proceeded to crawl across her lap until she was nearly covered. The dog was very heavy, but she enjoyed being surrounded by its warmth. Wendy saw the glimpse of gold and reached for the tag to read the dog's name.

Nana.

"Oh, so you're a girl? Doesn't surprise me one bit. I think you're a lovely, sweet-tempered girl." They sat like that, curled in a bean bag chair, hidden in the children's section, and Wendy thought this was the best day she'd had in a long time. She felt safe and warm and soon became lost in her thoughts.

Wendy counted the times the door jingled as it opened and closed and figured almost everyone had already left, but she had no desire to abandon the bookstore just yet. "Do you like stories, Nana?"

The dog's ears rose slightly. Wendy wondered if that was because she had stopped her petting.

"Well, I think you are in for a doozy." Wendy curled up and slowly and softly told one of the wildest tales she'd ever told. It was true she didn't know how much of her tale was true and how much was false, since it was based on her nightmares. But it felt nice to tell someone everything.

"And then the dark shadow flew into the young girl's room through the window. It stood over her bed and reached for her."

A soft cough interrupted her story. Wendy tried her best to turn to the person, but the weight of the large St. Bernard proved an impediment.

A young man leaned against one of the old wooden columns that supported the upper floor. Her heartbeat quickened at the sight of Peter. His tousled brown hair had hints of red. His eyes were a deep, mischievous green that twinkled with silent laughter as she struggled beneath the dog. He wasn't moving toward her or threatening her, so she decided it was best to play it cool, not let on that she recognized him as the one who saved her from the monster.

"She's quite taken with you." He chuckled softly, gesturing to Nana.

"Well, the feeling is mutual," she replied, watching him carefully.

"Didn't you come in for the job? I think everyone has already had their interview. You're up."

Wendy looked away and tried to deny it. Her cheeks flushed in embarrassment. "No, I'm not here for the job," she lied. "I, uh, came here to be a dog bed."

He scooped up the folded paper that had fallen out of her pocket and that now lay out of reach on the floor. One of his auburn eyebrows rose in skepticism.

His eyes scanned the paper, and they lit up at something he saw. "So, Wendy, you're not interested in the part-time job?" He waved the paper in front of her and she reached out and tried to snatch it away.

He laughed and continued reading. But then disappointment marred his expression, and her stomach turned. It was obvious he was a bit displeased by her lack of answers. He folded up her application and shoved it in his pocket.

Why would he do that?

Nana chose that moment to yawn and butt her head against Wendy's chest.

"Oof." Wendy responded when the head butt hit her a little too hard.

"I think she wants you to continue your story."

"No, that's okay. Maybe next time." Wendy tried to sit up, but the dog refused to budge so she just sank farther into the beanbag.

"Well, if you won't continue for her, maybe you'd do it for me," he said gently. "I like stories. Especially ones told by beautiful girls."

Peter's smile disarmed her and made her feel at ease in his presence. Nana seemed to like him, anyway. Her tail wagged when she looked up at him. And she was obviously a good judge of character. "Um, okay." Wendy blushed and tucked a strand of her strawberry blonde hair behind her ear and tried to pick up where she had left off. But she couldn't remember.

"So, once upon a time..."

"No. Not that one." Peter frowned and kneeled next to her. He reached out to bury his hand in Nana's soft dark fur and began to scratch. "The other one." His deep green eyes lifted up and met hers over the dog's head, and her breath caught.

"I don't remember where I was."

He glanced down at her lips quickly before looking back up and she felt herself trapped. Trapped under a dog and trapped with his gaze. His eyes searched hers, and he nodded his head encouragingly. "The shadow. The shadow had reached for you and..."

"No, not me. The girl," Wendy corrected. "It is a story after all. The shadow reached for the girl." But the way he changed that one word made her extremely nervous. She didn't want to finish the story. She wanted to escape the mesmerizing gaze of Peter and run away.

She tried to push Nana off, but the dog refused to budge.

Peter pinched his lips and made a soft commanding whistle. Nana's ears perked up, and she moved over to sit by his feet.

"So now...about the ending of my story. The shadow reached for her and..." he trailed off, offering her help up out of the sunken bean bag.

Wendy took his hand and he pulled her up until they were nose to nose. He didn't release her hands immediately. She had to pull away—gently though. She didn't fear *him*. Honestly, it was weird how safe she felt with him near, when she should be running away. She idly brushed off the dog's hair from her pants as she tried to regain her thoughts.

"The shadow?" he coaxed.

She usually spun her stories differently, always promising a happy ending, so she was going to give herself one here as well. "The shadow promised freedom, adventure, and love...if she'd but take his hand and fly away from there."

"Away from where?" His eyes narrowed as he stepped closer.

She inhaled and released the answer in a whisper. "Never mind, it's just a story."

He frowned before turning away from her and stalking over toward the counter. Had he been angry? Why? It *was* just a stupid story. He was the one who wanted her to finish the ending. Now she just felt embarrassed. She yanked up her backpack and slung it over her shoulder, heading toward the exit.

All of the interviewees had left, and the bookstore was empty. Mr. Bernard, the owner, was looking at the stack of papers and notes in front of him, still overwhelmed, from the look of it. Peter was leaning over whispering to him.

Her stomach dropped, as doubt filled her mind at what she saw. What was he telling the owner? Was he telling him not to hire her? Was it because her stories were a little odd? That she was odd?

He pointed in her direction and the owner gave her a surprised look. Yeah, he probably was. Wendy gripped her pack tighter and opened the door.

"Hey!" Peter yelled, but the door slammed and its jingling bell cut him off.

Wendy kept a brisk pace away from the shop, head low. Infuriated tears formed in the corner of her eyes, but she held them back. She heard the bookstore door jangle open down the block accompanied by another shout of her name. Without missing a beat, she ducked into the closest shop, which happened to be a secondhand boutique. She moved behind a rack of clothes and watched out the window as he ran down the sidewalk searching for her. Wendy gritted her teeth in frustration, because as much as she loved that store, she couldn't see herself going back.

Especially if he was there.

-15-

WENDY SPENT THE REST of the day looking over her shoulder. She wandered the park and stared at the displays in the windows until the stores closed for the evening, desperately wishing that the bookstore wasn't so close to her stomping grounds. Her stomach growled angrily, but she ignored it. She'd learned already that if she drank enough water from the public fountain, the pang would eventually subside. She was used to being hungry now. Just like she was used to being cold at night and stifling hot during the day.

She sat on a park bench and watched the bookstore. She never saw Peter return, which meant he could be anywhere in the city. She didn't like not knowing where he was—hopefully she could avoid him until she gathered enough money to move somewhere else. But that thought saddened her.

When the sky began to hint at nightfall she approached the hotdog vendor. He had been nice the last time she'd spoken with him, and hopefully he was feeling generous again.

"Hi." Wendy waved and shifted the weight of her backpack on her shoulder.

The aging African man smiled brightly at her. "Ah, I wondered if you'd come tonight. I saw you sitting over there." He pointed toward the park bench near the fountain and then wiped his hands on his red apron, winking at her.

"Need help?" she asked.

"Of course."

Wendy put her arm through the other strap of her backpack. She collapsed his red and white portable umbrella, and tucked it under her arm. She grabbed the white folding chair with her free hand.

She followed the hot dog vendor as he pushed his small wheeled cart out of the park and helped him load it into a nearby pickup.

"Ah, you sure know how to help an old man. What can I give you as payment—maybe the same as before?"

"Yes, please. If it's not too much trouble." Her stomach chose that moment to growl again, and the hot dog vendor laughed.

"Oh, it's no trouble at all. I can't sell my leftovers, so it works out wonderfully." He leaned over, opened up the lid of his cart, pulled out his tongs, and put together three all-beef hotdogs in silver foil for her. "Here you are, Miss Wendy." He handed her the dogs. "I hope to see you again."

Wendy couldn't wait. She opened up the hotdog and took a large bite. She smiled with a mouthful of food. "You will, Mr. Louie."

"Not Mister—just Louie. Remember?"

Wendy smiled again and nodded. "Okay. Thank you, Louie."

She turned to walk back to her bench, and he called out after her. "You take care of yourself, Wendy girl. Strange things happen around here after dark."

She shuddered but gave him a wave and headed back to the park. Oh, how she knew of the strange things that happened. But where could she go?

Wendy savored the first hotdog before diving into the second one. She wrapped the third in the two extra sheets of foil and tucked it into her jacket pocket for breakfast. This had been her way of surviving. Not stealing, just helping the locals and earning the things she would need.

While she helped Louie, the streetlights had kicked on, creating well-lit areas surrounded by shadows. Wendy picked up her pace as she headed past the fountain in the middle of the park.

The cold burned her lungs, but she made it to the fountain and her bench—directly under the lamppost. This bench boasted more lamplight than any other. She slowed as she stepped into the halo of light and let out a sigh of relief.

Wendy sat and pulled up her knees. Sleeping a full night wasn't safe. Catnaps during the day helped her stay awake during the night.

The clock over city hall chimed midnight, and Wendy stared off into the night, looking, searching for the shadows she knew to be out there—not the simple darkness everyone else feared, but the shadows that hunted—beyond her circle of light.

At first she thought she was imagining them, but she wasn't.

Wendy shifted her grip on the pocket knife, and try as she did to keep it away, the fear came flooding back.

-16-

SOMETHING MOVED IN THE darkness. It made no sound, but Wendy knew better. Just because you couldn't hear it, doesn't mean it's not there. A shadow emerged from a copse of trees.

Wendy froze, staring at the spot until her eyes burned from her unwillingness to blink.

There.

The shadow shifted, now distinguishable from the darkness of the trees. It was moving toward her.

"Go away. I don't see you. I can't see you. You're not real."

Her suddenly dry tongue stuck to the top of her mouth. She gulped and tried to swallow her terror. Her hands shook as she gripped the pocket knife and her flashlight.

The shadow slid along the ground, no solid form above it as it picked up speed and raced from a tree shadow to a bush shadow. From one patch of ground to another, the shadow played hopscotch until it neared the edge of her saving light. What kind of shadow was this one? Would it be one of the smaller ones that tended to tail her and follow her, or would this one morph into a monster like the one she'd seen eat the boy?

At the slight beeping noise, Wendy whipped out her flashlight and waved its beam along the ground in the direction of the shadow. But no flashlight would deter the ghostly predator tonight.

The beeping noise grew louder, faster, almost matching her pulse.

She stood with the flashlight in one hand and her knife in the other.

It was coming for her!

Just when the shadow was about to step into her circle of light, a hand gripped her elbow. She screamed, slashing behind her with her knife.

Her knife hand made contact with something solid. Cloth ripped.

"What the—!" a male voice cried out. Her assailant quickly let go of her arm.

Wendy saw two people behind her. The young man had on dark jeans and wore a black hoodie jacket. He held his hands up in the air and smirked, shaking his dark auburn hair out of his amazingly green eyes.

"You!" Wendy accused.

The petite girl next to him—blonde hair piled on her head in a messy bun—let out a stream of mild expletives in alarm at Wendy's knife. The watch on her wrist seemed to censor her words, chiming loudly like a bell. "Watch what you're doing! We're here to help you, you big oaf."

The girl from the lab. This was the first time Wendy had seen her face. She was beautiful—petite with small features. A pair of custom-looking mechanic goggles rested on her head, framing blue eyes, now lit with fury.

"Tink, calm down." Pete said.

"Peter, you tell me to calm down, when she practically tried to slice you in two? I say we leave her here. She's more trouble than she's worth." Tink's voice rose in pitch with every syllable.

"We startled her, Tink, that's all. It was only self-defense…right?" He looked up at Wendy. He held himself at a safe distance and cupped his hand around his forearm, pressing on the cut. He chuckled, but his eyes only briefly made contact with her before glancing beyond her, scanning the darkness. She watched him step farther into the circle of light.

The device in Tink's hands beeped louder the closer it came to Wendy.

Wendy made a motion as if to knock it to the ground, and Tink moved the device away. The beeping slowed.

Wendy turned to address Peter. "Why do you keep following me? What are you doing here?" Her hand still held the knife, but now she kept it low, by her thigh.

"I'm scaring pretty girls in the park in the middle of the night." He flashed her a charming grin.

"Oh, stop flirting, Peter!" Tink turned her beeping device in Wendy's direction again. "We could ask you the same thing. What are you doing here in the middle of the night?" She gestured to the bench and Wendy's knife.

"I, uh. I…" She turned to search for the shadow, but it had disappeared. Or it had retreated into another shadow. Either way, it wasn't moving toward her anymore. She felt tired, so tired of hiding and running and pretending to be someone she wasn't that she tried to shock them with the truth. "I live here."

"Well, then you should come with us." He smiled.

The words shocked her, but the sight of another shadow moving over his shoulder made her desperately want to trust the boy in front of her.

"I don't even know you," she whispered. "You're strangers. You saved me from that thing—and then you tried to kidnap me. I overheard what you were going to do. You were going to take me away."

"Tried is the key word here," Tink said. Peter shot her angry look, but she continued. "You're right. He could be some kind of crazed psycho killer trying to lure you away to your untimely death," Tink spat out. "But no, not Peter. Peter would never do that. Me, on the other hand..." she let the sentence drag. Tink fidgeted with her remote, and it continued to beep faster the closer the antenna came to Wendy's body.

"Stop it!" Wendy commanded, shoving the antenna away from her.

Tink ignored her and nodded at Peter with a one-shouldered shrug.

"I hate to admit you're right, but she shouldn't be left alone." She glanced around Wendy into the park and her face went white. Her voice dropped, and she mumbled something under her breath, but it was hidden by the sound of chiming bells.

A loud growl came from somewhere behind them in the darkness, and Wendy immediately imagined another monster coming out of the ground to get her.

Tink looked like she really wanted to leave, and she casually looked at her watch and noted the time. "Uh hey, yeah we need to run, if we want to make it in time."

Wendy bit her lip and heard a loud branch snap in the distance. She gasped.

"Peter. My name's Peter. Nice to meet you." The boy rushed out, offering his hand to her. "And Wendy, you need to trust me. Come with us...now."

She stared at that open palm and felt a moment of déjà vu. Somehow she knew she needed to grasp that hand or she'd regret it.

She thrust her palm into his hand and felt him grip it tightly as he pulled her off the bench, out of the protective beam of light, and into the night.

Tink clicked off her device and tucked it into her bag before following them. Peter and Wendy ran hand-in-hand through the park.

Once, Tink stopped. Wendy looked back and saw her pull out a silver ball that looked like a grenade. She pulled the pin and tossed it into the spot they'd just run from. A few seconds later, a flash of light illuminated the night. It flickered awhile, and they heard pained screaming.

When they neared the road, Peter let go of Wendy's hand, jumped deftly over a park bench, then turned and slid across the hood of a car. She was in awe of his ability to practically fly over any obstacles in his way.

Instead of weaving around a fire hydrant like she did, he jumped up and over it.

His dare-devil antics continued and he ran in front of an oncoming city bus. Just as the bus slowed to a halt, he was at the door, tapping at it impatiently, before the driver got the doors opened.

The driver yelled at Peter to back off, then pulled the lever and opened the doors with a hissing sound.

Peter grabbed Wendy's elbow and ushered her in before him. He swiped his bus pass for three fares just as Tink leapt onto the first step.

"Step on it, buster," Tink barked. Grabbing the handle, she closed the bus doors behind her.

The driver shot her a disbelieving stare, but she shrugged it off and marched to the back, muttering under her breath. More loud bells rang.

Wendy sat at what she thought was a safe distance across from Peter and Tink and studied them both. They were an odd pair—one tall and dark, the other short and fair. One relaxed and mellow, the other uptight and cranky. Then you throw a young, tired and confused runaway into the mix. What a bunch of vagabonds.

"So Wen-ndy…" Peter drawled her name. His eyes seemed to twinkle, and her heart fluttered. Oh, this was so not good.

"Pe-e-ter…" She answered back in similar fashion and waited.

Tink, clearly a bit peeved, spoke up and drawled out her own name. "Ti-i-i-nk."

Wendy started laughing. The girl was adorably rude. Wendy relaxed as they continued riding the bus toward the outskirts of town.

"So—" Peter continued. "You're welcome." He stretched his long legs out in front of him and crossed his arms behind his head. He grinned.

"For what?" Wendy asked, irritated at his attitude.

"For saving your life."

"When?"

"Just now."

"But you didn't do anything." She lowered her eyes, unable to bring up what she had seen before, from that other night—when his saving her life had been obvious. She wasn't ready to tread there, to the monster she saw. What if her sanity came into question? She sat back in her seat and stared out the bus window, watching as the streets passed by in a whirlwind of lights.

"Doesn't matter, just so long as you know." He leaned back and watched her through lowered lids while Tink pulled another odd gadget out of her backpack and opened the back. She seemed to be making some adjustments. She stopped abruptly and pulled out a bag of Skittles.

"What's that beeping box?" Wendy gestured to Tink.

Tink pulled out the green apple-flavored Skittles and handed them over to Peter, a few at a time. He gladly took the offending candy. "Oh that? That's my psycho detector," Tink said between mouthfuls. "And you totally made it go off the charts." She twirled her finger around her temple and rolled her eyes. "Cuckoo."

"Tink," Peter said her name with more than a hint of warning.

"Excuse me?" Wendy's temper went through the roof. "You're the one dressed like a mechanical circus freak."

Tink flashed a smile at Wendy, wiggling her eyebrows in response. "Why, thank you."

"Girls," Peter cried out in exasperation.

Wendy crossed her arms and glared at Tink. She didn't know how she'd offended the blonde. She wasn't sure she could convince the petite girl to like her—ever.

Wendy's head started to throb, and she pulled her knees to her chest. She pressed, rubbed her temples with both hands. *Please not now.* Pain, accompanied by flashes of white, pulsed in her skull. The headaches had come back with a vendetta ever since—since the night of the shadow beasts at the football game.

Peter watched her carefully, his brows furrowing with worry. "Are you okay?"

"Yeah, I've just got a headache."

Peter shot Tink a look, and she shrugged her shoulders, crumpling up the red candy bag into her pocket. "Do you get those often?" he asked.

"Monthly, I bet." Tink snickered before wilting under Peter's ugly glare.

"A lot lately," Wendy answered.

"Maybe it's a tumor?" Tink popped up cheerily. When no one laughed, she sulked in her seat.

Deciding to ignore Tink, Wendy asked, "Where are we going?"

"We're going to take you to a refuge for tonight. Then tomorrow, we'd like to talk to you about your living arrangements."

-17-

PETER TURNED DOWN A crowded backstreet, rank with the smell of garbage and urine. Wendy paused. She knew better than to follow handsome young men down dark alleys.

He pushed a large dumpster over to the side of a building, climbed on top, and gestured for her to watch. A fire escape ladder hung way above his head. Even on top of the dumpster there was no possible way for Peter to make that jump. Peter stood on the edge of the dumpster, ran toward the building, leapt into the air, and propelled himself off of the brick wall, turning midair to catch the bottom rung of the ladder. He grinned widely at her as the ladder slid down.

"My lady," he called out to her. She found herself grinning and running toward him. He pulled her up onto the dumpster. When she reached for the ladder, her foot slipped. Peter caught her, his arm tight around her waist.

She blushed and apologized as she regained her footing.

Tink spoke, but angry bells covered her words.

When Peter's arms left Wendy, the bells stopped.

"How did you do that?" She reached for the ladder again.

"Do what?" He shrugged.

"Well, practically fly to grab the fire escape, for one."

Tink called up to them from the ground. "It's parkour, you @%#." The bell noise covered her expletive.

"What's that noise whenever she talks?" Wendy asked Peter.

Tink speared Wendy with a glare from the ground and turned her back, mumbling under her breath, walking in circles. The tinkling bell noise continued, covering her words.

Peter laughed. "Oh, that's her censor band. Her own invention. Tink is working on her temper. The band monitors her vitals and can tell whenever she's about to lose it. Whenever she cusses, it matches her pitch with a bell tone in the same decibel."

"Oh, that's funny!" Wendy laughed at Tink, until loud chiming drowned it out. Then, she quickly changed her tune. "I mean that's...um...horrible?" The bell chimes got even more aggressive. Wendy had to cover her mouth with her hand.

Peter grinned. "It's okay. It is funny, but she's determined to correct this bad habit and become a lady." Peter pulled the ladder back up after him and followed her up the steps.

"Is she not coming up?" Wendy asked. Tink walked to the end of the alley, pulled out her remote box, and extended the antenna. Peter joined Wendy, pausing next to a window on the top floor. "No, Tink is terrified of heights.

She's actually terrified of a lot of things, but she tries to hide it behind her tough-girl attitude. Really though, deep down she's a sweet girl. I think you'll like her."

Wendy doubted that. She listened to the way he spoke about his blonde companion and felt certain there was something more between them. He wasn't going to elaborate on their relationship, and now wasn't the time to press.

Besides, even if he felt safe and familiar to Wendy somehow, the truth was they were practically strangers.

He slid open a window, pushed the paisley curtain to the side and disappeared into the darkness. "But about the um…parkour, as Tink said. I can teach you if you want."

"I think I'll pass." She stared into the window with trepidation. What was behind the curtain?

Peter leaned back out and grinned at her. "You coming? Or are you going to sleep on the fire escape?"

"Depends." She sat back down on the step, keeping a safe distance from the window. "What's in there?"

"Someplace safe." A light clicked on, and he pulled the curtain open so she could see into a small attic.

A crash made her jump and peer below. A cat yowled and darted out of the alley. Wendy jumped through the window into the small room and closed it behind her, locking it for good measure.

The attic, with its slanted walls and rough wooden support columns, felt surprisingly cozy for its size. Outdated wallpaper, a tattered futon, and a mismatched table and chairs were the only décor. A couple of old trunks, which had seen better days, stood stacked in a corner.

Wendy paused, taking it all in, while Peter immediately relaxed and pulled out a chair to sit in. Kicking both feet up on the table, he leaned back dangerously.

"Make yourself at home, Wendy." Peter stretched his arms wide, before folding them behind his head and grinning.

She had a flash of déjà vu when he smiled at her, and her head pounded suddenly. Unsettled, she rubbed her arms and moved over to sit on the futon across the room. "Why?" She narrowed her eyes, studying him.

The front chair legs touched the floor as he leaned her direction. "Why what?" His voice was soft, gentle.

"Why did you bring me here?" He'd been kind tonight, but too recently, he and his friends had held her in the science lab. Trust wouldn't come easy.

Peter folded his hands in his lap, looked down, and took a deep breath. "I don't know. You just looked like you could use an act of kindness."

That wasn't the answer she expected, and it left her momentarily speechless. Her mind ran through possibilities that left a crater of doubt. "You were following me," she accused.

His shoulders twitched, confirming her suspicions.

How dumb was she? She'd just locked herself in an attic with someone who had been stalking her, who'd charmed her into following him into a dark alley and would now keep her prisoner.

He looked up, his green eyes accusing her just as fiercely. "Why can you see the shadows?"

"I don't. I can't," Wendy choked out. "I mean, everybody can see shadows. Don't be stupid."

He smiled wryly. "Not the shadows you and I see. You know what I mean. And you were terrified of them tonight—ready to faint. Until I showed up.

"Them?" She repeated.

"It. Well…" Peter stumbled over his words. "Well, the shadows to be exact."

"Is that what I saw at the school?" she challenged.

"No, that thing was a morphling. Way more dangerous. They're hunters. The smaller shadows—are the seekers. For some reason, you keep showing up right in the middle of where they appear. But I think you'll be safe here for the night, and I know you need rest, so I'll go. We can talk more later." He stood.

"Go? Go where?" She panicked. Sure, she'd considered him her captor moments before, but that was when she thought he was going to imprison her. Now he was abandoning her, a lifeline quickly floating out of her reach.

Peter smiled reassuringly at her. "I'll just be outside." He popped his thumb out gesturing to the window. "Standing guard." He grabbed his leather jacket off the chair and left.

She stifled a sigh of relief as she stood to follow him. She still had to be sure. "Standing guard," Wendy spoke softly and leaned out the window after him, "or keeping me prisoner."

Peter leaned in close, and she caught a pleasant whiff of his aftershave. A small dimple appeared in his cheek, and she swallowed nervously. "No, Wendy, you've got it backwards. You've already captured me."

She knew he was teasing, trying to calm her fears, but the compliment warmed her cheeks. Who was he? Did she really care how he'd come to rescue her, when he was here now? She rubbed her temples.

He closed the window, ever so slowly, that pane of glass separating them with a soft *thud*. Peter tapped the glass and pointed to the latch. "Don't forget to lock it."

"What if you need to get in?" she asked much too loudly.

"Trust me. It's better if I don't." He peered through the window, and—something about those eyes—was it longing? Danger? Something else? She didn't know him well enough to read his expressions.

"Okay then." Wendy locked the window, and he sat on the top step, giving her his back. She grabbed the wool blanket she'd seen on the trunks, but when she glanced at the window again—he was gone.

She pressed her face against the glass and looked down and up, but he wasn't there. Strange. She had only looked away for a few seconds. There was no way he could have made it down the fire escape that quick. Besides, wouldn't she have heard his steps on the rungs?

Wendy sat in the chair facing the fire escape with the blanket wrapped comfortingly around her shoulders. She sat and waited up for him for close to two hours, but he didn't return. It bothered her that he'd lied—promised to stay and then left.

But finally, eyes heavy and body exhausted, head aching, Wendy moved over to the futon and fell into a deep and dreamless sleep.

"What do you think now?" Peter asked, his feet touching down on the pavement.

Tink jumped. "The shadow box is definitely reacting to her." She kept her voice down, even though they were out of earshot of the window. "But how is that possible? I thought it only reacted to shadows. This is out of my wheelhouse, Peter." Tink shook her head and rubbed the back of her neck. "Plus, she vanished after that night. Don't tell me she's been surviving on her own out here the last few days. I thought she had been taken."

"Well, I don't expect her to tell us right off the bat. We're strangers to her. We need to earn her trust, which is why I'm taking this slow. We messed up that night by not taking her straight to Neverwood. Then we lost her after she left her house, and now she looks ready to bolt again. We can't lose her again."

"But don't you think it's odd that she's shown up where a morphling appeared—twice? That girl is seriously messed up."

Peter tried to calm Tink by putting his hand on her head. "We're all a little messed up, Tink. It's why we do what we do."

She looked down and kicked a piece of trash. "You were right to bring her to the safe house, but we should leave her here and be done with her. She's not one of us, Peter. We can't start taking home every stray kid we find. They wouldn't understand our lifestyle."

"So should we let her roam the streets until she gets picked off by the next morphling she attracts? We know there will be more of them. She'd be safest with us."

"If she keeps attracting morphlings, I think we should dump her in the farthest regions of the state, but I doubt you'll go for that."

"No, I won't." Peter shook his head. "We've got to give her options, earn her trust."

"How are we going to do that?"

"Give her what she wants most right now. She wants to feel safe and secure. So we'll give her a job where we can keep an eye on her."

-18-

A SOFT TAPPING WOKE HER.

Wendy opened her eyes and saw Peter outside the window. Daylight streamed in around him, enveloping the attic with its warm morning glow.

Sometime during the night, Wendy had kicked off her boots, so she shuffled slowly to the window and gave Peter an accusing look. "Password."

Peter smiled and held up a white paper bag with a familiar golden arch logo. "Breakfast."

Wendy pursed her lips and raised an eyebrow at him, but then her mouth started to water at the promise of hot food. "Correct."

She opened the latch and Peter crawled in through the window, placing two still hot breakfast sandwiches on the table. She pulled out her leftover hotdog and shyly put it on the table as well.

Peter unwrapped a sandwich and slid the yellow wrapper in front of Wendy. The aroma of fresh biscuit, bacon, and cheese made her stomach growl. She hungrily scooped it up and took a humongous bite. Part of the biscuit crumbled, and she had to cover her mouth to keep all of the goodness within her lips. Peter either pretended not to notice or didn't mind her manners.

After she had chewed and swallowed, Wendy asked. "So what's below me?" She tapped the floor with her foot. "I saw the trapdoor in the floor but didn't open it."

"We're above an old print shop. The owners went out of business. It's a historic building and needs tons of repairs to get it up to code. Nobody has the money to renovate, so it sits empty."

Peter eyed his watch and jumped up, bumping the table.

"What's wrong?"

"You're going to be late for your first day of work." Peter picked up his sandwich, shoved the rest into his mouth, and climbed out the window.

"What do you mean?" She followed him.

"Bernard Books." His grin grew wider.

She stopped. "But I didn't apply."

"You didn't have to."

"Peter," Wendy said his name heatedly. "People don't just hire other people, without interviewing them or having an application."

"Bernard Books does."

"That's utterly ridiculous. Don't tease me like that."

Peter turned around on the fire escape, leaning on the window frame as she crawled through after him. "I'm not teasing you, Wendy. Who's to say you weren't interviewed? I interviewed you for Mr. B."

"But..." she waved her hands in front of her. "I'm not qualified."

He stared at her. "You love stories. You get along with the most important person in the world to Mr. Bernard—his dog Nana. And she likes you. I'd say you are more than qualified. I overheard most of the interviews from the loft, and I found you the most interesting of the candidates."

The way he said interesting, and hung on the last syllable made her look away in embarrassment. She could feel heat rising to her cheeks.

"But how? Why?"

He crossed his arms over his chest and pointed his thumb at himself. "Because, we go way back, me and Mr. B. And I told him that you were the best for the job. He would have told you in person if you hadn't run out the store."

"Is that so?"

"I want you to trust us. I thought maybe this was a good way of earning it. You start today at nine." He took off down the stairs.

She grabbed her backpack, slung it over her shoulder, and scrambled out of the attic after him. He was waiting for her on the last landing. When she got there, she noticed the dumpster had been moved and the ladder was pulled back up.

How had Peter gotten up there with breakfast? Tink wouldn't have pushed the ladder back up. Where was she anyway?

Not that Wendy missed her.

Peter breezed past her and jumped onto the ladder, his weight pulling it down with a jolt. He dropped to the pavement below and pushed the dumpster back over so Wendy could follow.

When she was safe on the ground, she made it a point to memorize familiar landmarks—she needed to be able to find this place again. She didn't recognize any of the buildings or street names.

From the alley, she and Peter jogged to the bus stop. They made it just as the bus pulled up. He paid for both fares. The trip to the bookstore—without Tink's monologue—was much more enjoyable than the walk the night before.

Peter sat close to Wendy on the bench seat. Whenever the bus would shift or hit a pothole, his leg would brush against hers, setting her own leg into a frenzy of nervous tingles.

"Where's Tink this morning?" she asked.

"At our secret hideout," Peter answered seriously.

"What? You have a secret hideout?" She didn't believe him. "Where is it?"

"If I told you, then it wouldn't be a secret anymore. It would just be a hideout, and that doesn't sound as mysterious, now does it?"

"Oh."

"Besides. You don't really want to go to the secret hideout, because once you do, you'll see how awesome the place is and decide you can't possibly ever leave. Then you'll do the girl thing."

"Girl thing?" Wendy asked, her voice filled with irritation.

"Yes, you know. The girl thing." He wiggled his hands for emphasis.

"This I've got to hear." Wendy crossed her arms. "Please elaborate."

Peter laughed and pulled his foot up to rest on his knee. "Oh, you know. You'll start acting like a girl and put things away and organize stuff, and we just can't have girls messing up our secret hideout."

"Our? So there's more than one who know about this hideout."

"Of course, but they're all boys." He answered as if that was enough explanation.

"But Tink is there...and she's a girl."

"Well, Tink doesn't count."

"Ah." She had a feeling Tink would hate to hear Peter say she didn't count. But it bugged Wendy too. She didn't like being excluded from things because she was a girl. She shifted in the seat.

Peter's odd sense of humor was becoming familiar to her, but then he'd say something like this, pushing her away and making her feel like a stranger. She scooted as far away from him as the seat would allow and stared out the window. Her breath made little patches of misty condensation on the glass.

She was cold. Moving those precious few inches made her miss their connection, but he had hurt her feelings, and she wasn't quite sure how to respond.

Peter moved next to her and draped his arm across the back of her seat. He leaned in, and his breath tickled the side of her neck as he whispered. "Don't be upset. Tink predates the secret hideout, so she kind of has to be allowed there. I'd love to take you."

She turned to look at him, and their faces were almost touching. Peter's eyes flicked to her lips before he dragged them away to meet her gaze.

"Really?"

"Yeah, except that I can't." He actually seemed sad that he couldn't.

"Because it's secret," she repeated.

Peter shifted again, without moving away this time. In fact, he maneuvered himself even closer. Color rose in his cheeks, and he looked down in shame. "No. The real reason is because Tink really... really..." he emphasized each word, "does... not...like you. She has threatened to burn the place down if," his voice took on a higher pitch, "that Wendy girl sets foot in it."

Wendy punched him in the shoulder teasingly, and he made a pained noise in response. "Peter. You could have just said that in the first place."

"No, I couldn't. Then you'd know that Tink doesn't like you and you'd end up hating her. I probably shouldn't have told you...'cause now you will."

"Tink doesn't exactly make her feelings toward me a secret." Wendy caught the distress etched across his face. He really was trying to protect his friend. She sighed. "And that does make it hard to like her." Peter's shoulders dropped before Wendy finished. "But it's impossible not to."

Peter squeezed her hand and gave her a quick kiss on the cheek. "I knew you'd understand." He stood quickly, seconds before the bus pulled up to their stop.

Wendy, still stunned by the kiss, had to shake her head to clear it. Understand what? That Tink was unique? His care for the petite firecracker of a girl was quite obvious. But what was she supposed to make of the kiss on her cheek?

"Come on, gorgeous, you don't want to be late," Peter called from the steps. And he jumped onto the sidewalk and took off running.

"Wait up!" Wendy grabbed her backpack and ran after him. Peter seemed to have boundless energy. His path to the bookstore resembled that of the little boy from the old Family Circus comic—meandering even as he made his way toward the book shop. He'd loop around a pole just to come back and run backward with Wendy.

Wendy found his energy infectious—and maybe that was his plan. Peter winked at her as he nimbly dodged the walkers without even looking. She laughed. How good that felt! Her abs hurt from laughing by the time they made it to the front of the bookstore.

Mr. Bernard, shop keys in hand, walked up with Nana just as they arrived.

"Oh, so you decided to take the job. I'm glad to have you," he said.

Nana huffed and leaned heavily against Wendy's legs, demanding attention. Wendy reached down to scratch her head.

Mr. Bernard chuckled. "Nana's never been wrong about somebody, and she likes you."

"Well, I hope so."

He smiled and pushed the door open, beckoning her in. Peter flew by them both and ran up the stairs to the loft where he had been watching her from the day before. His head disappeared up the stairs, and she felt a little saddened by his departure.

"Today, I'll start you on the register and teach you opening procedures for the shop. I'm pretty flexible, so we will see if the opening or closing shift is more to your liking." He spoke over his shoulder as he headed to his office in the back.

She followed, taking note of the small office with an antique desk. It looked like Mr. Bernard spent most of his time in here. Old coffee cups, magazines, and notebooks littered around the office. The bookshelf couldn't possibly hold any more books. Vertical, horizontal, and in every crevice, the shelves were crammed with books of all shapes and sizes. Off to the side of the bookshelf stood a safe bolted to the ground. He knelt down to open the safe and pulled out a till, full of cash and rolled coins. Mr. Bernard closed the safe and carried the cash drawer out to the register, and then he turned the key to the on-position.

He spent a few minutes going over transaction procedures as well as cataloging what was purchased throughout the day. This was a small-scale bookstore, and they didn't have an electronic check out system to track inventory. It had to be manually calculated.

"It doesn't get busy during the fall, but I try to schedule a few local authors for readings and such. Still, you'll have plenty of time to do your reading for school."

Wendy just nodded and continued to follow him around the store. She was a bit bummed that there wasn't more to the job. He showed her the back storage room with an old desktop computer and more boxes of books.

"Your main duty will be to clean up after story times and whenever the young families come in browsing. Lots of books get put back in the wrong places. We can't have our murder mysteries shelved with our poetry, now can we?" He chuckled to himself.

Wendy just smiled wanly.

After a few more hours of too-easy training, he left Wendy to organize and straighten the shelves while he went to do bookkeeping. Alphabetizing was a breeze for a book-aholic like her, and she found the time passed quickly, as long as she was able to stop glancing up at the loft, where Peter disappeared. A few times, she caught him watching her as he leaned over the banister. Her face flushed when she met his gaze. He watched her like a hawk, a hungry hawk. Hungry for what exactly? She wasn't sure, but he definitely knew how to make her heart skip a beat.

The door jingled, and she walked to the front to find the two girls who had come in to apply yesterday. One was busy checking her phone for messages, and the redhead leaned against the counter, snapped her gum, and rang the silver bell impatiently.

"May I help you?" Wendy asked politely.

"I'm Desi, and this is Penny. We're just checking to see if Mr. Bernard hired someone yet." The girl with the red hair turned to Wendy, and a look of disappointment flittered across her face. "Oh...I guess he did."

"Yes, he did," Wendy answered simply, uncomfortable saying anything more.

"Isn't that what you wore yesterday to the interview?" Desi snapped her gum and wrinkled her nose in disdain.

Wendy looked down at her rumpled clothes from the day before, and she could feel their condemnation. She straightened her shoulders, held her head high, and looked them square in the face. She had no reason to be ashamed of the clothes she wore. She may not have a home or a lot of money, but that would change with hard work.

And what she did have was her pride.

Penny looked up from her phone and her eyes went wide when she finally connected the dots. "Oh, I've seen you around the park. I recognize you. You're homeless, aren't you?"

Did these girls not understand manners?

"Shh, Penny! That's not polite." The other girl swatted her friend in the arm.

"Ouch. Well, I think she lives in the park, Desi. I've seen her sleeping there often."

"I'm not homeless," Wendy answered with more emphasis than needed. Both girls stared at her. "I'm not homeless," she repeated.

"Are you a runaway? Did you get kicked out? I bet you have a record. Does Mr. Bernard know this? Did you tell him?"

When Wendy didn't immediately answer, Penny continued. "I guess you didn't. Someone should notify the poor old man that he's likely to be robbed because he hired a hobo."

Wendy's temples started to hurt, and the headache was back, meaner than ever. All she saw were flashes of white. The drone of the girls' accusing voices faded out. She saw a room, bright lights, heard the sound of a compressor, felt a jarring stab. Her hands locked onto the counter top, because she knew if she let go, she'd fall. The book next to her fell off the counter and clattered to the floor.

She felt a warm presence against her back. Peter's right arm came around her waist to steady her. It was an intimate gesture for someone she had just met, and it probably sent all the wrong signals to the girls, but at that moment she didn't care. She leaned backward and let Peter's strength hold her. Without it, she'd probably have fallen already.

Penny's and Desi's mouths dropped open when they saw Peter, and they looked a little dejected at the fact that their eligible bachelor looked to be taken already.

Peter smiled at them. "Can I get you anything? Coffee, tea, some manners perhaps?"

That snapped them out of their befuddlement. Desi coughed, grabbed Penny by the jacket sleeve, and marched out of the bookstore, the door slamming behind them.

As soon as they left, Wendy pulled away from Peter, and let herself lean fully on the counter, pressing her face against the cool wood.

Peter's strong hand gently pushed her blonde hair out of her eyes. He leaned forward to whisper to her. "Are you okay? Wendy? Please talk to me."

Wendy had a perfect view through the bookstore window and into the park.

She could see them.

Standing perfectly still in broad daylight. Bold, unaffected, fearless—as if to mock her.

She counted them.

Seven perfect, unmoving shadows.

LOST GIRL

-19-

COFFEE HELPED. WENDY'S JITTERY hands had problems grasping the ceramic Bernard Books mug. Still, she realized simply wrapping her hands around the cup as it sat on the table calmed her. Well, maybe it was the coffee. It could also be the fact that Peter hadn't left her side and was even now rubbing his hand along her back.

"What just happened, Wendy?"

She shivered. Okay, this time it was from his touch and definitely not from being terrified out of her wits.

Peter quickly pulled away. He must've mistaken her shiver as revulsion. Immediately, Wendy missed his closeness. He sat there with her, not saying a word, although she knew that he wanted to ask her a million questions. She hesitantly glanced up and met his green eyes. "I saw them. The shadows...there were a lot." She pointed out the window and wasn't surprised to see an empty park.

She expected to see pity, or the wary look of someone trying to study her, to see if she was crazy. But in Peter, she hoped for a friend who understood. She needed him to believe her. He stood and stared out the window where she had pointed.

It was obvious he hadn't seen the shadows, and she prepared herself for the rejection. But a look of contemplation battled with some other inner turmoil as he glanced back at her.

Her heart pounded, and she willed him to believe her. He had to. He pulled out his phone and studied the screen for a second and let out a long, audible breath. He put his phone away.

Peter reached forward, squeezed her shoulder and then gently commanded, "Stay here."

She let out a sad laugh. "Uh, plan to."

He smiled, the corner of his mouth lifting as he left. It was a placating smile, one people gave to reassure small children. The shadows had disappeared or moved on, and now Peter was outside with them. Was he really going to follow the shadows?

Her neck itched, as it always did when she felt weird like this, and she absently scratched at a small scar on the side of her neck.

Not wanting to be caught sitting down on the job, Wendy carried her coffee cup back to the desk and proceeded to wipe down the tables and straighten the chairs. A few customers came in over the next hour, one looking for bird books, another a gift for her grandson's birthday. Someone else wanted a copy of the school's summer reading list. Wendy found all of them without having to bother Mr. Bernard.

Nana had frequently come and leaned against her for company. Another hour passed, and Peter hadn't returned. Wendy walked to the back of the shop and peeked into Mr. B's office. He faced the old typewriter and the *clickety-clack* of the keys filled the small room. She knocked but he didn't hear her, so she entered and stood in front of his desk.

She'd seen him throughout the morning bustling about the store, carrying old books into his office. An oddly assorted stack sat precariously on the end of the desk, and she pushed them back—books on flying, mermaids and Indians, pirate ships and tropical islands.

Mr. Bernard turned in his seat.

A sketchbook lay open on the desk, and there, in pencil, was a young man with a mischievous smile. The young boy, wearing pants and shirt made of leaves, looked oddly familiar.

"Oh, Wendy. Sorry, dear.

"Mr. Bernard, I'm sorry to bother you. I knocked but you didn't hear."

"That's no trouble at all." He pulled his glasses off and rubbed his tired eyes before replacing his glasses on his nose. "I get so lost sometimes while writing that—even if you used a bullhorn—I probably wouldn't hear you."

"Oh, so you're writing a book?"

"Yes, I am. It's my first one, and it's the reason I hired you. I needed more time to finish up my manuscript. Sorry for not checking on you, dear. How are things going? Been busy?"

"Sort of." She wasn't sure how to answer since she didn't know how busy they normally were. "Um, Peter hasn't returned yet from an errand."

"When did he leave?"

"About three hours ago."

"Ah." Mr. B yawned but didn't seem worried at Peter's absence.

"Well, I was wondering if you knew his cell number."

"Where would I get his number?"

Wendy frowned in confusion before asking. "Maybe from his employment application?"

"Like the fully filled-out employment application you turned in?" He chuckled.

She flushed with embarrassment.

"Oh, well. You're right." Wendy backed out of the office. "Sorry, I just was worried about him. Please don't be mad at him for being gone so long. I was hungry, and he offered to get lunch. I just...I don't want you to fire him."

Mr. Bernard's laugh started out small but grew into a full belly laugh.

"Oh, I wouldn't worry about that. Look at the time! You've had one full day. Why don't you go clock out, and I'll see you on Wednesday. Put the service bell out, and I'll be out there in a few tics."

"Okay, Mr. Bernard." She left his office door open, went up to the front, and slid her time card into the old-fashioned clock. Next to it, she found a well-worn *Please ring for help* sign and propped it up.

Wendy grabbed her jacket and backpack from under the counter. She stood there by the front desk worrying her bottom lip. What was she supposed to do? Should she wait for Peter? Had something happened to him or did he just forget about her?

Part of her kind of hoped she could crash back at the same place, but she couldn't just assume. She'd be fine on her own. But just the thought of having to be alone again terrified her. Not with the shadows out and about.

She had walked past the desk phone numerous times today and avoided the temptation to call her family. But she didn't think she could hold out any longer. Wendy reached for the phone and dialed John's cell. On the third ring someone answered. The voice on the other end wasn't her brother.

"Hello?" the feminine voice answered. It was her mother.

The wall broke. All of the pent up emotion she didn't know she was blocking and holding back came pouring out after hearing her mother's voice. Tears burned in her eyes.

She couldn't control the desperation in her response. "Mom!"

"Wendy?" Her mother started to sob in relief. "Are you okay? Where are you?" The phone became muffled as she heard her mom cry out, "George, it's Wendy!"

The phone switched hands and she heard her dad's voice. "Sweetie, please come home. We're sorry about the clinic. We won't send you there, we promise. Whatever you need. We can work this out...as a family."

Her heart began to swell with hope. Family. She could go home. She could sleep warm and safe in her bed tonight. All she'd have to do is tell them where she was. Then she hesitated when she saw something in the distance. It was just a shadow of a cloud passing over her, but it made her pause.

There is no place that's safe for her. Not from the shadows. Not after she saw what the morphlings did to that boy. She couldn't bring that thing to her parent's doorstep. She couldn't expose her family to the dangers that seemed to follow her. Not until she had more answers. Not until she knew she could protect them—from what followed her.

"I...I can't Dad."

"What? Why not?" George's voice dropped.

"Give me the phone," Mary demanded. "Honey, please. We miss you. We're sorry. Just tell us where you are and we will come get you."

It pained her to pull the phone away from her ear. It was a blow to her heart to hang up on her mother's frantic voice. But she needed to do what was right. She needed to keep them safe and to do that—she needed Peter.

Wendy turned around and wiped her tears away on her jacket sleeve. She looked up when she heard a familiar voice.

"Hey, dork. There you are," Tink called out. "You ready to go?"

The front desk phone started to ring and Wendy intuitively knew her parents must have redialed the number. She glanced at the caller I.D and it confirmed her fear. She was dumb. She shouldn't have called from here.

The phone rang a second time.

"Are you going to answer that?" Tink asked.

Wendy looked over at Mr. Bernard's office and he seemed oblivious to the ringing. "Uh, no." It rang again and she unplugged the phone from the outlet and the ringing stopped. "It's been sales calls all day." She picked up her jacket again and looked at Tink. "You said we're going somewhere? Where's Peter?"

Tink rolled her shoulders and frowned at Wendy. "He got busy with something but didn't want to worry you, so he sent me."

"Well, where is he?"

"Neverwood."

"What's Neverwood?" A twinge of excitement ran through her. "Is that the secret hideout?"

Tink waited a few seconds as if deciding the best answer. "Uh, sure...of sorts. You should think of it as a reform school."

Huh. Tink who would burn the place down if Wendy stepped foot in it had come to be her personal escort?

Wendy raised her eyebrow, not buying the girl's obvious lie. "Didn't seem to really reform you, did it?"

"There's nothing wrong with me. I'm perfect. You, on the other hand," Tink waved her hand in a circle in front of Wendy, "have a whole mess of problems. And Neverwood is the only place you're going to find any answers."

Answers. Yeah, she wanted those, but there was something about the name that made her hesitate. It sounded like a prison...or another clinic. "I felt pretty sure you didn't want me there, Tink. Maybe I'm better off taking my chances alone."

Tink pursed her lips. "I definitely don't, and I'm not the only one. The room above the bakery is probably available to you still." She turned to walk away.

But if she could get some answers...

"Wait...I'll go."

Tink turned around, her mouth shifting into an annoyed frown. "Figured you would. Let's go." Tink stopped walking when she heard Mr. Bernard come out of the back room. He was humming softly to himself while tying his work apron around his waist.

Tink's body stiffened. She craned her neck and watched Mr. B as he picked up a book and headed over to the register. He saw Tink and gave her a welcoming smile.

"Hello there."

"Hi," she whispered back, giving him a curious stare.

"If you're here for a job, I'm sorry to say that I filled the position already." He smiled warmly at Wendy.

Tink's lips pressed into an irritated line. "No, wouldn't dream of working here."

"Then maybe you're here for a book? I'd recommend anything on our front table for young girls like you. Do you like teen vampire romances?"

"No, I'm more of a War and Peace girl. Minus the peace," Tink snapped. She grabbed Wendy's elbow, dragging her out of the store. Her whole mood had turned sour as she motioned toward her scooter for Wendy to get on.

Wendy held onto Tink's jacket as tightly as she dared. The girl rarely stayed in her own lane, whipping around cars at breakneck speed and tailgating. She never signaled.

Wendy figured she was much safer in the park battling her own demons, than on the back of an electric scooter with Tink.

They drove through town but stayed on the outskirts, following the road that bordered the scenic waterfront. After a few miles, Tink slowed and turned up a gravel path until they stopped near the top of a hill in front of a dilapidated house.

Tink parked her scooter, and Wendy hopped off first and explored with her eyes. The front of the house looked uninhabitable with faded blue clapboard siding and broken windows that had been hastily covered with mismatched boards. Dead ivy clung to a broken trellis, and garbage littered the surrounding area. Wendy was pretty sure she saw a sleeping homeless person next to the garbage cans.

Tink walked around the garbage where the man slept. "Don't pay him any attention." She led Wendy across the front porch. Once she'd pushed a doorbell next to an ornate wooden door four times, she waited. A few minutes later, a little hidden door within the door—five feet up—

opened and a face appeared. Only the eyes were visible behind the grille.

"Password," a young male voice called out. Wendy had said the same thing that same morning to Peter. It seemed so long ago now. Was Peter inside somewhere?

"Pickled Codfish," Tink answered.

"Nope," the young voice answered.

"Tootles, that *is* the password," she argued.

"Nuh-uh, it's been changed."

"Since when?" Tink demanded.

"I changed it myself just now. It's up here now." It was hard to see, but it looked like he tapped the side of his head.

"You can't change a password on the spur of the moment without telling anyone," Tink challenged.

"Yes, I can. I'm in charge of the door. And I say it changed."

Tink leapt for the peephole, and Wendy heard an *Eep!* from behind the door.

"Listen to me, you little dirt bag. If you don't open this door, I'm going to throw your little duff into the ocean and feed you to the fishes. Do you know what hungry little fishes do first? They eat off your toes, then your fingers. Now open the door!" Tink punched the door angrily. Her swear bracelet went off, ringing loudly as she jumped around and shook her fist from the pain. @!*&

"Tootles," Wendy cajoled softly. She waited for the young boy behind the door to reappear. "Tootles, since you've changed the password and you didn't tell anyone, you need to give us a riddle instead."

"Says who?"

"It's in the Door Guardians' Handbook. Chapter three, paragraph six. If a password has been changed without the knights having been notified, then a riddle must be issued."

"It says that, does it?" the boy asked.

"It does."

"Oh, I like her, Tink. Can we keep her?" Tootles said excitedly.

"No, we can't. Now get on with the clue, boy," Tink snarled, nursing her sore hand.

"Well, then let me think. Oh, I've got a good one. What's black and white and—"

"A newspaper." Tink grinned. She turned and whispered to Wendy, "It's like the only riddle he knows."

"That's not fair. You didn't let me finish the riddle. I get to tell a new one now."

"Hey listen, pipsqueak. I guessed your stupid riddle. Now open the door."

But he didn't answer. And the door was still shut tight.

"All right," he said, back suddenly and sounding really sure of himself. "A homeless person has it, a rich person doesn't need it, and if you eat it, you'll die."

"What kind of riddle is that?" Tink growled through the door.

Tootles laughed, "Slightly said I was doing it wrong and making it too easy on ya, so he gave me a proper riddle."

"Slightly!" Tink yelled. "Open the door and tell Tootles he better run for cover."

Scuffling sounded through the door, and maybe what sounded like a metal chair being dragged away from the door. Intense dark brown eyes peered through the hole and met Tink's. "You heard him. Answer the kid's riddle."

"I don't know the answer, Slightly." Tink stomped.

"It's nothing," Wendy answered, stepping into view so that Slightly could see her. "The answer is nothing. Poor people have it, rich don't need it, and if you eat nothing, you'll die."

It was hard to judge an expression when only seeing a few inches of his face, but she thought he smiled.

"Correct. You may enter."

The peephole closed, and a large bolt slid into place. The door opened, and a very large teen about seventeen or eighteen stood there in a blue jersey with a white number three. He was huge. Linebacker huge with slick, dark hair, and he wasn't wearing shoes. When he turned to close the door, Wendy noticed he had a slight limp.

Tootles, probably about eight years old, jumped off a metal stool and ran in front of Tink, who pretended to take a swing at the boy.

"Ah, you can't catch me!" He squealed and took off running farther into the building.

Tink dropped her bag and sprinted after the kid. "Come back, kid. You've got an appointment with the fishes." A scream of laughter rang out through the hallway.

Wendy remained next to the large muscled young man she assumed had to be Slightly. He was slightly larger than she expected, so the name suited him.

He turned to look at her, and she swore a blush rippled up his cheeks. "Um, welcome to Neverwood." He swept his arm outward as they walked into the main room, as if showing off something grand.

But she could see it—a rundown building with tattered curtains and couches with stuffing falling out of them. It smelled like something was rotting away in a hidden room somewhere. Had she walked into a halfway house? She stayed close to the exit.

When Wendy refused to budge, he hit himself in the head with his palm as if he'd forgotten something. "Ah, don't be frightened. I forgot it's your first time. We don't get many planned visitors. Just the odd vagrant, or spelunker looking for hidden antiques. This way."

He led her down the hallway Tink and Tootles had run through. They came to a stone fireplace, the largest she had ever seen. Wendy heard a loud scraping noise coming from the fireplace—was it beneath the logs and grate? Slightly stopped next to the stairs and pulled the frame away from a family portrait to reveal a hidden computer panel. As soon as he punched in a code, she heard the grinding noise again. The back of the large fireplace sunk inward, revealing a long tunnel.

They could hear laughter and Tink's censor box echoing from within. They must have passed through just moments before.

"After you." He closed the frame. That's when Wendy noticed someone familiar in the portrait.

Slightly picked up on Wendy's interest. "Yeah, she doesn't look anything like that anymore, does she?"

Wendy stared at the picture of a young girl in a pale blue debutante gown, head-to-toe frills and lace, long hair curled past her shoulders. What threw Wendy was the smile.

Tink didn't smile like that—hadn't since Wendy had met her anyway.

"Is this Tink's home?" Wendy asked. Being here suddenly felt awkward. Would it be obvious to everyone that they didn't like each other?

"Uh, well...her dad owns the building. Her family—one of the founders of the Neverwood Project—put lots of money into fixing it up and making it a safe haven for kids like us.

"You said one of the founders. Who are the rest?"

Slightly's smile dropped. "Well they were all pretty prominent scientists in their field."

"Were?" Wendy asked. "Why the past tense? Where are the founders now?"

Slightly sighed. "Gone. They've moved on in their lives. They forgot what was important to them. Except for our first founder. He's like a Dad to all of us," He pointed to Tink's picture again. "You might actually meet him one of these days. But he's pretty busy running Neverwood and trying to stay one step ahead of the Red Skulls. So if you have any questions, feel free to ask me, Peter, or Tink."

At Slightly's mention of Red Skulls, Wendy lost her footing. Slightly grabbed her arm to steady her. She prayed that he couldn't feel the small tremor that passed through her body. She had to take a deep breath and try to focus her attention on where they were walking. She had heard the name Red Skulls before, at school, from Peter, but there was something else about that name that shook her to her core.

They stepped into the fireplace and the wall slowly closed behind them, trapping them within the darkened hallway. Slightly, unfazed, continued to walk down the tunnel. Cement surrounded them and a string of lights flickered above them, creating a haunting illumination— fodder for her nightmares.

After a good hundred yards, Wendy followed Slightly out into a completely different house. Her jaw dropped at the beauty of the marble floors, the immense winding staircase that divided the main hall to split off in two directions.

"We're only visible by helicopter, and we are in a no fly zone. Neverwood is over twenty thousand square feet, complete with three full-sized kitchens, a gym, a medical center, and a pool. It's completely safe. The dorms are that way," he pointed up and to the left, "and the class-rooms are this way." He pointed to the right.

He led her down a hall into one of the main rec rooms. "The main entrance, the rambler house, is the one you came in, a façade meant to detour unwanted attention."

Wendy made it to the lower rec room and paused to gaze out the floor-to-ceiling windows at the most amazing view of trees. She felt like she was in the middle of the woods.

Tink's voice above drew her attention to a loft area which looked like a little workshop filled with computers, monitors, and various gadgets and machines. On the side wall was a large sign that read *The Hideout.* Wendy supposed it had been a club name at one time, but now it was just a cool decoration.

Around her, lights and sounds flickered from various arcade games, and air hockey tables stood near the center of the room. Twin brothers played ping-pong, and they simultaneously raised their hands up in greeting. A few other boys loitered around the room—one boy with light red hair was reading a book. Someone tossed a pillow at his head, and another called him Fox. Such an odd name.

Fox looked up and waved.

Wendy politely waved back.

Tootles ran upstairs on the far end of the great hall and knocked on a door.

"It's not much," Slightly said, "but it's home."

Wendy studied him. *It's not much?* It was fantastic.

"Tink has a security system in place with infrared cameras and motion detectors, so no one can track us when we're within the walls."

"So…is the door password just fun for Tootles?"

"No, Tink shorted something out yesterday, so security's down at the moment. She's up there now getting the system back online."

Wendy glanced up at the booth just as Tink slammed her fist down on the table. Bells sounded loudly. "I almost had it."

"She'll get it," Slightly said. "She's a genius, it's in her blood."

Wendy was about to ask about the relative, but Slightly led her back to the foyer and up the marble stairs.

They stopped at a beautifully crafted set of double doors, carved to resemble a forest. Her hand reached out and touched the base of a tree. "It's gorgeous." She had never seen doors so big. It looked like she was about to walk into a wooden painting.

The forested door opened with a jerk, and a kid with a surly expression strode out. His dark, irritated eyes widened in shock before looking away. He pushed past her roughly.

"Excuse you," Wendy gaped at the boy who had ignored her, as if she were a fly on the wall.

"Hey, I'm talking to you." Wendy yelled after him, but she was met with silence and his retreating back. "Who is that?" Wendy asked Slightly.

"Oh, that's Jax."

"What's his problem?"

"Oh...ah," Slightly pondered for a second and then shrugged his shoulders.

Slightly didn't seem inclined to elaborate on Jax's disposition but instead ushered her into the room before him. The door closed with a soft click, and she was alone in an office, surrounded by books.

Oh, not alone. Peter stood with his back to her, leaning against a mahogany desk. His shoulders looked tense, and he was muttering angrily to himself. He hadn't noticed her.

Wendy cleared her throat.

He jumped, turning to face her, and his right hand reached up to swipe at his hair.

She had surprised him and that made her smile, but she was done with waiting for answers. "So you didn't come back with lunch."

"Yeah, I got caught up chasing shadows. I'm sorry I sent Tink. I would have sent someone else, but she was the only one you knew."

"She changed her mind about me staying here, huh?"

"I'm afraid we don't have a choice anymore. You're not safe out there."

She tried to let what he was saying sink in, but it was easier to just ask. "When am I going to get the truth?"

"What do you mean?"

"Oh, come on, I'm not some naïve kid. I know what I saw that night. Quit hiding the truth from me. I deserve answers."

"Wendy, wait." He moved toward her, but she backed away from him, so he held his position. "We haven't been lying...exactly. We've been trying to protect you."

She laughed at the idea, but then her humor trickled away as her voice became raw with emotion. Her hand started to shake. "I tried to tell my parents the truth—what I saw—but they planned to send me away again...to *protect* me. I had to run away from home, from them, because of you."

Her voice rose in pitch and volume as her anger took over. "I've been living on the streets because of you. I lost everything...because of you! I think I'm done with being protected."

"Shh, Wendy," Peter spoke softly from his spot in the middle of the room. He dropped his gaze toward the antique rug he stood on, and it was a few moments before he met her eyes again. His own eyes filled with guilt. "If there was some way I could have prevented all of that, I would have. We didn't want to take you against your will, but you weren't awake for us to ask. And then you disappeared—from the lab *and* from your house, and we didn't know where you went." He took a tentative step toward her.

Then another one.

Wendy studied Peter's face and saw only sincerity. Of everyone she'd met so far, he was the one who displayed his emotions openly.

"I looked for you, I swear. I assumed the worse. That you had been taken by them."

"I don't understand any of this Peter...who's them?"

"The Red Skulls. The shadows seek out kids, and then the morphlings hunt them down. You saw what a morphling can do, and the Red Skulls can barely control the beasts."

Wendy's world crumbled around her as two planes, real and imaginary, suddenly collided. For years she'd struggled. What she'd seen and felt argued with what she knew had to be true, and she was desperate to cling to what she'd grown up believing. "I was really hoping that I hallucinated that morphling, thing, whatever. In fact, I'm still kind of hoping that I'm dreaming. That at any moment, I'll wake up at home and all of this," she waved her hand around, "will just be a bad dream." Her voice sounded childlike to her as she formed the words, but deep down Wendy already knew the answer.

"Hey," he came over to her. "I told you, I keep the bad dreams away. Those smaller shadows don't seem to be much of a nuisance. You only have to worry about the morphlings. We use these"—he held up a pair of digital goggles with blue lenses and handed them to Wendy—"to see them. We're still not entirely sure whose side the shadows are on, though. For the most part, they're harmless. They tend to gather whenever a morphling is about to appear."

"A morphling—I can't forget what it looked like, but—what is it really?" She couldn't find words to describe the beast she saw, so she tried to use her hands.

Peter smiled, "Uh, they're hard to categorize. Part shadow, part shape-shifter. Very deadly."

"And you hunt them down?"

He nodded. "Each of us here has a talent that makes us uniquely qualified to hunt down the morphlings and protect the innocent."

She shivered at the memory of her own confrontation. "And where does it come from?"

"From a place that shouldn't even exist anymore. A place we saw burn down years ago. Somehow it survived, and these things are coming from it."

"Where?"

She could see the fear deep within his eyes. "Neverland."

Her hands shook as she took the specs from Peter. Something wasn't right. Why would that word scare her as much as it did? She didn't know what it was, but she tried to convince herself she was just picking up on his own fear of the place.

She pulled the specs up to her eyes and looked through them. Not much changed except for the blue tint it gave the room.

"But you see them without the special goggles." He made it sound so significant.

"What I wouldn't give to never see them again."

Peter's eyes suddenly filled with sadness. "I knew one other person who could see the shadows without the specs, although I didn't believe her at the time."

"Really," Wendy felt a moment of excitement at the thought of meeting someone else like her. She had so many questions. "Can I meet her?"

Her question clearly caught Peter off guard. He shook his head and turned away. "No...you can't."

"Why not?"

He rubbed a spot on his chest and stared off into the distance. After a moment, he closed his eyes and sighed. "Because she died a long time ago."

Wendy felt horrible. Guilty. From the look on Peter's face, he mourned her passing. "I'm sorry, I didn't know."

"Her ghost taunts me." Peter's voice was firm, his fists clenched angrily at his sides, his eyes burning with fire. "Like a constant reminder of my failure. I can't outrun my past. I couldn't save her...or the others."

"What do you mean, Peter?" Wendy asked as the pounding began in her head. The floor felt like it was moving beneath her, and the room started to spin.

"The kids left behind at Neverland."

-20-

WENDY'S FACE WENT WHITE as a sheet at his admission, and she looked like she was about to collapse. She stumbled back, retreating from him. He reached out and caught her arm, then led her over to a chair. Her hands were clammy between his warm ones.

"I shouldn't have shocked you like that. It's my burden, not yours. Your first day here, and I've already frightened you." He swallowed. He wanted to punch something.

Self-loathing was taking over again. Peter was blowing it...not explaining things right. Jumping in and telling her things out of order and confusing and scaring her in the process. This is what Jax had warned him about. He never thought before he spoke. He jumped to action when the situation called for caution. He didn't guard his emotions, was too easily shaken.

It's why Jax wanted Peter to step down as their leader and support him as the new one. He thought Peter wasn't being firm enough, couldn't rein in the boys, because he couldn't even rein himself in.

And here he was about to drive a wedge between Wendy and himself and scare her off into the night again, where she could be snatched by the morphlings. How in the world she'd made it this long on the streets astounded him.

That's why he'd arranged the job for her—where he could keep an eye on her. Just that afternoon, the shadows had been stalking her again—in broad daylight. The number of them hovering around! She was a magnet.

Still, for some reason, they never took her. They always seemed to be waiting.

For what exactly, he didn't know.

When he'd "gone for lunch," he chased the shadows back to the river where they dove under water, where he could no longer follow. He hadn't realized how much time it had taken, but one glance at his watch reminded him he had left Wendy alone. He sent Tink to bring her to Neverwood, where he could truly keep her safe.

And now he was about to chase her away.

His jaw hurt from clenching his teeth, but then a gentle hand reached out and touched his shoulder. He closed his eyes and breathed in her scent. Just the feel of her hand touching him was calming.

He opened his eyes and saw the worry etched in her face—in her blue-green eyes. Her eyes were like the deepest part of the night sky, where mysteries hid within the stars. Peter desperately wanted to know the depth of Wendy's soul. Already, he saw her insecurities and doubts, and he wanted to chase all her fears away.

She was hiding things from him, too, but that was okay. He would be patient with her—if he could convince her to stay.

Here he was, telling her horrifying things about his past—giving her every reason to walk away—and she was trying to comfort him? She was incredible. Maybe Jax was right, and he wasn't fit for the job.

"It's okay, Peter. I've been through a lot, and yes, I'm having a hard time believing what I'm hearing, but it's not scaring me. In some ways, what you're saying is a relief. It means I'm not alone." Her words lifted his heart. She was a fighter. He just needed to give her the tools to survive.

"You'll never have to be alone again, Wendy. You can stay here with us. I'll teach you everything you need to know about how to fight the shadows." He held out his hand to her.

Wendy looked back at the door.

Peter held his breath, waited for her to make her decision. She turned uncertain eyes back to him, and he smiled at her, trying to hide his disappointment.

But Wendy placed her hand in his and breathed out softly. "Yes, teach me to fight the shadows."

Peter's heart soared, and he felt like flying. He couldn't hide the smile that crossed his face. "Of course, and I promise I'll take it slow."

-21-

"WHEN DO WE START?" Wendy asked, feeling exhilarated.

"Let's get you settled, and then I'll get a schedule made up and assign you some instructors. We've got to get you up to speed." Peter moved over to the desk and ruffled through some papers.

"What exactly do you do here, Peter?" *He wasn't in charge, was he?*

"I...uh...I run the Neverwood Academy."

"What? You're way too young for that."

"Well, I only run it when our founder is away. Which has been more and more often lately." The laughter she'd seen in his eyes was replaced by sadness and worry. His brow furrowed, and she stepped around the desk and gently touched his arm.

"I think...he trusted the right person for the job. He wouldn't have given it to you if he didn't think you could handle it."

Peter glanced at the door and sighed. "Thanks, but not everyone has the same faith in me that you do."

Wendy wasn't sure what to say. Peter opened the doors and stepped out, and she had to run a few steps to catch up to him. He turned down a hall and stopped at double metal doors decorated with two crossed fists—one holding a ball of light, the other a knife. They opened to reveal a large three-story room with a climbing wall, ropes, an obstacle course, and various locked weapon cabinets.

"This is our training gym, where you'll learn self-defense and combat techniques." Two boys with boxing gloves sparred on the mats in the center, while another climbed the rock wall, and a third ran laps.

They kept going, passing a door with a flower and snake design.

"That's our medical center."

"So far, the two rooms you've shown me aren't really convincing me to stay," Wendy said lightly.

"Well, most of the medical center visitors are only there because of injuries they get in training."

"Oh," Wendy said in relief.

"Field injuries are much more severe—done by the morphlings. Those boys don't usually make it back to Neverwood."

"Ohhhh." The weight of that explanation made her stomach sink.

The next room had long wooden tables and chairs facing a large screen. "Our younger kids take online classes with tutors. We don't allow many outsiders into our academy—it's safer for everyone. Those who do work here have been with us since the beginning. They know who we

165

are, know our cause. You'll recognize them by an N tattooed on their wrist." He turned his own wrist over and showed her where to look. It was part of a compass rose with only the N highlighted. "We're not alone like you might think. There are many outside the Academy who will always help a lost boy. Look for the Neverwood symbol, Wendy."

"I see," Wendy said. Everything seemed so dire.

Peter continued the tour, showing her the kitchens and the rec room which she had already seen. Wendy absorbed as much information as she could, but she found herself wearing down. She yawned.

"Hey, let's get you to bed. You'll start tomorrow with lessons."

Wendy nodded. "That sounds wonderful."

"You'll be in the girls' hall. And besides Tink, you're the only one, so you've got the hall to yourself." Wendy eyed the closest door, which was covered with crime scene tape.

"Let me guess," Wendy pointed to the door. "That's Tink's room."

"Yep," Peter rocked on his heels, arms crossed over his chest, and chuckled. "As well as the next one...and the next."

Wendy looked at the next door down and saw My Little Pony and Hello Kitty stickers on the door. "I think when it gets too messy, instead of cleaning it, she moves on."

"Isn't that what parasites do?" Wendy laughed.

"I heard that, you *&%@!" Loud, ringing bells chimed from behind the taped doorway.

Peter made a pretend scared face. "Oh no, we've awakened the monster." He gestured to the hall of beautifully carved doors. "Pick one. Any one."

At each of the rooms, the doors were carved with different symbols or scenes. She saw clouds in the night sky, a mermaid in a lagoon, a flower.

"Who carves these?"

"They've just always been, since the founders built the house. Each lost boy has found one of the doors significant to their life in some way. Choose the door that speaks to you."

Wendy studied every door and found herself reaching for one with a squirrel. It wasn't so much the squirrel but the acorn in its paws that made her feel a connection to the room. Her hand reached for the iron door handle and turned it. The door swung open easily.

She reached inside and felt for the light switch. Wendy's breath caught as the room illuminated. Everything about the room was something she would have picked, given the choice. A white four-poster bed with a soft white and rose duvet. A white vanity with silver mirror. A bookcase filled with heavy hardbound books.

She walked to the bookcase and picked up a book of fables. She'd read this book hundreds of times. How could the architect have known?

"Is it a match?" Peter asked. He stepped into her room and looked around.

"Are all of the rooms like this one?"

He shook his head. "No, each one is unique."

"What's in your room?" Wendy asked.

He smirked at her and raised an eyebrow. "Wouldn't you like to know?"

Wendy put her hands on her hips, and he grinned.

"Get some sleep, Wendy. Your first class is early tomorrow."

As he shut the door, Wendy panicked at the thought of being alone in a strange house and strange room by herself. "Peter wait," she called before she could stop herself.

Her door opened, and his head peeked inside.

"I'm...I'm..." She couldn't bring herself to say that she was scared of her nightmares again, of what she would see in her head.

"Don't worry," Peter answered. "I'll watch over your dreams."

As soon as the words fell from his lips, she relaxed.

The door closed again, and Wendy looked around. She found that the dresser already had clothes. Not a lot, but a pair of pajamas and socks, which she donned. She went to the window and opened it, feeling a soft cool breeze come through. She looked out into the night and shivered.

One day, she'd feel safe enough to sleep with an open window. But tonight would not be that night. She closed the window, locked it, and pulled the curtains.

Soft scratching noises came from her door. Wendy listened until they stopped. She flung open her door, just as, across the hall, Tink's shut with a thud. Confused, Wendy began to pull her door closed when she spotted a red, black, and white sign swinging gently back and forth on it.

She couldn't help but laugh at Tink. Somehow, the dig Tink sent her way made her feel accepted. Wendy adjusted the crooked DANGER! HAZARDOUS WASTE sign before closing her door with a gentle click.

-22-

L OUD POUNDING WOKE Wendy, and she rolled over to see the clock on her bedside table.

Six a.m.? She found a robe to cover her pajamas before she answered the door.

Jax stood there, an irritated look on his face. Up close, he was way more attractive than she'd originally given him credit for. Maybe it was the gold stud in his ear that made him look like a rebel. Or maybe she had been too preoccupied with Peter's handsome face to notice. Jax's black jumpsuit and his black hair accentuated his striking features, making him look even angrier than he was—she hoped.

"You're late," he said.

"For what?" Wendy tried to stifle a yawn but failed.

"Training. Peter assigned me to instruct you, although I have no clue why. Be at the training gym in ten minutes."

Jax marched off.

"Wait, I haven't even showered. I'm not ready."

He paused and turned back. "No time. Bottom drawer. You'll find everything you need. You now have nine minutes or you'll find an empty gym."

She saw the back of his dark head and growled. She rushed back into her room and tugged open her bottom drawer. Sure enough, a gray training uniform lay folded in there. When was the last time she'd moved this fast? In less than a minute, she wore the suit, traced one of the white and black stripes on the sleeve. A glint of silver grabbed her attention—a bracelet. It took a second to find the button that opened it, but once it was around her wrist, it snapped shut with a hiss.

She stepped into the hall and closed her bedroom door. This morning she wasn't in the mood for the sign on her door. She spun and glared at Tink's. What did her room say about *her*?

Wendy drew closer and pulled the crime scene tape aside. A fairy. What? Tink seemed the complete opposite of a fairy. Weren't fairies supposed to be sweet and grant wishes? Yeah, this must be her spare room. One of the others must belong to her.

She didn't have time to waste. Wendy jogged down the hall and back to the training gym, finding it after only one wrong turn. She shoved the doors open and stepped into a completely dark gym.

The door closed behind her with a thud, encasing her in inky blackness.

"Hello, Jax." Wendy's voice sounded odd to her as it bounced off the brick walls.

"Lesson one," Jax's voice echoed around her. "Everyone is your enemy."

"I'm sorry...what?" Wendy turned in circles, trying to get a fix on his location. Something about what he said made her feel sick to her stomach. Where had she heard that before?

"Rule two, remember rule one." Something flared in the darkness, a glowing ball of light, which illuminated Jax's right arm and the side of his angry face. "Rule three, if you break rule one, be prepared to pay the consequences." His face became brighter as his fist rose and the ball came closer to his face, and then it darkened as the light rushed her.

Wendy screamed and dropped to the mat just a second before the ball of light took off her head. Gasping for breath, she rolled to her back and watched it hit the wall and disappear.

"What's wrong with you!" Wendy got back to her feet and yelled at Jax. "You could have killed me." Darkness once again enveloped her. Bright spots from staring at the ball invaded her vision.

"Rule one!" Another flash of light and another attack.

Wendy dodged the light ball by jumping to the side. Hoping to avoid more blinding spots, she closed her eyes. She waited for the ball to dissipate before opening her eyes and listening for Jax, this time, keeping her mouth shut.

She heard just a whisper of sound.

Turning slowly, she was able to make him out faintly in the darkness. Wendy crept along the ground until she could crouch behind one of the obstacle course pieces.

Why was he trying to hurt her? She glanced toward the door and wondered if she should make a break for it.

Too late.

Jax rounded the barrier and his hand glowed again. A shot of light hit her square in the chest.

She squeezed her eyes shut and waited for the explosion of pain, but she felt nothing. Her hand searched for an injury, but her shirt wasn't even damaged.

Jax's hand whipped out and bonked her on the back of her head. "Aaand you're dead." He pulled a remote out of his pocket and aimed it at the ceiling. A second later the overhead lights kicked on, bathing them in blinding light.

Wendy blinked at him, confused. "I thought you were trying to kill me."

"Relax, a light blast is harmless to humans...if it's on low."

Jax saw her look of confusion and grabbed her by the bracelet. He held up her wrist, palm facing her. A similar half-inch silver bracelet wrapped around his own wrist. "This is a light brace. With a flick of your wrist—" He flicked his wrist, and a small silver lever flipped down into his palm. A ball of light formed at the lever's round wand tip. "Let the light orb form within the palm of your hand. The longer you hold it, the bigger and brighter it will become."

He let the ball fly toward a wall, and it dispersed in a burst of colors.

"It's just a specially altered form of light. Its reflective coating helps illuminate and keep the light in a shape as it flies—it's nearly weightless."

Wendy studied the contraption on Jax's arm and flicked her wrist, surprised when the rod on her brace slid into her palm. She gently ran her fingers over the tip and felt the small circle. "So kind of like a bubble wand but it captures and reflects light."

"Ridiculous. It's nothing like…" he thought about it for a second and his face began to turn pink. "Okay, yeah. It's a little like a bubble wand." He formed another ball of light in his palm and, this time, very carefully cupped it in front of her.

She reached out and felt the film that covered the ball. "How is the light generated?"

Jax made the wand pop back into the bracelet and turned it over. "It uses your energy to power it, so it can wear you out. Excessive use will drain you. This is the first and easiest weapon to use against a shadow, but try to avoid it in public. Most people are unable to see the shadows, but a crazy person wielding light bombs, no matter how harmless, is bound to draw attention."

Wendy tried to create a ball of light and nothing happened. She looked up and saw Jax's frown deepen. He gave her a searching look.

She stepped back and flicked her wrist, trying to envision the glowing orb, but she barely felt a tingle in her fingertips.

"Why doesn't mine work?" she asked.

He shook his head. "Because you're not one of us. It's a lost boy thing, something that only we can use. It's part of our genetic code. See?"

"Then why train me in something I can't use?" she huffed.

"Because it was a test. I thought for a second that you—" he trailed off, his teeth began to grind and she watched his jaw muscle tic. "Never mind, I was wrong." He glared at her. "Lessons over for today. Don't let yourself think it went well...it didn't." He strode toward the gym door, turning back at the last minute. "Don't get settled in. You don't belong here."

Wendy's heart sank as she watched him retreat, the darkness of depression beginning to consume her. She pushed back those thoughts and tried to focus on her future. She unclipped the light brace, left it on the bench, and headed back to her room.

Every part of her wanted to crawl back into bed and pull the covers over her head. Instead she combatted it by opening the curtains and letting as much light as she could into the room.

She grabbed a clean set of clothes and headed out. Tink was just leaving her room.

"Showers?"

"Upstairs, second door to your right. There are towels in a laundry basket inside. They're clean, just not folded."

Wendy walked up the stairs and found the bathroom easily. As soon as the shower steamed up the room, she peeled off her clothes and let them fall to the floor in a heap. She stayed under the hot streams for what felt like hours, hoping the water would wash away all of her restless emotions. She opened a new bar of generic hotel soap and scrubbed her body until the little bar was gone. Wendy washed her hair three times until the hot water ran out. Even then, Wendy didn't want to get out. She just slid to the back of the shower and let the water beat against her skin. It had been forever since she felt truly clean, and she was enjoying the accommodations here at Neverwood, even if she did have to put up with people like Jax.

Someone knocked on the door, but she didn't answer. She thought she heard it open, but Wendy never looked up. The water stopped spraying and something soft landed on Wendy's head—a towel.

"Get up, lazy bones," Tink sassed. "Here are some normal clothes. You can thank me later, by not saying thanks." Then the door slammed closed.

Wendy pulled herself up and put on black stretchy pants, an oversize pink sweater that went past her hips, and fuzzy, warm socks. Tink had even been kind enough to include a comb. Wendy brushed out her long strawberry blonde hair and blew it dry. It fell in soft waves past her shoulders. She'd forgotten how pretty her hair was when it wasn't covered with dirt.

She headed downstairs to the main rec area. As she walked into the room, her skin prickled at the stares of all of the boys. Tink, obviously immune to it, headed back up to the loft to work on the computers.

A skinny teen, wearing an oversized jersey and glasses, sat on the floor by the coffee table with Tootles. They were poring over school books—the older boy evidently tutoring the younger.

The ping-pong twins sat on the other couch playing a PS4—some kind of racing game.

"You're here!" Tootles jumped up, knocking books off his lap, and ran to hug Wendy around the waist, his fists bunching in her shirt. "I have more riddles."

"I love riddles." She really had missed him. The skinny tutor stood, pushed his glasses up the bridge of his nose, and watched her as if waiting for something. The twins stopped playing their game, and she saw a blur of motion as they merged into one person.

"Whoa! What happened?" Wendy shook her head. "I thought there were two of you." Was she hallucinating again?

"Isn't it the coolest?" Tootles climbed up the couch and jumped off the armrest. He landed on the boy's back and held on like a wrestler trying to put a sleeper hold on him. The boy smirked, and in a second blur, there were once again two of him. One of them grabbed Tootles from the back and gently launched him into the air to land on the couch with a bounce.

"Again, again!" Tootles yelled.

The second twin tilted his head, cracked his knuckles, and feinted left at Tootles—the other boys laughed as they watched. Then with another blur of movement there was only one. He held out his hand to Wendy and gave her a wry smile.

"We've never been introduced. I'm Ditto."

"Ditto?"

"Yeah, it means to duplicate or repeat. And that's what I can do. I can temporarily duplicate myself."

The skinny guy coughed and rubbed the back of his head. "We've been working on seeing how long he can control his other half—they actually work in conjunction pretty well."

Wendy did a double-take as she stared at the scrawny guy. Did she know him? When he started to move closer to her, she noticed his limp—Slightly!

"Yeah, but it wasn't always like that," Ditto admitted. "It's kind of disconcerting. Like dual tunnel vision, but I've gotten better at handling it."

"When I first came, and you were playing pool against yourself, you didn't say much. I thought you were just upset," Wendy said.

Ditto's face turned red. "I don't like talking when I replicate. Not saying that I can't. I just prefer not to."

Wendy stared at Ditto, and he backed away from her. Her discomfort must've made him feel awkward. She sat on the couch, and Tootles scooted close, gazing up at her.

Wendy pointed her finger at Slightly. "And you...you change too. I'm not crazy. I've seen it."

Slightly bit his lip, and Ditto punched him in the arm.

"Do it, Slightly. Shift to the Bulk." Ditto turned and grabbed Slightly's glasses and taunted. "Come on man. She's seen you as the Brain and the Bulk, let her see you morph."

Slightly reached for his glasses, but Ditto split in two and the glasses appeared with him across the room. Back and forth, he tossed the glasses, and Slightly's frustration level was on the rise. "Don't break those. I need them, Ditto." Slightly quivered with anger and then he grew taller and wider until he towered over Ditto and resembled the large linebacker she had first met.

Slightly laughed and lifted Ditto, his feet kicking and knocking over a barstool. As he dragged Ditto across the coffee table, books and papers scattered.

"Ah, put me down, Slightly." Ditto's voice came from both Dittos' mouths simultaneously, creating an echo. Which explained his hesitance to speak.

Tootles laughed and threw the couch cushions at the closest Ditto. Then he disappeared and reappeared on the other side, grabbing more throw pillows and tossing them. *Okay. Tootles can teleport.* Within minutes, the boys destroyed the room, and a larger than normal fox had appeared out of nowhere and was running among the furniture and yipping in excitement.

Wendy looked up to the booth.

Tink watched her from the balcony.

"You're…You're all…" Wendy stood to survey all the boys and turned around without looking. She bumped into the coffee table and lost her balance, falling into the hard wooden surface. As quick as she could, she jumped up and tried not to act like she'd just made a fool of herself from her surprise.

"Awesome!" Tootles chimed in from across the room. In a flash he was by her side holding her hand, interrupting Wendy's thoughts. That was probably for the best.

Because awesome was definitely not the word she would have chosen.

"H-how?" she squeaked out.

"It's in our genetic makeup," Peter's familiar voice drifted over her shoulder. "There's something special about each of us.

"Us?" Wendy turned to look at Peter and waited for him to sprout a tail.

"Yes, them...you...although I'm not sure why you yet."

Wendy shook her head. "No, you're wrong. I-I...I'm not like you. I'm normal. I just have bad dreams." She began to pace like a caged animal.

In this moment, she wanted to believe Jax—not Peter. She didn't want to belong here. This was her worst fears come to life—that she was different. She looked to Tink for backup, but the girl just shrugged at her.

"I don't think so," Peter said slowly. "You can see the shadows, which makes you special."

"You just haven't realized your potential yet," Slightly added. He had de-bulked and was standing before her once again in his oversize jersey and spectacles.

"I bet it will be amazing," Tootles piped up.

"She doesn't belong here," Jax said as he entered the room. "Tink was right. She's not one of us. She'll just slow us down." He walked over to the mini fridge, grabbed a glass bottle of ginger ale, and used the counter to pop the top.

Something in her rebelled. One thing was sure: she didn't just want Tink and Jax to dismiss her. She wanted answers, wanted to know why she'd been able to see the shadows all her life. But she'd believed for so long that she was just crazy. And now, she was causing dissension between Jax and Peter.

Wendy shook her head. "I think you made a mistake bringing me here." She felt the cushion sink next to her as

Peter sat down. She whispered under her breath so only he could hear. "I think I'm causing more problems just by my presence." She hated being the center of an argument.

"I admit, I make a lot of mistakes, but bringing you here—Wendy, that's not one of them. I believe in you. Now you need to believe in yourself."

Her heart fluttered at his acceptance of her, but she still had doubts. "This is getting increasingly difficult to swallow. My whole life, doctors have told me everything I see is fake, but here you say it's real. It's hard to believe what I'm seeing with the boys too. It doesn't seem humanly possible."

"That's because they're not." Jax took a final swig of the pop and tossed the bottle in the receptacle. "They're not human."

She snapped her head up. He'd said "them." Was he not like them either? She wanted to question him, but Tink's voice called down over the wall. "We've got active dead zones popping up in Washington County."

Peter jumped up from the couch, and the boys in the room looked to him for direction. "Ditto, Jax, Slightly, you're with me on this one."

"What does that mean?" Wendy asked.

Ditto, more pale-faced than she'd seen him, put on a light brace. "It means shadows are congregating—and where they congregate, a morphling appears. It's a race to see who can get there first. Hook and his Red Skulls or us." He looked resigned, prepared to step into battle.

She briefly wondered which was worse—meeting a Red Skull or a morphling?

"Tink, I need you to stay here with Wendy," Peter ordered.

"I'm not a freakin' babysitter!" she screeched. Tink charged down the stairs, shouldering her bag. "I'm going and that's it." Her censor band began to have a field day.

"I'm fine by myself." Wendy said. No one seemed to hear her over their rush to get armed and out the door.

"Tink," Peter gave her a pleading look.

"I'll stay, Peter," Slightly said. He pushed his glasses up his nose and turned to give Wendy a tentative smile. "She should stay with someone she knows."

"Okay." Peter's frown turned into a smile. "Wendy, you're in good hands."

The four of them left without much fanfare. Wendy began to worry as soon as the door was closed. She paced. She bit her nails.

Slightly rubbed the back of his head.

"Are they going to be all right?" Wendy asked.

"Of course. Peter's the best at this. Hey, why don't I show you the control room to help take your mind off what they're doing?"

Slightly didn't take her up to the loft, but instead, led her to the main control room. This one didn't have a crafted wood door. A heavy metal door with a key card scanner barred their way.

Slightly swiped his card and then motioned her in, over to the bank of computers. They sat down and, after a few quick strokes on the keyboard, a map of the city appeared on a big central screen. "We have antennae on the roof, and they can tap into all of the major cell towers. We're tracking the dead zones created by the shadows. For some reason, shadows mess with the radio waves. The more shadows in an area, the larger the dead zone."

She watched the screen. A certain colored area lit up yellow and disappeared. A few seconds later, it reappeared, only in a different shape. Was this a dead zone?

"Tink scans and follows the dead zone. For instance, normal dead zones are usually in valleys—or they're at least stationary. But a dead zone caused by a shadow moves. We monitor the signal strength, zero in on the mobile ones, and then we switch to the mobile unit."

"That's the box thingy she uses." Wendy felt like she was catching on.

"Yeah, it's portable—also not as accurate." Slightly rolled his chair over to the cabinet and pulled a key out of his pocket to unlock the door. He pulled out the smaller portable device.

Something bothered her. She was still missing a key piece of information. "So why can't everyone see the shadows like I can?"

"I don't know. Maybe you've got a special gift?"

"What about Tink?"

"Tink can't see them without her special goggles either. She's special, but in her own right."

"What about all of you? How come you all..." she trailed off.

Slightly looked a bit embarrassed. "Well, we're a bit different. D.U.S.T. changed us—D.U.S.T. was a program run by Neverland."

"Neverland. Peter said that's where the shadows are from."

He nodded. "They took us as kids and gave us PX-1, some experimental drug. As we aged, we mutated. Sort of freaky, but this is who we are.

"And is Neverland still experimenting on kids?" She scratched at her neck again as an unsettled feeling overcame her. Her mouth went dry and she found it difficult to slow her breathing, which had picked up unexpectedly. Why was she scared?

"I don't think so, but I couldn't say for certain. I know Neverland creates nightmares, and unleashes them to do the corporation's bidding. Soon, they'll do it for the highest bidder.

"Why doesn't the government stop them?"

Slightly laughed and eyed her. "How can you stop what you don't believe exists? Especially if you can't see it. There was only one man that knew how to fight Neverland—Mr. Barrie. He created Neverland Corporation. But when his shareholders forced him out, he saw it coming and went with Plan B: Neverwood."

"What about Neverland? Don't they know you're here?"

"No, we're hidden and well protected." He grinned and started to click away at the screen. He pushed off in his rollaway chair and stopped before another monitor.

"Here are the schematics for the school. We control all of the security, including holograms that hide our location from the Red Skulls." Various boxes and colors lit up the screen indicating every defense system in the school. And there were plenty.

"Our system is based on hiding and misdirection," he said. "If a morphling makes its way here...then BAM!" He pointed to a red switch on a panel and made an explosion motion with his hands. "I turn this place into a giant disco ball of light that will make the shadows scatter." He pointed his finger in the air and did a sixties dancing pose. "Except no music."

"What about the Red Skulls?" That name...it made her neck prickle. Differently than it did when she'd seen them at the school that night. Not just because they were dangerous. Something else.

"Well, if they get through my traps, then the boys will take care of them. And nobody wants to mess with the lost boys."

"I guess I'm not following. How can a handful of teen boys—even if they do have special powers—take on a heavily armed militia?"

"We are getting stronger, and our numbers are growing too. Jax is fantastic at training in hand to hand combat. He's the best. He's taken each of the boys and really trained them to use their abilities."

Wendy was uncomfortable at the obvious idol status Slightly bestowed on Jax. "Do you trust him?"

"Of course," Slightly asked, clearly offended. "He's one of us, he's a lost boy."

If only she could say she trusted Jax. She wanted to, she really did.

Something beeped on the computer screen, and Slightly groaned. "Oh, this doesn't look good. They're on their way back and heading here fast." Slightly hit a button, and an alarm sounded throughout the school.

Wendy watched the map as a fast blue dot darted toward their location. It wasn't using roads. "How is it possible that—"

She looked up and the room was abandoned.

-23-

CHAOS ENSUED AS LOST boys started pouring out of their rooms and classes, heading to the main hall. Wendy ran out to find Slightly, but he had already disappeared.

Unsure what to do, she jogged down the stairs and stayed back on the steps to watch the main door. It seemed the lost boys really were a trained mini-army, because they had gathered in groups at each of the main exits.

She felt helpless and small in such a crisis situation. Did she even have anything to offer? What should she do? One of the lost boys, Fox, started to glow yellow and his motions became faster, as if he was bouncing out of his skin. Another boy's eyes became black as night; she heard Fox call him Onyx.

Wendy shivered in fear, not wanting to discover what Onyx's special ability could be.

Slightly appeared behind her. His phone buzzed and he answered it, listening for a few seconds. Then he motioned for the boys closest to the tunnel to run down and open it. Echoes of feet came rushing back and a disheveled Tink and Peter rushed in, carrying a body between them. When they shuffled him, his head fell forward.

Ditto.

"Get him to the medic room!" Slightly shouted.

A blur of motion, and Fox was at Tink's side, helping shoulder Ditto's weight. Wendy barely saw him move. Onyx came to help and relieved Peter. Both boys followed Slightly down the hall.

Tink leaned against the wall and slid down, her legs collapsing under her. Her hands shook and she covered her eyes.

Peter turned and kicked the door. When that didn't satisfy him, he kicked it again. And again.

"Where's Jax?" Wendy asked, feeling a surge of panic.

"He stayed behind to lead them away from us." Peter turned. A bloody, red scratch ran the length of his face.

"What happened, Peter?" Onyx asked.

"It was a morphling," Peter answered. "They gathered and attacked another innocent. We didn't get there in time." He stormed past the boys. More questions and concerns flew at him, but he jogged upstairs and ignored them all.

The door opened again and an angry Jax stepped through. He glared at the surrounding kids and barked at them, "It's fine. We weren't followed." He stomped upstairs after Peter.

It looked like Jax was going to have a few choice words with his fearless leader.

Wendy went over to Tink, who had finally gotten up, her small body trembling. "Are you okay?"

Tink wiped her nose on her sleeve and nodded. "Yeah, it's just those things are scary, and it got ahold of Ditto before we even knew it was there. Peter was able to wrench him away. It wasn't a very strong one. But still."

"Is Ditto going to be okay?" Wendy asked.

"Yeah, yeah. Just a scratch, so the venom wasn't a high dose, but he'll have nightmares for a few days." She looked worried. "I uh, need to get back to work." Tink brushed past her and headed upstairs.

Tootles came up to Wendy and slid his hand into hers. She looked down at the small boy and felt her heart swell. He was scared. He kept flickering in and out of sight, and he was using her hand to ground himself.

Finally, something she could do. "Tootles, are you hungry?" His small head bobbed up and down. "Good, so am I. Show me where a starving girl can get some food around here."

Tootles led Wendy to the main dining hall, where a buffet dinner was set up. She picked up her dinner roll, cut it down the center, and turned it into a talking bread puppet. His squeals of laughter lifted the tension in the dining room. More and more boys brought their plates over to sit by Wendy and join in the fun. For the next hour she told stories and jokes, trying to make the young boy laugh.

Fox had quite the talent for storytelling too. And the kid with black eyes, Onyx, did amazing impersonations.

Her hand went to Tootle's back and rubbed it fondly. He leaned over and put his head on her arm. He was so young to be here without family.

After they'd eaten, Tootles tugged on her arm and led her from the dining hall to see his room. Toy trains decorated the walls and the floor—probably the reason behind his name. When it was time for bed, he pleaded with Wendy to tuck him in and say prayers. She wondered whether he had a mother out there somewhere.

Tears filled her eyes as she thought of her own family and bedtime routine. After listening to a long story, Tootles fell asleep. Wendy let herself out of his room.

She wandered past the recovery room and peeked in to see Ditto sitting up in bed. Slightly and Tink were both talking to him. He kept shaking his head and trying to get up.

"We're fine. I'm fine. Stop being a nanny goat!" Ditto flung the blanket off the bed. He appeared to be recovering fine, so she headed back to her room but stopped when she came to the office. She heard raised voices— Peter and Jax arguing about something.

It wasn't her place to interfere, so she hastened toward her room. But then she heard Jax say her name.

She went back and pressed her ear to the door.

"Send her back to where she came from! She's no use here, and she doesn't need to be learning our secrets."

"Back to the streets?" Peter's voice rose in protest. "After you suggested she come here?"

"I was wrong. I admit it. But I suggested the refuge, not Neverwood."

"Give me your reasoning, Jax. I need to know why."

"I have a bad feeling about it. That's all"

190

"Is this one of your intuitions again?" Peter asked. "Because those hunches have saved our hide plenty of times with the Red Skulls."

Silence followed. Wendy held her breath.

"Jax, I can't ask her to leave. You know that."

"That's because you have feelings for her." Jax's voice rose again. "You're not thinking like a true leader."

"And you are? Sending a girl out unprepared when the shadows seem to be following her around. No, she's safer here."

"Safer for who? Not us. I tell you this girl will be our undoing," Jax snarled. "Maybe she'll just choose to leave on her own."

Wendy pulled back from the door at the sound of footsteps, but she wasn't fast enough. The door opened and she faced Jax's dark angry eyes. He closed the door so Peter didn't see her.

"Spying?" He raised an eyebrow.

That night, she lay in bed wide awake for hours. When she finally fell asleep, it was to be plagued by dreams...of shadow monsters, and a building burning, and drowning.

-24-

THE NEXT MORNING JAX knocked and demanded in a gruff voice for her to get to the gym for more training. She waited for more accusations to fly at her, but he didn't even stay to talk.

This time she was prepared to walk into darkness, smart enough not to announce her position. A ball of light flew in her direction and she dodged it, grinning at her accomplishment. Except that she remembered she'd had no other plan of attack.

"Hard to attack when you leave your weapon behind," Jax growled as he sprung up behind her. He hit a button on his brace and the gym lights came up. He picked up her abandoned light brace from the bench.

"What's the point? I can't use it," Wendy argued.

Clearly irritated, Jax shoved the brace back into her hand. "Maybe it's because you don't believe you can do it."

"Yesterday you said that I couldn't use it because I'm not like you. Has that changed?"

"Maybe, do you believe yet?"

She sighed and snapped it back on her arm. "What does this light ball do to the shadows?"

"It makes the morphlings lose their shape if they haven't shifted into anything more solid. If they're hit with a strong enough blast, they'll dissipate instantly. They can re-form, but it gives us time to get away."

"Is light the only weapon against them?"

"In their pre-morph shape. After that it's all physical, but they're not your only problem."

"What can you do?" She eyed Jax.

"Excuse me?" He looked irritated by her question.

"Um," she faltered, "it seems everyone can do something...what's your gift?"

His eyes grew dark and he cracked his knuckles. "Believe me, you don't want to know."

"I do, actually," she pressed.

It seemed to make him even angrier, but then he shook his head and dropped his gaze. "I used my gift once and people—too many—died. I've promised myself I'd never lose control of it again. So don't ask."

There was heaviness in the air. Was it guilt?

"Why don't you want me here?" she pressed, changing the subject.

He seemed startled. "Because it's not safe."

"For who?"

"For us," he said.

Wendy looked around the gym, "That seems pretty cryptic and doesn't give me a reason to leave. What aren't you telling me?"

"Plenty. I *know* your kind."

"No you don't." Wendy answered.

"I know you better than you know yourself," he grinned.

"That sounds pretty stalkerish." She stepped away from him, giving him room.

"The Red Skulls *will* find you—eventually—and you will lead them right to Neverwood's doorstep." Jax seemed adamant.

"I'd never do that."

"You would, given the right motivation," Jax said firmly.

"Nothing would make me betray Neverwood," her voice filled with false bravado.

He stared her down. "Hook is ruthless. He's worse than the morphlings or the Red Skulls. He just has to find your weak spot and then," he picked up an air-filled ball, "apply enough pressure and—"

POP!

Wendy jumped.

"We're all dead or worse...back at Neverland."

He gave her his back, which made Wendy angry. How dare he accuse her of betraying them when she just got here.

"Test me," she demanded.

"What?" He turned surprised.

"You heard me." She brought her fists up into a fighting stance. "Do your worst. Try and make me talk."

He actually laughed. "If you actually went toe to toe with me, you'd be running for the hills." He paused in thought. "Maybe I should show you what you're up against. Give you a taste of how ruthless the Red Skulls are."

Wendy gulped and wanted to withdraw her earlier challenge.

Jax lunged at her. She screamed when he slammed her body against the wall, his hand wrapping around her throat. She stilled, her back pressed against the cool wall. "The Red Skulls only understand one thing—violence."

Wendy clawed at her throat, pulling at Jax's thumbs, trying to loosen his grip, but he was relentless. She was stunned by his sudden switch to aggression.

"Stop!" she gasped. "Please stop!"

He whispered against her ear. "Tell me where the lost boys are, Wendy. Lead me to the one called Peter."

He wasn't applying as much pressure on her throat as she'd thought. It was just enough to scare her—her own struggles against him were what was cutting off her wind-pipe. That thought steadied her.

"Never." She stopped fighting and relaxed. She stared into Jax's eyes with a resolved calm. His eyes bored into hers, and she saw a hint of underlying panic at her lack of response.

"Try, Wendy. The Red Skulls are pirates; they will not take it easy. Fight."

She shook her head.

"Hook will come. He will kill everything you hold dear, everyone you love. Even your family."

An image of her mom, dad and brother flashed in her mind. The thought of their deaths frightened her enough that she froze, her body going limp.

Jax took her fear for acceptance, his hands loosened around her neck, and he stepped back with a look of shock. He ran his hands through his hair as he studied her.

"You have to fight, Wendy. It's easy in a controlled environment, where you know it's a test, but can you really handle conflict in the heat of the moment?"

She was feeling a bit braver and rubbed her throat. "Of course. I can handle most surprises."

She moved away but was caught off guard when Jax spun back and pinned her to the wall with his body. She squeaked in surprise, but all sound was cut off when his warm lips pressed against hers, forceful. Their lips ground against each other in pain, and his hand found her lower back, pulling her toward him.

No! Wendy reached for his wrist, twisted it, and pressed a button on the brace. His light brace released a blast of light right in his face.

While Jax was blinded, Wendy brought her foot up and kneed him.

He doubled over in pain.

Wendy lunged to the side, but his hand caught her foot and she fell onto the floor mat. He dragged her back and kneeled on top of her. His strong hands pinned her wrists to the mat beside her head.

"Let me go!"

The corner of his mouth worked up into a grimace of pain before it slid into a smile. "That was excellent, Wendy. You're very resourceful under pressure." Another pained look. "Even using the light brace against me."

"Don't ever kiss me again!" Wendy hissed. She tried to buck him off and roll away, but he was too heavy.

Jax's hands tightened on her wrist and he leaned down, his face and mouth mere inches from hers. "Relax, this was just a test." He smiled. "I promise if I'd kissed you for real, you wouldn't say that a second time." He pulled back, his eyes fixated on her lips.

Her heart began to race, and Jax glanced up at her wrists, rubbing his thumb gently across the underside.

"Your pulse just picked up at the thought of me kissing you." Jax eyed her lips and leaned forward again.

Wendy sucked in her breath and closed her eyes, unsure if she was scared or excited.

Lights! Bright overhead lights blinded her as Tink entered.

She froze when she saw Jax over Wendy on the mats. "Well, well, well. What do we have here?" She put her hand on her hip and snapped her gum in her mouth.

-25-

WENDY'S FACE WAS ON fire—she was sure
her cheeks were bright red.

Jax sighed and got off the mat, leaving her to
scramble to her feet in front of the gloating Tink. This was
not how she expected her second day at the Neverwood
Academy to go.

Tink's gum snapped loudly again, and she lifted an
eyebrow at Jax. She stalked slowly around and looked
him up and down. "I didn't think she was your type, but
then again, we all have our secrets. Don't we? Like where
you keep disappearing to in the middle of the night?" she
challenged.

Jax snorted. "You're right. She's not my type, and the
other is none of your business." He marched out, the gym
door slamming behind him.

The slam of the door felt like a slap in the face. Wendy
tried to straighten her hair, since her ponytail was skewed
and had almost come undone.

Tink had watched Jax leave, and now turned to give
Wendy a calculating look. "So when you're done fawning
over every boy at our school—"

"That's not what it looked like," Wendy interrupted. "He was training me."

"In what, mouth to mouth resuscitation?" Tink snorted. "Look, I get it. He's hot, and there are a lot of guys here and only two available girls. Things can get awkward pretty easily. Just be careful."

"What are you doing here?" Wendy grumbled, her face a mass of red.

Tink put her hands on her hips and studied Wendy. "I'm your next instructor." She wasn't dressed in a training suit like Jax. She was wearing green shorts and a black and green plaid shirt. She was shorter than Wendy by at least three inches.

"What are you going to train me in—fashion sense and sarcastic comebacks?"

Tink's green eyes sparkled mischievously and her smile grew, "Better, my young Padawan. Soon, you'll be a master insulter like me."

"Yes, Master Yoda," Wendy grinned.

Tink turned and gave Wendy an ugly glare at the insult, but then she started to laugh. "Did you call me Yoda because I wear so much green?"

"And because you're short."

"Nice," Tink laughed. "I approve. Let's blow this place and get ice cream."

Wendy looked at her watch. "It's seven thirty in the morning."

"Perfect time for it, don't ya think?"

"How's Ditto doing?" Wendy asked.

"He's Ditto," Tink snorted. "He's pretending he's not scared, but soaking up all of the attention he's getting."

Tink and Wendy made their way to the kitchen and into the large dining room. A buffet of warmers filled with eggs, hash browns and French toast, lined one wall. About twenty boys of varying ages were downstairs this morning, most looked to be from thirteen to mid-twenties.

Tink cut through the room, headed straight for a warmer, and flipped the lid back. A blast of humid air and the mouthwatering smell of bacon hit Wendy's face. Tink grabbed tongs and crammed a napkin full. Wendy mimicked Tink and followed her through a swinging door and into the industrial sized kitchen. With purpose, Tink made her way to the walk-in freezer, pulled it open, and stepped inside. Seconds later, she returned with two pints of Ben and Jerry's Ice Cream. She tossed a Cherry Garcia to Wendy and then grabbed two spoons out of a drawer in the center island.

"This way." Tink nodded and left through another side door. They were in a back hallway. They walked in silence up the stairs to the crime-scene-taped door, and Tink opened it.

"Welcome to the brain—my brain." Tink turned with a pleased smile, showing off her extremely messy bedroom. Clothes and electronics littered every available space, except for a desk with a Mac. The computer desk was spotlessly clean. "From here, I can control all of Neverwood's defenses without having to be in the control room." She sat on her unmade bed, opened up the carton of ice cream, crumbled the bacon into bits, and sprinkled them on top before taking a bite. Her eyes rolled back in her head with joy. "You've got to try it."

Wendy wasn't convinced, but she didn't want to insult her instructor, so she sat on a chair covered with what she hoped were clean clothes, opened her napkin, and broke off a corner of a piece of bacon. She put it on her spoon of ice cream. Wendy wrinkled her nose preemptively as the cool spoon touched her tongue, and she ate. A few chews later, she bobbed her head in agreement. "Mmm. It is good."

"Told you," Tink quipped. "Ohh, brain freeze!" She grabbed her blonde head and then shook it. "But enough about ice cream. I need to know what your intentions are."

"Regarding what exactly?"

"Peter," Tink seemed focused on her ice cream and didn't look at her.

"I don't understand."

"GAH!" Tink said. "What don't you understand? It's not that hard."

Wendy wasn't really in the mood for ice cream anymore. Tink's plan was a little too obvious: offer ice cream and pretend to be buddy-buddy just so she could interrogate her. "Well, I barely know him."

"Exactly!" Tink pointed her spoon at Wendy. "And it's best if you keep it that way and not make things complicated."

"How so?" Defensive, Wendy realized she'd read Tink right. And Jax surely didn't want her here—at least she thought that's how he really felt. Two of them—two of

Peter's closest friends—hated that she was here. What was she supposed to do with that?

"Peter likes you. I can tell," Tink added glumly. She poked her spoon in her ice cream. She hadn't taken a bite in a while.

Wendy's cheeks warmed at Tink's admission of Peter's feelings. Her heart sped up. "And that's bad because...?"

"You distract him. Peter is the only one keeping Neverwood running right now and you...don't really belong here yet. You don't really know who Peter is and what he can do. You don't know the real Peter."

"What are you talking about, Tink? What are you not telling me?" Wendy was beginning to hate everything about this place. Today was becoming one of the worst days ever.

"Listen, and listen well. You're just a surrogate. You remind him of someone he couldn't save...a long time ago. He's been beating himself up over that for years. But let's get this straight. You're not this girl. She died. Peter's developed a bit of a savior complex since that day. He's projecting those feelings onto you—trying to save you—but I have to ask myself if you're worthy to be saved."

"You know nothing about me!" Wendy argued. "You know nothing of my life, or my circumstances, or the nightmares I've lived through."

"Listen, growing up in middle suburbia with a family is a way better life than what any of us ever got here. This is our family. This is all we have."

"If you knew anything about me, then you'd know I don't need to be saved. I can save myself." She'd had enough of Tink's barbs. She stood and tossed her half-eaten pint of ice cream in the trash, and only wondered for a second if the girl would take it out later. "Thanks for the girl talk." Wendy glared at Tink. "Let's not do it again any time soon."

Trying to leave gracefully, Wendy's foot became tangled in a pair of jeans. Tink just laughed.

Wendy slammed the door and headed downstairs, her hands clenched into fists. Man, she really wanted to punch something.

How come everyone doubted her? Was it because she doubted herself? She really was starting to believe that she had made a mistake coming here. Jax was right. She didn't belong.

Maybe the shadows weren't really after her. She'd been seeing them for years. If they were after her, they'd had plenty of chances to try and nab her. The more she thought about it, the more likely it seemed that Peter had made a mistake about her.

About everything.

-26-

WENDY SPENT MOST OF the day in her room, eventually she wondered out and headed downstairs. She collapsed on the couch in the rec room next to a seemingly recovered replicated Ditto and hoped no one could see she'd been crying. It was late evening and Slightly was sprawled out on another chair across the room as the three played a video game.

"So how are you feeling?" Wendy asked the Ditto sitting closest to her.

He dropped the game controller and became one person and grimaced a bit. "Great, except I didn't sleep well."

"Bad dreams?"

He swallowed and looked at her. His red-rimmed eyes filled with fear. "The worst." He rubbed his eyes. "It will go away in a few weeks."

"Yeah, I have them too." Wendy offered up.

"Mine are worse," he challenged. He continued to click the controller and jerked his whole body as he tried to dodge an incoming attack.

Wendy laughed and tucked her legs under her. "Can you beat dreaming about being trapped as a building burns around you?"

Ditto nodded his head and gave her an odd glance. "Yeah, that's exactly what I dream."

Slightly added, "Mine are running. I'm running through the woods and someone is hunting me."

Her hand went cold as she looked over at Ditto. Slightly stopped playing the game to stare at her. Her voice was barely above a whisper. "How does your dream end?"

Ditto licked his lips and answered. "Well, I'm obviously saved at the last minute."

Slightly nodded his head. "Yeah, me too. How about you?"

Wendy felt like she was going to throw up. She'd never told anyone about her dream and how it ended. "I drown."

Wendy couldn't look at the guys. She glanced at the 60-inch TV and recognized the video game on the big screen—the same one her brother played. In fact there was an extra headset on the coffee table. Someone was talking frantically on the other end.

She watched the four-way split screen as one soldier fought an enemy base by himself. The other three avatars stood frozen, taking damage and getting killed. Wendy looked at the screen and read the name of the player who was fighting the losing battle alone.

Lt. J-Dog.

205

"John?" Wendy gasped, feeling her knees go weak. With trembling hands she reached for Ditto's extra headset and brought it up to her ears.

"Slightly! Ditto! Man, where are you guys? We're getting creamed again. You better not have abandoned me for some girl," John's voice came over the headset.

Wendy watched his lone avatar try to take the enemy base, not knowing he'd been abandoned. A second later, three of the screens faded red, as Ditto's two characters and Slightly were killed off by the other team.

Her mouth was dry and she swallowed, trying to speak. "John?" her voice rasped. Tears started to pour down her cheeks. She turned around and saw Ditto scratching the back of his neck and refusing to make eye contact. Slightly's shoulders were hunched, and he wouldn't look up from his shoes.

"Wait...what? Wendy, is that you?" Her brother's voice spoke back in disbelief. She swallowed, about to say more, but Tootles ran through the room and tripped over the game system.

It came unplugged. All she got was static on the other end.

She turned and stared accusingly at the boys in front of her. "It was you...both of you. You were playing that night, with my brother. He said your name." Wendy pointed to Slightly. "I thought he was just giving you instructions. And you...she pointed up to the screen name of Ditto. "I recognize your voice."

Ditto and Slightly's faces had gone white, and they nodded, confirming what Wendy had already known.

"You've been following me, spying on me since before the football game? It was no accident; you were there that night. You lied to me—even figured out my worst nightmares to play them against me. Trying to get me to trust you. You are all sick!"

"No, that's not it, Wendy." Slightly jumped up from the chair. He seemed excited.

Peter joined them, tuning into the commotion. "Are you all right?" He tried to wrap his arms around her, but she pushed him away.

"No, no I'm not," Wendy cried out. Tears welled in her eyes, making his face swim before her. "I think I'd like to be alone."

Peter's jaw set in a firm line and he nodded in understanding. She headed out of the room.

Slightly called out after her, but she held up her hand to cut him off. "Don't say anything. I don't want to hear it." She made it to her room where she lay down on her bed and cried until her lungs burned. Her heart ached for her family. John had sounded so surprised to hear her! It made her chest hurt all the more deeply. She wanted to go home. Even if she did have weird similarities with some of these guys, she didn't belong here. Not with people who lied to her.

What were the chances of meeting so many people from Neverwood on the same night by coincidence?

Those weren't odds she trusted.

It might break her heart to leave Peter and Tootles, but she couldn't stay here. Not now. She grabbed her backpack, filled it with the few items she owned, and left the room.

Tink was leaning against her own door waiting for her. "It's time for your next class."

"That's not going to happen, Tink," Wendy spoke angrily. "I'm leaving this place."

"And going where?"

"Anywhere that's not here." Wendy headed toward the exit.

"You're serious? And after I just started to like you too," Tink scoffed.

"I'm not a prisoner," Wendy chastised. "Peter said I'm welcome to come and go as I please. Are you saying that's not true?"

Tink's lip stuck out in an angry fit. "No, but by walking out that door, you're endangering not only yourself, but all of us at Neverwood."

"I never said I wanted to be here, that I would become one of you. I came here because you offered me a safe place to stay."

"We're not Motel 6," Tink's voice rose. "If you leave—don't come back."

"Well, maybe I would have chosen to stay if you guys had told me the truth from the beginning." Wendy adjusted her backpack and headed down into the main rec room. She grabbed a couple bottles of water off the counter to toss in her backpack.

Tootles snuck up behind her and watched as she grabbed some granola bars and other snack foods laid out for them. "You're not staying with us, are you?" His bottom lip trembled.

Wendy turned to kneel behind the bar and out of sight of the others. Hopefully, no one else had heard. "No, Tootles, I don't belong here. You do though."

He wrapped his hands around her shoulders and squeezed. "But I was hoping that you'd stay and be my mom and tell me stories and tuck me in at night."

Movement from above caught her attention, and Wendy looked up to see Peter sitting in the loft above, looking down on her. His expression was unreadable, but it was obvious that he could hear them.

"No, Tink can be your mom." Wendy hugged the small boy back, and she felt the crack in her heart widen.

"Not Tink. She's terrible at telling stories. Her stories always end up with everyone being dead."

Wendy snorted, "Oh, come on. They can't all end like that."

Tootles' bottom lip pooched out. "Trust me, they do. Her latest story was about a bird named Wendy that was eaten by an eagle."

Wendy started coughing, and she could even hear Peter chuckling from the loft.

"Well then, I'll tell you what."

"What?"

Wendy looked around. She opened up the cupboard under the sink and found a paint stick. She grabbed a blue magic marker from the counter top and wrote two words on the stick. "This is a magic stick. What does it say?"

"Story wand."

"The next time the story doesn't end the way you want. You wave your magic story wand and bring the Wendy-bird or whoever else you want back to life. And whoever is telling the story must change the ending until it's one that you like. Got it?"

His fingers wiggled excitedly. "Got it!" He grabbed the paint stick and ran out to find Tink.

Wendy stood and looked up.

Peter sat on the banister, dangling his feet over the edge. His hair looked damp, as if he'd just showered, and he wore a clean blue shirt which made his eyes look different—deeper, sadder—in the light. "Wendy, I—"

"Peter was right. You are good at telling stories." Slightly had leaned over the bar counter to look at Wendy as she stood up to dust off her knees and hands. "Thanks for doing that for Tootles. He really wants a mother."

"Then take him home, Slightly," Wendy demanded. "To his family." Even though she spoke to Slightly, her voice aimed for Peter's ears.

"He's one of us. We're the only family he's got, and if he leaves, the Red Skulls will find him and take him. I can't have that. As long as he stays within these walls, he's safe," Slightly answered.

"So in other words, you've made him a prisoner out of fear," she yelled. The others looked up at her from their spots in the room. The mouth of one of the younger boy dropped open at her words.

Tink immediately gave Wendy the stink-eye and tried to calm him down. The twins jumped up simultaneously. Jax had entered the room and stood by the door, watching her with half-closed eyes. He might pretend not to care what was going on, but he stood right in the middle of the doorway.

"Excuse me," Wendy said rudely.

Jax didn't move, his arms crossed over his chest. She could see his fingers curl as if he was getting ready to jump on her.

"I thought you didn't want me here?" She whispered so only he could hear.

"My feelings may have suddenly changed. Maybe I'm waiting for that second kiss," he whispered back.

"Not going to happen." Wendy's cheeks felt warm.

His eyes drifted up, and Wendy turned and watched Peter give Jax a nod to let her pass. When Jax moved, she breathed out a long sigh. She could see the exit from where she stood. "Be careful," he murmured.

"You're protected here at Neverwood," Slightly called after her.

"But who will protect me from you?" Wendy answered. She entered the dark hall and jogged to the fireplace door. She pulled the large sliding deadbolt on the door and an immediate door alarm went off. Tink's censor box rang loudly from the main room. She must be scrambling to silence the alarms. The thought almost made Wendy smile.

Wendy rushed through the abandoned house, out the door, and down the steps.

She looked out into the dark night. A storm had come up and it was pouring rain. She gripped her backpack and headed out into the volley, letting it pelt her, soaking her only clean and dry shirt. She started walking. Maybe if she got to the main road, she could find a bus stop and use her last few dollars to get back to the park.

She was saddened when no one tried to stop her. Well, that wasn't true. She was disappointed Peter hadn't come for her.

-27-

AFTER A FEW BLOCKS of hiking in the rain, Wendy found a bus stop. Within moments the bus came around the corner. Perfect timing. She dug in her backpack and took out enough change to pay.

"Where you headed?" the friendly driver asked.

Wendy was the only person on the bus so she sat in the middle, facing front. "Doesn't matter," she mumbled as she stared out the window, searching for signs of movement in the darkness.

He closed the doors and drove off.

"What are you doing in this area so late?"

"My uncle owns a boat he keeps docked by the waterfront," she lied easily.

"A boat, eh? I own a boat. What kind?"

"A white one." She leaned her head back against the seat.

After a few more failed attempts at conversation, the driver stopped with the onslaught of questions and just drove his route. Wendy figured from the map on the small board inside that this route would take her about a mile from the park.

Did she want to go back to the park? Not really. Maybe she should go home? No. Not after Jax said the Red Skulls could hurt her family. She didn't want to endanger them. That didn't leave her any other option.

"This is the last stop for the night, miss." The driver turned in his seat. "Do you want off here? I'm not supposed to but if you need I can drop you off somewhere else. I can—as long as it's on my route back to the bus barn."

Wendy sat up. She had missed the stop for the park altogether. She looked up at the map and tried to place where she was—by the St. Mary's Catholic Church.

"This is fine," Wendy answered. She stood and waited for the doors to open. Something moved just at the edge of her vision, and she froze on the last step. Was it a trick of the rain, a part of her imagination?

"Is everything all right, miss?" The driver's palm rested on the handle, waiting for her to exit so he could close the doors.

Was everything all right? Her skin tingled, and she had to force her hand to let go of the railing and take the first step onto the pavement.

She moved into the circle of light cast by the street lamp and waited as the bus pulled away from the curb. She should have taken his offer for him to drop her off somewhere else, but where?

Wendy ran toward the Catholic church and ducked into the large entryway by the antiquated wooden doors with the brass lion knockers. She pulled out the sleeping bag from her pack, unzipped it, and wrapped it around her. With her back pressed to the wood, she pulled her backpack against her legs. Here under the safety of the church and guarded by the lion doorknockers, she would wait until morning.

Life was so much better before she'd learned about morphlings. She'd almost rather still think she was crazy. But she wasn't. She was apparently sane. Just sane with unreliable-or-absent memories. She was broken. And she needed to fix herself before she could fix or help the others.

Something large flew by and cast an ominous shadow along the sidewalk in front of the church.

"What in the world?" Wendy whispered and watched again. She grabbed her flashlight, tightened her grip on the sleeping bag in front of her neck, and tiptoed down the front steps of the church. She shined the beam all around the treetops. Her heart raced and her hands shook. But she didn't see or hear anything, so she went back to the church steps.

There, standing on the top step was Peter, his hands in his jacket pockets, looking like he just stepped out of a magazine.

"You would really leave without saying goodbye to me?" He walked off the top step and into the light. His hair and clothes were sopping wet. His eyes looked wounded.

"How did you get here?" Wendy turned to scan the street for a car or Tink's scooter. She hadn't heard any vehicles approaching.

He shrugged in a teasing manner and smiled. "I flew."

"I see," Wendy said. "As the crow flies, huh?"

Even dry, with the sleeping bag wrapped around her shoulders, Wendy still shivered from the rain. Or from Peter's closeness—she wasn't sure.

He stood in front of her now, gazing down into her eyes. The rain poured down his face in rivulets, but he didn't seem to notice.

"No, not crow. I'm faster than a crow." One corner of his mouth lifted, revealing his dimple. That dimple made him seem oh so much more charming.

That dimple could be her undoing.

"You were right," he said. "We *were* watching you. That's because two weeks earlier, the shadows were swarming your house. Your house was a dead zone. I'm not sure why, but I put my best team on it. We didn't know if a morphling was coming, but two more times, the dead zone moved around your house. I did it to protect you, but I have a crazy feeling that the shadows are actually gathering to help you." He sighed. "Now *I* sound crazy."

His body trembled slightly in front of her, but he didn't draw any closer, and he didn't touch her. How was it that she wanted him to? She wanted him to kiss her, really kiss her. To feel his lips pressed to hers and to hear him say she meant something to him.

"Wendy," her name fell from his lips.

She met his eyes. The water dripped from his face to hers, and he leaned in. He pulled her into his embrace. His body heat slowly merged with hers as he nuzzled closer to her. Her heart filled to overflowing. She wanted this moment to be locked away forever in her memory, but knew it couldn't last.

"Please. Don't leave me," he whispered against her cheek.

"You can't save everyone, Peter. You can't save me." She started to cry, her tears mingling with the raindrops.

"I can try." Peter buried his head into her neck, and she could feel his lips press against her skin in the gentlest of caresses. Maybe it wasn't a kiss, maybe it was just him whispering something she was unable to hear in the rain.

He took her hand and pulled her back up the church steps and to the door. After shaking off the excess water from the bag, he wrapped it around them both, and he sat in the corner, pulling Wendy against his side.

He didn't speak. He didn't ask questions. He just held her protectively against his side and hugged her.

They sat and enjoyed the silent comfort that came from being close to someone. No words were exchanged. No apologies were given. Words would only complicate things.

Wendy leaned her head against Peter's chest and listened to his heartbeat. It only took a moment for the coolness of his skin to warm up. His clothes were still wet, but at least he was warm. Peter nuzzled the top of her head with his cheek.

"Sleep, Wendy. I'll watch over your dreams."

"I remember you saying that once before."

"And I'll do it again."

How easy it would be to let herself fall in love with Peter. But then she remembered she couldn't trust him, and as painful as it was, she resolved not to fall in love.

But in her dream she could fall in love, so Wendy let herself dream.

And like she'd done in her dreams many times before, Wendy dreamed she was flying.

Peter held Wendy in his arms and tried not to jostle her as he pulled his specter goggles on over his eyes so he could scan the perimeter. Even though he didn't need them, it was always easier to use them in inclement weather.

Once again he could see the shadows, skirting the light and floating among the trees. Through the goggles, they looked like blurred shapes in light blue. Always at about the same distance, never leaving but never coming any closer to Wendy. They didn't seem to want to harm her, but he kicked himself for not bringing Tink's scanner.

He wasn't going to leave her unprotected again, not when the shadows' presence always attracted a morphling. Ugh. How he hated them, wanted to kill every single one of them.

Wendy moved as she snuggled under his arm. He took a deep breath and could smell her honey and vanilla shampoo. He pressed his mouth to the top of her head in a gentle kiss. What was it about her that made him so possessive? Was it her innocence, her laughter, her fighter instinct? He almost laughed out loud and woke her when he remembered the time she'd sliced his arm with a knife.

At the same time, though, she was childlike in her fears; she'd whimpered in her sleep at the safe house. Quite a few times, as he checked on her and listened outside her door last night, he heard her cry out in fear. But he never could make out what she said.

About an hour later, her REM cycle started, and Wendy began to kick out and twitch. "Don't let go of me!" she cried out in fear. He wrapped his arms around her tighter.

Peter froze. His body began to tremble as her words brought him back to his own personal nightmare—to that night on the boat. He closed his eyes and whispered. "Never."

-28-

S OMETHING WARM PRESSED AGAINST her face, and at first Wendy thought it was Peter. But then a rough, wet tongue lapped at her cheek.

She opened her eyes to a Saint Bernard eagerly sniffing her face.

Wendy grunted. "Nana?" Confused, Wendy sat up, her sleeping bag slipping off of her shoulders.

"Oh, Wendy child. What are you doing here so early? Don't tell me you slept here on the steps."

Wendy looked up at the ever-chipper Mr. Bernard. He was carrying his umbrella and holding Nana's leash.

Everything was wrong. She wasn't on the stoop of the Catholic church; she was sitting in front of Bernard Books. She looked to her right and Peter was gone. How did she get here? Where was Peter? Then the horrible realization came to her, and she felt like she was going to throw up. Had it been part of her imagination? She wasn't going to work at the bookstore, but then she showed up here. It must be a sign.

Wendy stood and quickly began rolling up her sleeping bag. "Um, I had to take the early bus this morning and ended up getting here…a few hours earlier than I'd thought."

"Oh, I see," Mr. Bernard said, opening the front door and setting his umbrella in a stand. "Well, come on in, come on in. I'll fix that by giving you a key." He headed back to his office and she followed. "That way, if you ever get here early again, or miss the bus home at night, you can just let yourself in and take a nap on the couch." He flung his jacket over his chair and rummaged through his desk.

"Key, key, key. Where's my spare key?" He pulled out multiple keys of various shapes and sizes until he found the small brass one. "Now for a key ring." He dug in a small tin cup until he found an old keychain with a charm. He attached the key and handed her both. "There's a shower and bathroom upstairs. Use it whenever you like."

Wendy stared at the key dangling from the keychain in her hand. "I'm not sure what to say other than thank you."

"Nothing, Wendy."

She fingered the small keychain charm and held it up to Mr. Bernard. "What is it?"

"Oh, that. That's a pan flute. I got it at a gift shop when I visited a small island in the Pacific for research on the book I'm writing."

"A pan flute? How interesting."

"Glad you like it. Don't lose your key," he warned. He opened up the safe and handed her the till and then immediately got started on his book. Nana curled up in the corner of his office on an overstuffed dog bed and went to sleep.

Wendy went out to start her morning routine. When the drawer was counted, front steps swept off, daily papers brought in, and the morning coffee brewed, she found herself at a loss. She decided to straighten the shelves, lining the books up with the edge.

With nothing left to do until the first customers came in, she poured herself a cup of coffee—one sugar, one cream—and sat by the front window to people watch. She absently picked up a pad of paper and a pencil and began to sketch. It had been a while since she'd drawn, but before long she had a decent image of Peter's face.

She glanced at the clock on the wall. Was he coming in today?

She wanted to ask him about last night. About whether or not he'd been at the church with her. But the front door never opened, and Peter never stepped through. By lunch time she was starving, and she hadn't thought to bring a lunch.

Mr. Bernard came out of the back office with Nana and pulled out his wallet. "Hey, Wendy. How about I make you a deal?"

"What's that, Mr. Bernard?"

"You take Nana for her walk, and while you're out, pick us both up some lunch at one of the vendors. She needs to go out, but I'm on a roll with writing. My main character is just about to encounter the pirates." He handed her a twenty.

"What do you want to eat? There's pizza, hotdogs, tamales..." she asked, glad for something to do.

"Oh, whatever you get, just get me the same." He handed her Nana's leash and waved her off. She watched as he quickly shuffled back to his office.

Wendy looked at the twenty-dollar bill in her hand and then down at Nana, whose front paws were shuffling a doggie two-step. She really was antsy to do her business. Wendy put out the small sign that said "Ring for Help" and opened the door for Nana, who bolted out onto the sidewalk.

"Whoa, Nana! Slow down." But the dog didn't listen. She just made a beeline for the crosswalk, and then stopped to wait for it to turn white. How the dog knew when to walk and when to wait was a mystery, but as soon as the walk symbol appeared, Nana dragged her across the road and down the path to the middle of Kinderly Park.

Nana's nose glided over the ground on the hunt for the perfect spot. She pulled Wendy off the stone path and into the trees. "Oh, come on, Nana. That looked just as good a place as any. Oh, thank goodness," Wendy exclaimed when Nana found a place to pee.

Unfortunately, it lasted for all of two seconds, and the dog was off again chasing after a squirrel.

"Down, Nana. No, Nana," Wendy commanded. But the dog only continued to yank her arm. She tried to readjust her grip on Nana's leash, so her hand wouldn't get ripped off at the wrist, but Nana bolted again.

The leash slipped out of Wendy's hands.

"Noo!" Wendy darted into a thicket after the Saint Bernard, but she couldn't make it very far.

Frustrated, she kneeled to see if she could crawl in. The Saint Bernard was the size of a small bear, so of course she should be able to follow her same path. The problem was the thicket itself. It was full of thorns—Nana had a nice, thick coat to protect her skin. Cautious, Wendy held up the branches and passed through the thicket and into a small clearing.

Nana was jumping up and barking at something in the tree.

"What is it, Nana?" Wendy asked softly as she picked up the leash from the ground. She tucked her wrist through the strap and wrapped it around her arm. If Nana wanted to run away again, she would have to take Wendy's arm with her.

Something dark was caught in Nana's teeth. Wendy reached down to remove it, thinking it was a bit of black cloth, but it wasn't corporeal.

A black, misty smoke clung to her canines.

Was it burning? In a hurry, Wendy swiped her hand through the dog's mouth, but the misty shadow swirled around her hand and disappeared, leaving a dark wet smear across her fingertips.

"What is this?" She looked closer. It looked like blood, except the color was off, wrong. It was almost black.

Nana's barking turned into a deep threatening growl. Alarmed, Wendy looked up and noticed a dark form sitting on a branch among the leaves. It was large, much larger than a squirrel or even a raccoon.

It moved suddenly, floating to the next branch. Wendy would've dropped the leash again if her arm hadn't been wrapped in it.

A shadow. The way it floated and quivered told Wendy that something was wrong. Had Nana injured the shadow?

Well, there was no way they were going to stay and find out. Wendy turned and dragged Nana out of the clearing and back through the thicket. The dog wouldn't come easily, but Wendy was desperate. The shadow reached out toward her, its hand elongating, stretching as if to touch her.

"Go! Run, we have to run." She tried to run but she was only being pulled toward the tree by Nana's insistence to chase the thing down.

"Please, Nana," Wendy begged.

Finally the dog looked at her, sensing her distress. Her ears perked up and her head tilted to the side.

She tried a new tactic. "Treat?"

Nana barked and eagerly ran for Wendy. Wendy's fear made parting the thicket much easier, and they ran out onto the sidewalk and across the park. They hurried into the bookstore, and she shut the door and closed the shutter on the window. Nana was exhausted and wanted her water bowl, so Wendy reached down and unclasped the leash.

She went to the bathroom sink and tried to wash off the dried blood.

But it wouldn't come off. It looked like permanent marker stuck to her skin, and then it slowly faded into her skin.

Cages.

Kids screaming.

Memories that weren't hers plagued her.

"Nooooo!" She squealed and turned the hot water on and scrubbed till her hands burned. Finally she could take the pain no more, and she turned the water off.

"It's not real, Wendy," she told her reflection. "Stop imagining things. You're normal. You didn't see black blood, and it definitely did not absorb into your skin." She pressed her wet hands to her face and took a few deep breaths. She had to be losing her mind.

After twenty minutes she gathered her courage and stepped out of the bathroom. The bookstore was still empty.

She went and checked his office door. She had forgotten his lunch, but there was no way she was going back into the park. Digging in the desk drawer, she found a few takeout menus and ordered Chinese for two. Fifteen minutes later, she was dropping off the still hot sesame chicken and egg rolls in his office, but he wasn't there. She didn't know where he'd gone, so she left his food on his desk with napkins, a plastic fork, and a can of coke.

Wendy decided to head up to the loft with her food and sit on the small couch. The coffee table was covered with various magazines and stacks of books that needed to be put away.

Is this what Peter was coming for when he met her at the bookstore? There didn't seem to be any evidence of him working up here—or anywhere. Unless his work required reading. Wendy took a sip of her cola and reached for a book on rare diseases. Another one was on genetic research. Another book was an anthology of medical journals on children with special gifts.

Did this have something to do with the lost boys? She was still confused by half of the things that Slightly and Peter talked about, but then she didn't want to know. She had enough to deal with inside her own dark mind.

Wendy ate half her food and put the rest in the mini-fridge in the loft, straightened the books and her mess, and headed down stairs. Mr. B still had not returned, and his food was cold. She really hoped he hadn't gotten tired of waiting for her and gone out to get his own food. Guilt assailed her as she realized that was probably exactly what he did.

The afternoon came and went. It was closing time, and she wasn't sure what to do. Nana had to go outside again and Wendy was nervous to venture back into the park. What if she saw something else? What if her next hallucination sent her to the psych ward? Why did she find that thought funny?

Wendy left a sign on the door that said *Back in fifteen*, locked the door behind her, and headed with trepidation toward the park.

Thankfully, Nana was quick with her business and was as eager to get back to the bookstore as Wendy.

By the time she'd waited an hour past closing and Mr. Bernard never returned, she did the only thing she could. She closed the bookshop. Wendy flipped the sign to *closed* and locked herself inside.

What was she to do? She couldn't take the dog with her. For one, she had nowhere to go, and two, she felt much safer with Nana beside her. She would just have to stay here in the bookstore until Mr. B came back.

By ten o'clock, she was terrified something had happened to him. She wandered back down to his office and looked inside. Nothing looked disturbed. Well, it was hard to tell what mess was purposeful and what mess could've been from a struggle, it was so piled and stacked with stuff. His jacket was still where he had left it, across the back of the chair. But nothing seemed amiss.

Wendy took Nana's dog bed out of the corner and carried it upstairs to the loft. She placed it near the couch and coaxed Nana to lay down. Wendy curled up on the soft leather couch and let her hand burrow into the thick fur of Nana's neck.

"Don't worry, girl. He'll come back," she whispered. "He'll come back. He won't forget about us."

She just wasn't sure if she was referring to Peter or the bookstore owner.

-29-

H E DIDN'T COME.
Unsure what to do, Wendy got up the next morning and packed away her sleeping bag. She changed in the small upper bathroom and started getting the store ready to open. She moved the dog bed back to Mr. B's office and took another hard look around. Was there a clue? Was she missing something?

It was 8:58 a.m. She sat at the front desk, her gaze flicking from the clock on the wall to the phone sitting next to her. Did she dare call 911? He certainly hadn't been gone forty-eight hours yet, and she didn't really know much about him. She had no idea where he lived, what his number was, or if he had any family. All she had was the dog. Proof that he had disappeared. He wouldn't have left Nana behind.

But what if the police started asking questions about her? She didn't have an alibi other than walking the dog. She was a homeless kid who had only been working here a few days. They'd immediately suspect her. Then she could end up in prison. Was it worth it?

Well, they got meals in prison, right?

Wendy picked up the phone and dialed nine and a one. She was about to press the one again when the door opened, the bell rang loudly, and Mr. Bernard walked in with a newspaper under his arm.

"Mr. Bernard?" Wendy gasped holding the phone up to her ear.

"Oh, Wendy, good morning. It is such a glorious morning, isn't it?" He turned to look outside and breathed a deep sigh of pleasure.

"Mr. Bernard, are you okay?"

"Of course I'm okay, why wouldn't I be?" A surprised look crossed his face.

"Well, you sent me for lunch yesterday, and when I got back you were gone. And you didn't come back."

"I, uh...I didn't?" He scratched the back of his head. "That doesn't sound like me."

"You forgot your dog," she said softly. It was obvious he didn't remember. He seemed a bit scattered.

"Oh, well, I knew she'd be in good hands. Nana likes you." He shuffled into the bookstore and looked around in appreciation. "You did well, Wendy. Everything looks great. You're such a good girl. I'm very glad I hired you."

"It's in the mini-fridge," Wendy called after him as he headed to his office.

"What is, dear?" He seemed a bit panicked.

"Your lunch from yesterday."

"Yesterday?"

"Uh huh, Chinese food."

"Oh, yes. Chinese food always tastes better as leftovers. It was smart of you to put it in the fridge."

Mr. Bernard entered his office and closed the door, just as Nana tried to enter. She whined and pawed at the metal doorknob but it didn't open. Dejected, she lay down in front of the door and set her large head on her paws.

Wendy stared at the door and felt the same way Nana did. Helpless. Something was wrong and she didn't know what. She hated feeling left in the dark.

Seeing that Mr. Bernard forgot, she went to the door and flipped the sign to open. Of course the zillion customers waiting outside chose that moment to come barging through the door to buy up all of the books. Well, she wished there were a zillion. She would have been satisfied with one or two. Instead, all that sat outside on the front walk were a couple of hungry sparrows.

Business was slow. More than slow—it was dead. She knocked on Mr. Bernard's office door and asked if it was okay to change the front display window.

He grunted his approval. Was he sleeping? It sounded like he was asleep.

She took down the display and dusted all of the books and pulled down the chairs and tables. It looked like it had been quite a while since the display had been changed. It was decorated for summer, but a fall scene was in order.

Around noon Wendy knocked on Mr. Bernard's door and asked if she could take her lunch break and have a longer one so she could pick up a few items for the front window display.

"Oh yes, go ahead and take as long as you need. If you're buying things for the window, take a twenty out of the drawer and bring me receipts. It will be nice to have new vision for our store."

Feeling proud and excited, Wendy took the bus to the It's All a Buck store and spent some money on white lights, crates, and fake leaves.

She had a purpose and she wanted to please her boss—that felt different. Nice. After she carefully arranged the display, she picked out some of their newest and hottest books and set them upright in the leaves.

She stepped outside and smiled. It was awesome. Fall had come to Bernard Books. Heading inside, she waited and watched and saw that her new display made people slow and look in the window. She had two come in and browse the store, but only one purchased. Well, that was better than nothing, she guessed.

Mr. Bernard gave her two thumbs up. That was the start of her week, and the next day followed a similar routine—without ever running into Peter or Tink. She decided the good outweighed the bad. She'd keep the job.

Painfully sometimes, the hours dragged on. Each time the door jangled open she half-expected Peter or Tink to walk through it. Frequently, she felt as if someone was watching her. She'd glance up and go to the loft, searching for Peter, but it was always empty.

The more hours that passed without her seeing them, the more she realized that she wanted to see them. Needed to see them, because it was all beginning to feel like a dream.

Wendy couldn't help but let her thoughts drift back to her last night with Peter. Had she dreamed it? Surely, she would have remembered taking a bus to the bookstore. That night left her with more questions than answers.

She tried to take the bus back to the waterfront and find the path that led to the old house, but she had gotten so turned around she couldn't find it. It was as if the building had disappeared. Once again, it all felt like a dream. She had imagined Peter and Tink. She tried not to dwell on the thought that she was imagining everything. It wasn't good for her self-esteem.

When Wendy earned her first paycheck, she was ecstatic. Especially when Mr. Bernard cashed her check for her himself and gave her cash.

Money! She had money! She could buy new clothes, get a haircut, buy groceries. Oh, all of the stress that had mounted on her shoulders felt like it was melting away. She grabbed her backpack and headed to a small outlet mall to hit the clearance racks. Setting herself a budget, she picked up quite a few pairs of jeans, shirts, and under-clothes. Walking back to the bookstore, she stopped at a gas station and picked up a pay-as-you-go cell phone. Her fingers itched to call home and hang up just to hear her mother's voice, or to slip her number to John in case of emergency, but she didn't. She tucked her phone in her pocket.

Wendy carried her bags to the back of the store and put them in the closet. When she came to the front she spotted a small notecard by the register. She could hear Mr. Bernard typing in his office. A customer must have come in, and he hadn't heard the bell or the door.

Great. Wendy felt guilty for leaving the store and losing a customer, but she had to rein in those feelings. She wasn't on the clock, she was off. She was allowed free time. But seeing the card, she couldn't help but investigate. She walked over and lifted up the small white envelope.

Her name was written in black ink on the front.

Feeling a bit of trepidation, she tore open the envelope and pulled out the card. Inside was just one sentence.

Don't trust anyone.

-29-

HER MOUTH WENT DRY. She found it impossible to swallow around the fear lodged in her throat, which quickly turned to anger. Wendy crumpled the notecard and tossed it in the garbage. Who would have sent such a horrible note? Was it meant as a threat or a warning? After trying to ignore the message, she went to her knees and dug it out of the trash and read it again.

Then a third time.

After the fourth read-through, she still couldn't figure out who'd sent it. Her eyes drifted to Mr. Bernard typing away in his office. Could it be a warning from him?

Either way she had to decide what she was going to do with it.

She shivered and tossed it back into the wastebasket. Then she tied up the bag and went around the back of the building to the alley where she threw the whole bag into the large dumpster. As the lid slammed, it startled a flock of pigeons in the alley. The flapping filled her ears as they flew off, amplifying her terror.

Wendy was just about to exit the alley when a black Hummer pulled up and drove slowly past the bookstore. Just like the one she'd seen at school. Wendy pressed herself against the brick wall and watched it drive down the street and do a U-turn. It parked facing the bookstore. The engine turned off, but no one got out of the car. Hard to be sure with the glare of the sun, but she thought there was only one person in the vehicle.

Wendy stayed in the alley for five minutes and waited. The driver never moved the car or got out. It looked like the same car the Red Skulls had that night at her school. Peter didn't trust them. Why were they here watching the store?

Were they back for her? Should she try to sneak inside and warn Mr. Bernard? She tried to shrug it off. It was probably just a suburban soccer mom in a really big car.

She decided to slip away, to see if they indeed followed her. A group of five teens walked noisily past the bookstore, and Wendy timed it so she slid right into the middle of the group and stayed with them, keeping her head down.

They were loud, and a few boys tossed a football, before they crossed the street and headed toward the park—the place she had been avoiding since her last encounter with the shadow. Wendy groaned.

Still, if they got close enough maybe she could walk by and see who was in the driver's seat.

A blonde with a ponytail squealed as one of the boys tried to trip her. She took off chasing him. Wendy had to catch herself as she fell into another of the group. The boy plowed into her and tripped her up.

"Sorry!" the boy yelled and continued running backward.

They were now close enough to the Hummer that she could see inside, and the driver's seat was empty. No one was in the car at all.

Wendy told herself she was being overly paranoid. She parted ways with the group as they headed into the park, and she re-crossed the street and headed back to the store.

The front door jangled as she entered, and she was so relieved about not being followed that she forgot her trepidation about the note. Until she put her hand into her jacket pocket and felt something inside.

Her hand shook as she pulled out another small card. This one had no envelope.

She could barely read the words as they blurred in front of her tear-filled eyes.

I'm watching you.

The next morning Wendy was outside washing the front window, when she noticed a dark-haired boy, about fourteen, staring into the store next door looking at a small brown bear. His striped shirt was ragged, and he looked tired and hungry. He gazed longingly at the toy in the window before walking off down the road.

A shadow flew up behind the boy, then peeled off and rushed for her.

She made a mad dash inside and slammed the door on the shadow and turned the bolt for good measure. The inky blackness floated on the other side of the pane before dropping down to slowly push under the door. A pool of black liquid ran in from under the door and Wendy used her jacket to try and block the miniscule gap.

It wasn't working.

Panic took over and she ran to the back of the store. This was it. She was doomed. Any minute a morphling would appear and she would be—she couldn't finish the terrifying thought.

Wendy hid behind the bookshelf and tried to find some way to defend herself. Chills ran up her arms and she turned just as the shadow appeared in front of her. She held up her hands to stop it, but the shadow pushed into her body. She threw her head back, willing the thing to get out of her. She gasped as an icy feeling spread through her and her eyes rolled back. That's when she saw them. The visions.

The boy, kicking and flailing.

The Red Skulls, hauling him away into a room. Fear had control of her, her chest thrumming, irregular and dangerous.

What was happening to her?

Wendy looked up and was able to focus as the shade passed out of her body. It waited, floating just a few feet from her. Her breathing was erratic, but the shadow didn't make another attempt to attack her. It beckoned for her to follow.

It flew a few steps then waited. She took a deep breath, and followed a few steps before stopping. They continued the strange pattern right to the front door. Wendy's hand unlocked the door and flung it wide open. The shadow brushed past her out the door, heading in the direction the boy had gone.

Another shadow followed from across the street. She wasn't sure what to make of the shadows, but she finally understood that they were trying to help her, to communicate with her.

Grabbing her phone out of her pocket, she checked her cell signal. Dead zone.

They were here, which meant a morphling was coming.

Wendy grabbed her backpack, put her head down, and tried to follow the young boy. He was already at a good distance. She shouldn't be too obvious.

She had jogged for two blocks before she caught up to him. She slowed and continued walking, her head still pounding from those visions.

The images brought pain, fear, grief. She shoved the memories aside. Too painful.

The boy crossed into the park, and Wendy decided it was best if she circled around and came at him from the other direction. She waited at the crosswalk, and when the light turned green she walked into the road. Still pondering the image, like it or not.

The boy.

The name.

Suddenly, it came to her. She recognized him, but didn't know from where. She froze in excitement. Right in the middle of the road.

"TEDDY!" Wendy cried.

A loud horn blasted to her right, followed by the screech of brakes.

Wendy raised her arms to protect herself from the imminent impact.

Something hit her in the waist, and she flew through the air. Crack! Pain knifed her skull as her head connected with the sidewalk.

Wendy blacked out.

-31-

"COME ON, WENDY!" A male voice demanded angrily. "Open your eyes."

She tried, but her eyelids weighed too much and her skull throbbed. She was broken. She knew that. There was no use putting her back together. As much as the voice calling to her seemed familiar, she couldn't find the strength to obey.

"Darn you! Why do you have to be so stupid? I knew you couldn't handle yourself alone...useless."

The voice wouldn't stop talking, and she tried to block it out and retreat back into the darkness.

"I'm warning you. Open your eyes or you're going to regret it."

She didn't want to. She wanted the pounding in her head to go away. The farther she retreated into the darkness, the less pain she felt. She heard the sound of a click followed by a whoosh as if a minuscule air compressor had turned on.

No. That sound she recognized. That sound terrified her to her core.

"Girl. Open those eyes. Now!"

241

She felt the cold barrel of the injector and the pain that followed. Her eyes shot open and her back arched as her body was shocked with an intense stimulant. Her whole body seized and immediately began to tingle, head to toe.

She gritted her teeth as the face came into focus.

Jax.

"W-what—" She licked her lips to try and speak again. "What did you give me?"

"Adrenaline. Although not the normal kind." Jax still stood over her as she lay in the grass off to the side of the park.

She tried to sit up, but he pushed her back down onto the grass. "Not yet. You need at least a minute—if we have it. You shouldn't move after a heavy concussion." He turned, scanning the area, and Wendy studied Jax's profile. He was on edge, the muscle ticking in his jaw.

She was so confused. He had obviously saved her from being hit by the car. But why was he even here? Was he watching her?

Oh. The notes. They were from him.

People were beginning to gather around and watch her. Pulling out phones, aiming their cameras toward her.

"This is not good." He turned to give everyone his back, pulling up the collar of his jacket. "We have to go now."

He slid an arm under Wendy's legs and another around her shoulders and then she was up in the air, being carried away. Away from the angry driver yelling at her from the car. The mob of people recording them with their phones and snapping pictures.

With every jarring step, her jaw seemed to rattle loudly in her head. When Jax had walked to the other side of the park, he put her down on a bench.

"You've been following me," she accused. "What was with the threatening notes?" Wendy hissed under her breath.

The pain was slowly fading, and her thoughts were starting to make sense. Wendy stood and moved away from him.

"Right. You don't owe me any explanation."

Nothing. He checked her for other injuries while scanning the crowd.

"You are so frustrating!" she hissed. "Why are you here?"

He paused in his work and looked back up at her. He flashed her a smile, showing his even white teeth. "Because Peter sent me to watch over you. You've never been alone. Someone's always been within shouting distance. Even if you couldn't see us."

"Why you? You clearly don't like me."

"No, that's not true." He sighed. "I'm not thrilled about my current assignment. I thought maybe if you left and went home, I could too. I need to get home."

Wendy snorted. "Believe me, I wish I could. I'd go home in a heartbeat." She paused and then looked over at him. "I was following a boy, and I think he's in trouble..."

Jax looked over his shoulder at her and was about to say something when two large black Hummers pulled up across the street. Doors opened and men dressed in black army gear stepped out. They pointed in her direction.

A high school cross-country team rounded the corner just then, cutting the men off.

One of the men knocked a girl over, heading toward them. "Get out of our way! Stupid kids."

Jax's face filled with fear. "Run!"

Wendy panicked and her legs failed her. An adult with the joggers shouted for them to stick together and run harder. Jax grabbed Wendy's arm, half-dragging her after him into the throng of joggers. They stayed with them for twenty yards until the trail rounded a copse of trees. Jax ducked into the bushes and she followed. He pulled her down beside him and shushed her.

She wouldn't have made a peep. If Jax was afraid, that was good enough for her. The men came down the path and stopped when they got near the trees.

Please don't look this way. Keep moving.

All four men were about the same height, muscular. The way they carried themselves spoke of military training.

The leader held up his arm, and they slowed, stopping only meters from where Wendy and Jax were hiding. He touched his ear and spoke into a mouthpiece.

"We're here. Where did they say the target was?" He paused. "Roger that."

After a few quick hand signals, the men continued up the path toward the center of the park. Wendy and Jax stayed put until they could no longer hear or see them.

Jax looked angry. "We need to get you as far from here as we can. Follow me."

"No."

"What did you say?" Jax clearly wasn't used to being disobeyed.

"I said no. I'm not going with you." She stood and walked out of the bushes, away from him.

"Get back here," Jax hissed and started to break through the bushes to come after her.

"Stop!" Wendy warned. "Don't come near me or I'll scream."

He froze mid-bush and studied her, trying to decide if she meant it.

"There's a boy here somewhere. I saw the shadows following him. I've seen what will happen—here," Wendy pointed to her head, "if I don't help."

She left him and skirted the perimeter of the park, ducking into a different copse of trees. Then she picked her way along the hidden back trail back toward the middle of the park.

Something crashed in the foliage in front of her. Bushes rattled and twigs snapped and it was rushing toward her.

Wendy didn't have time to hide before she heard angry bells. Tink. She waited in the middle of the clearing. Sure enough, Tink's blonde ponytailed head appeared, wearing goggles and grumbling. Right on her heels was Peter, and they were carrying the body of the young boy between them.

The boy she had been looking for. Teddy.

"Is he hurt?" Wendy ran over to them as Peter and Tink froze and gawked at her.

Peter adjusted the arm draped across his neck, and Tink started moving again. "Wendy, what are you doing here? It's not safe." More crashing noises made him move forward too.

Tink struggled under the weight of the young boy. "They're close." She stared at Wendy. "If you're here to help, grab a leg. If not, then get out of the way."

Peter's jaw clenched as he shuffled the weight of the boy he was carrying. His eyes weren't leaving Wendy's face. "What happened to you?"

Her hand immediately went to the large bruise on her head. "I was almost hit by a car."

Peter paled, his eyes widening in fear. He almost lost his grip on the boy. His fear turned to anger as his turbulent eyes scoured her for more injuries. "Where's Jax? He was supposed to be protecting you. I'm going to kill him."

"I'm fine," she snapped. Wendy avoided looking at Peter as she went to help lift the boy. They began carrying him again—not a fast walk, definitely an awkward one. If their eyes met, would he see right through her brave attitude? Recognize her fear?

She couldn't let him know how seeing him again almost brought her to tears.

Peter grunted between clenched teeth. "I'm so sorry, Wendy. I was trying to give you space." His pace slowed. "But, I didn't protect you."

"Peter, get moving. If you don't, I swear to heaven I will not be there the next time you pan again," Tink huffed.

"Pan?" Wendy looked up at Peter.

Peter closed his eyes. "Wendy, I will explain things. I just can't right now."

$@*&! The bells rang, covering Tink's voice, but then the noise abruptly dropped off as a large shadow formed from the ground behind them.

"Shoot it before it morphs!" Tink yelled.

Peter raised his light brace and shot a light beam into the shadow. It dissipated but quickly reformed.

Jax sprinted into the clearing, rushed up behind it, and his brace turned into a light sword. He sliced it through the shadow, splitting it into two. It dimmed but floated along the ground and coalesced again.

An inky form rose from the shadow and morphed into a bear with unnaturally sharp teeth and claws that dripped black liquid.

"Watch out for the claws!" Peter yelled. "Don't let it cut you, or your mind will be poisoned." The put Teddy down and turned to face the morphling.

That must be what happened to Ditto. Wendy scrambled away from the bear.

"What is that thing? What's going on?" Teddy woke up in a panic and chose that moment to run past the beast. It swung out and sliced the kid across the leg before Jax could stop it.

Teddy curled up in a ball, crying out in pain as he grabbed his leg, which now oozed black.

CHANDA HAHN

"Don't worry." Wendy pulled her jacket off and used
it to staunch the blood flow. She tried to keep an eye on
the morphling as she tended to the terrified boy. Grabbing
him under the arms she pulled him as far as she could
away from the beast.

The fight didn't seem to be going in the boy's favor.
Peter's light brace was damaged by a hit from the beast's
paw. He was left dodging the claws while Jax tried to distract it. Peter unhinged his brace and tossed it to Tink. She
caught it midair and kneeled down by her pack.

"This is wrong," Tink said worriedly. "They never attack during the day because they're not as strong.
Something's off about this." She yanked various objects
out of her bag, picked up wire cutters, and began to splice
wires. Her deft fingers opened up the light brace. Could
she repair it?

The morphling disappeared in a mass of shadows and
reappeared behind Wendy. A cold claw latched onto her
leg and she cried out as the beast dragged her across the
ground, her hands scrambling for purchase.

She flipped on her back and saw the cavernous hole
between the roots of an oak tree. "No!" Wendy cried as
the morphling tried to drag her into the depths.

"Don't let it get into the hole!" Peter yelled.

Wendy's fingers clenched onto the tree root and she
locked her arms around it as the morphling shrank in size
to slide into the dark retreat. It tried to pull her with it
and she screamed.

Jax attacked it from behind with a blast of light.

248

A screech rent the air as the morphling turned on him. Its ginormous paw struck Jax across the arm, ripping through his shirt.

Peter darted toward his friend but wasn't fast enough to dodge the beast. A good swipe sent Jax flying across the small clearing into a tree trunk. Wendy heard the thud as his body made contact and fell to the ground. The beast turned on Peter and rushed him.

"There. Done, and I upped the power level but it may overload instead." Tink turned and didn't have anyone to hand the brace to.

Wendy grabbed it without thinking and tore in Peter's direction, desperate to get to him before the beast did. She wasn't going to make it.

Wendy clamped the brace on her own wrist, flicked it, and dove in front of the morphling.

But the brace started to malfunction. It beeped and fizzed out, smoke curled out from the side panel.

"Wendy no!" Tink yelled.

Wendy ignored Tink, and the broken bracer. She focused on Peter.

All she had to do was Believe.

Her hand grew warm, her fingers tingled as a giant ball of blue energy formed in her palm. It hurt, her whole hand was on fire, but she held the ball until she could no longer contain it. And then she released it with a scream of pain.

The light shot straight into the morphling's chest. It roared in agony as the light flooded into him. The morphling began to glow, and cracks formed along its body.

With another roar, it exploded into a million pieces of black ash that sank to the ground.

"How the @&% did you do that? You shouldn't have been able to. Not with a broken brace!"

Peter slowly got off the ground, shaking his head as if to clear it. He gave Wendy an elated smile. "Who are you really, Wonder Woman?"

Wendy looked over at Teddy, where he lay on the ground, groaning softly. He was alive, but seemed to be nearly unconscious...again.

Tink on the other hand, was stiff as a board, a Red Skull's blade pressed against her throat. Where had he come from?

Two more soldiers appeared from behind Tink and surrounded them, glowing white knives in their hands.

"Red Skulls." Peter stepped in front of Wendy, keeping her safely hidden behind his broad back.

"Don't move, or the girl will get a nice crimson necklace."

"Let her go," Peter demanded. "She doesn't need any more jewelry."

"You destroyed the morphling? How did she do that?" a soldier asked.

The leader tightened his grip on Tink and silenced the gaping soldier with a single glance. "You tried to steal something that doesn't belong to you," he said to Peter. He motioned to his soldier who then leaned down to pick up the mostly unconscious boy. "It's not nice to steal."

"I say finders-keepers." Peter taunted with a smile.

The Red Skull frowned.

Tink's eyes were wide with fear and fury. "Anytime now, Peter." She said in a singsong, her foot tapping her impatience.

"I've got this under control, Tink."

The last Red Skull lunged forward to challenge him.

Peter moved forward like lightning, their two weapons clashing.

Peter fought with a short knife, and the Red Skull wielded a much more brutal looking one. Wendy couldn't believe they were fighting hand to hand. She thought militia used guns, but then it made a strange sort of sense in a crowded city. Guns would draw unnecessary attention. More proof that the Red Skulls were used to staying under the radar.

Peter ducked as the soldier swung toward his head. He rolled across the ground, easily popped back up, and ran toward a tree. The soldier was right behind him, but Peter didn't stop. He took three running steps up the tree and then pushed off and flipped, landing behind the Red Skull and conking him on the head with the back of his knife.

The soldier went down in a heap.

The Red Skull holding Teddy set him down to challenge Peter. Teddy showed no signs of waking up.

"You won't get past me as easy as you did Bakerton," the Red Skull threatened. He changed his stance—martial arts. How would Peter's parkour and quick thinking help him now?

"So if he's Bakerton, what's that make you? Pie man? Pumpkin eater?"

The man smiled, revealing missing teeth. "I'm your worst nightmare."

"Yeah, I have nightmares of my teeth falling out too." Peter said. "Regular flossing and daily brushing will help."

Toothless rushed forward.

Peter shifted his stance, twisting slightly and pulling the punch toward him. He twirled the man's arms into a painful wrist lock. Then Peter leapt up into the air, wrapped his legs around the soldier's face, and flung himself backward. His hands grabbed the ground and he smashed his adversary into it with a grunt of pain.

Only the leader remained. His knife was still pressed to Tink's throat.

"You okay, Tink?" Peter called out.

Tink grinned and, with her free hand, reached down and hit a switch on a black box on her belt. The magnet ripped the knife from the leader's hand and attached it to Tink's belt.

Addled that he'd been disarmed, the Red Skull didn't see the tiny, powerful fist that connected with his jaw. And a second later, the knife was pointed at his own throat.

"Yep, I'm great. Now what were you saying about buying me jewelry?" She waved the knife across the man's throat.

"Now who's playing around, Tink?" Peter laughed.

Tink made a face and pulled another little contraption from a pocket—a portable taser. She touched it to the Red Skull. He jerked and fell to the ground. Tink moved closer and Peter leaned down, bringing his knife to the man's throat.

Wendy was so pumped for Tink and Peter that she wanted to cheer.

Until she felt the cold steel of a gun barrel press to her temple.

-31-

"**M**OVE AWAY FROM THE captain, or the girl is going to get it," a deep voice warned. Wendy heard the click of the hammer being pulled back as the gun pressed into her temple. "Unless you've got some trickery up your sleeve that can stop a bullet."

Wendy went absolutely still and looked to Peter for help.

Tink's joyous smirk fell from her face as she looked at Wendy. "No, we don't," she answered. "But if you pull the trigger on that one, you'd be doing all of us a favor." Her eyes narrowed.

Wendy's face paled at Tink's out of place comment.

"The boy for the girl." Peter moved away from the brown-haired boy.

The Red Skull holding Wendy yanked roughly on the back of her jacket. He pressed a small device to her neck and Wendy felt a pinprick as it drew her blood. The device beeped and the soldier tightened his grip on her.

He smirked at Peter. "Naw, I think I'll take this one. You keep the boy." His voice held more cockiness than before. What had he seen?

Wendy's captor yanked her backward.

"Wha..?" She cried out and her feet tripped over a tree root as the Red Skull pulled her into the bushes. Peter and Tink were arguing. "Let her go, Peter! Help with this kid!"

A few seconds later, Peter charged through the bushes after her, but the Red Skull shot at him and he dove for cover.

Now she had her feet under her, but she struggled to keep up as they were running back toward the Hummer. They crossed into the crowded park.

People screamed when they noticed the gun. Her captor fired at Peter again. Everyone scattered.

Peter jumped out of the trees and rolled along the ground.

Wendy fought as the Red Skull dragged her toward a Hummer. She wouldn't get another opportunity like this where the soldier's attention was divided.

She tried to stop abruptly, but received a blow from the handle of the gun. Her cheek stung and she started to fall forward.

"Get in there!" He yanked open the passenger door and held her at gunpoint. "Move it or I'll shoot."

Wendy stared down the barrel of the gun and into the hate-filled eyes of the Red Skull. "Then shoot."

"Not you." He aimed the gun at a young woman shielding a baby stroller with her body. "Her...or maybe I can take them both out."

The young mother screamed in terror and held the stroller tighter. The baby started crying.

"Stop. Okay. I'll go."

Wendy slid into the front seat and kept her eyes on the gun as the Red Skull kept it trained on the woman in front of the car, until he was in the driver's seat. He hit the door locks, and Wendy's hands immediately went to the latch trying to let herself out.

"Ah ah ah. That won't work." Just as the Hummer roared to life, something hit the roof with a loud thump. Peter jumped onto the hood as the Red Skull hit the gas.

He crashed into the windshield.

Wendy screamed as Peter almost slid off the car, but his body torqued midair, and he spun around to land across the hood.

"How did he do that?" the guy growled. He reached for the gun and aimed it at Peter's face. "Let's see him dodge this."

Wendy grabbed the hand that held the gun and pulled, causing the driver to swerve the Hummer onto the sidewalk.

Peter slid across the car again but maintained his precarious position by holding onto the driver's side mirror. The Hummer plowed through a newspaper stand and into a blue garbage can, which went flying into the air.

The gun fell onto the floor and slid under the driver's seat.

"You know it's not nice to litter." Peter yelled through the windshield.

"Why will you not die?" The driver gripped the wheel tighter and veered back onto the road, weaving through traffic.

But no matter what he did, Peter was able to hold on.

"Watch out!" Wendy cried as the Hummer swerved straight for a woman on a bike. The Red Skull wasn't interested in slowing. He sped up.

Peter looked over his shoulder and read the Red Skull's intention in his eyes. He smiled at Wendy and began to slide down the front of the Hummer by the grill.

"Peter, no!" she cried, but he didn't hear her. The Hummer sped up, and just as it crashed into the bike, Peter wrapped his hands around the woman and held on.

Wendy watched as the world slowed down. Peter and the woman slid up over the hood of the car. They hit the windshield, causing a spider web of cracks, and then they rolled up and over the Hummer. She heard the thump, thump, thump as their bodies bounced across the roof.

"NOOOO!" She shrieked and spun to look out the rear window. She didn't see where they landed. Did they slide off and get hit by another car? Was he dead?

Wendy felt as if her heart grew three sizes and got lodged in her throat.

"You killed him. You killed Peter and that woman." Wendy began slapping and clawing the Red Skull, who swore at her and pushed her back into her seat.

He backhanded her in the same spot as her swollen bruise, and she saw stars. For a moment, there was only pain. Wendy fell against the door, and the glass felt cool against her cheek. She was slipping into unconsciousness, but she fought it.

With everything she had left.

Within minutes they were out of town and heading along a small highway along the river.

She stared out the side view mirror and saw another Hummer race up behind them. The others had joined them. No escape now.

But this Hummer didn't fall into line behind them. It continued its frenzied speed—not even looking like it would slow down. Wendy buckled up.

"Oh, so you're resigned for the ride now."

The other Hummer rammed them from behind.

"What the—" The Red Skull almost lost control of the vehicle, but he recovered. He adjusted the rearview mirror, and his face paled. He reached for the radio and held it up to his mouth. "This is Lt. Hastor. Careful with your driving, Stanton."

Static was the only thing that greeted him on the other end. His face paled, and sweat trickled across his brow. He gripped the steering wheel as the other Hummer pulled up to the left of them on the two-lane road.

Hastor recognized the driver. "You little traitor. Wait until the captain hears of this. You're dead." He yowled and rammed into the other Hummer.

Wendy palmed the dashboard and looked over Lt. Hastor to see who he was referring to, but the SUV surged ahead and moved in front of them—barely missing an oncoming car. Hastor had an evil grin on his face as he floored the gas pedal.

He was trying to ram the other Hummer off of the road. She watched the speedometer—fifty, fifty-five, sixty. They were on a city street.

"Stupid insubordinate son of a b—"

The brake lights in front of them lit up. Hastor hit the brakes, but not hard enough. They plowed into the Hummer and the airbag went off.

Pain wracked her body, and she couldn't breathe. Air. She needed air. Her door was pulled open and cold air rushed across her body, but she still couldn't inhale.

"Hold on, Wendy. I'm coming."

She recognized that voice. It was Jax.

A large army knife appeared in front of her, and Jax sliced into the airbag, deflating it. She gasped as the pressure released her. She turned to look at Jax as she fumbled with her seatbelt. He was covered in blood—a cut along his scalp. The airbag of the other Hummer had scratched and bruised his face.

The buckle wouldn't release. Jax moved her hand out of the way and sliced through the belt. He pulled her from the car.

She tried to glance at Lt. Hastor, but all she could see was blood.

Jax carried her off to the side of the road. She asked him, "You're one of them, aren't you?"

He carefully brushed her hair out of her eyes and answered her. "No...and yes." He got up and went to the back of the Hummer and pulled out an emergency kit. Opening it, he grabbed a flashlight and clicked it on.

He flashed the light in and out of her eyes and checked her response time.

"The driver." She swallowed. She was finding it very hard to swallow. "He knows what you did. That you saved me. He said when the others find out...that—"

"They won't find out."

"He'll tell them." She could feel her panic rising.

"Wendy, he's dead."

She let his words sink in. Death wasn't something she had wished for Lt. Hastor, but then she remembered Peter and the woman on the bike. Hastor had turned the gun on an innocent young woman and her baby.

A slow angry tear slid down her cheek. "Good."

Jax nodded. "I'm glad too. Because if the crash hadn't killed him, I would have had to." He pulled Hastor's body from the first vehicle and dragged him over to the rear, leaving him on the ground by the passenger door. His face was stone, his emotions hidden.

He pulled out a small silver case and clicked it open. Inside were small tubes: clear, green, blue, and one that looked almost gold in color, next to an injector. Wendy couldn't pull her eyes away from the injector. She knew what it was. She had seen one, heard one long ago. A memory perhaps, but the more she focused on it, the more her head hurt. Instead, she focused on Jax.

He quickly tended to her wounds.

"How...how long were you one of them—a Red Skull?"

Jax began to dab at her face, gently wiping the blood from her cuts. It stung. "For a while."

"Does Peter know?"

He shook his head no. "It's complicated," Jax growled. "It's better if he thinks I'm dead. Wendy, they have someone very important to me, and they're using them as leverage."

"What do you mean?" Wendy reached up and touched the side of her neck.

"There's something big going on, and someone has to stop Hook—I'm just now figuring out why you're a part of it. Why the shadows keep gathering to you. They're attracted to you, but yet they don't call the Red Skulls. It's like they've been watching you, Wendy, waiting. But not anymore. Something's changed now. They'll come for you."

A loud static noise from the Hummer's CB-radio interrupted him. "Hastor? Do you copy? We're almost to your location."

Jax started to hide the evidence of the bandages. "When they get here, you can't be anywhere near here." He looked around. They were out of town, down one of the main roads by the river. There weren't many safe places other than the woods.

"Me? What am I supposed to do? We're miles from the city."

"I expect you to run and survive. Head into the woods, backtrack for a few miles, then you should be able to follow the road back to town. Go with Peter. Neverwood is your best chance at being safe. And don't get caught. If you get caught, that means I murdered a man for nothing."

"You're not coming with me?"

Jax put a vial in the injector gun and handed it to Wendy. Then he closed up the silver case and put the emergency kit in the back of the Hummer. "Trust me— they won't hurt me. I'm too important to them. They've been pulling my strings for too long though. I have to go back—cut the strings once and for all. And it's better for all of you if I distract them. If they think the lost boys did this, they will attack and kill every one of you."

He walked around to the first vehicle, placed his light brace on the ground, and stomped on it multiple times until the light went out. He got back into the driver's seat, set the silver case on the seat beside him, and buckled in. He laid his head on the steering wheel to feign uncon-sciousness.

In the distance they could hear the sound of a large en-gine racing in their direction. The other Hummer. Jax pointed to the injector gun in Wendy's hand.

"In the neck, pull the trigger once and it will do the trick. But you need to take the gun and run. You can't stay here."

"Neither can you! Please, if they find out what you did, they'll kill you."

Jax shook his head. "It's time for me to go back. I can do more good by going back with them than staying here."

The injector, though smaller than a Ruger pistol, felt unbelievably heavy in her hands. She didn't think she could do it. "What is it going to do to you?"

"It's going to knock me out, but if you don't get going, they'll see you. It's what they use when capturing the boys. It won't hurt...much."

His calm explanations gave her strength.

"They'll see the second airbag in the other car, Jax. They'll know someone was with Hastor when he died. They're not going to be fooled."

Headlights reflected in the rearview mirror, and Jax swallowed nervously. "Knock me out, Wendy. We're running out of time. You have to run and take the injector gun with you or they'll suspect."

"I can't do it." She held the injector up to his neck, but her hands were shaking so hard, she couldn't steady the gun.

Jax grabbed the gun, put it up to his own neck. "That kid, Wendy, the one we saved today. I recognize him. He shouldn't be alive, he shouldn't be here." He shook his head. "But then neither should you." Closing his eyes, he pressed the trigger. The gun jerked. She heard the hiss and watched as his eyes rolled back in his head. His body slid forward. She reached across him for the injector gun but ended up knocking it on the floor.

The Hummer rolled to a stop nearby.

She ducked low and scrambled around in the dark until her fingers found the cold metal. *It sure wouldn't hurt to grab the silver case with the other vials as well.* She tucked the case under her arm, carefully closed the door without latching it, and ducked as she heard voices approach the rear vehicle. Wendy crawled to the front of the vehicle and kneeled. There was no way she could run for the woods now.

She heard the far Hummer's door open and someone yelled out, "Hey, Hastor's dead." Footsteps sounded on the pavement, and a few pieces of stray gravel stung her as someone ran up to Jax's vehicle.

"It's Jax!" There was a pause, and she assumed someone was reaching in to check his pulse. "He's alive!"

"What's Jax doing way out here? Is he back from his assignment?" The first voice answered. "Wonder what the captain's going to say about this."

"What do you think happened?"

"Looks like Hastor rear-ended him."

"Questions later. Right now we need to clear the trucks and get rid of evidence. Could be a passerby called the police already. We can't have them finding anything."

Wendy slid the injector gun into her waistband, its metal cold against her back, and stayed hidden. She pressed against the grill of the Hummer in the deepening darkness as the two Red Skulls moved Jax into the third Humvee. They unloaded what looked like weapon cases and medical equipment out of both vehicles before they came back and she heard water.

That smell! Not water. Gasoline.

Two pairs of black boots approached. She bellycrawled under the Hummer. No choice.

She covered her nose with her shirt as the clear liquid pooled off the car and ran underneath, right to where she was hiding. The gas started to soak into her shirt and jeans. They were going to light the cars on fire. No way she'd get out in time.

Unless she ran right now, out in the open, and headed for the woods. Even though it was getting dark, they'd see her for sure.

But her only other choice was to stay underneath the gasoline-soaked Hummer and wait to go up in flames. Maybe she'd die instantly when the car exploded. Either way she was toast.

Oh, why hadn't she run?

Wendy crawled out of the pool of gas onto dry cement. She didn't know what to do but stay down beside the vehicle. The soldiers moved to the back of the second Hummer, and she heard the sound of a match scraping. The hair on the back of her arms stood straight up.

"Ah, dang! The match went out."

"Try another one."

Another match lit and immediately went out.

"Get the other box from the kit. These ones are no good."

She was so terrified that she started seeing things in the dark. No, not the dark. A shadow was moving in front of her. Her heart was beating so loudly in her ears she didn't hear the second match light. The shadow moved lower and lay beside the Hummer with her. It beckoned her to follow it.

Should she?

Jax said he thought they were trying to help her. Peter had said something similar once.

What choice did she have anyway?

Wendy followed.

They slowly crept away from beside the Hummer, pausing occasionally as the men came nearby. But the shadow got her safely to the edge of a ditch. Then the shadow gestured oddly—trying to show her something? Oh. A drainage pipe.

Not giving a care about what could be down there, she slid on her belly down into the ditch and backed into the pipe feet-first, just as the Red Skulls found a dry set of matches. Her eyes locked on the small match in the tips of a soldier's hands, watched in fascination as it flew in an arc, up, up, then down onto the trail of gas. Hungrily, the flames followed the fuel. Within seconds, fire engulfed the first truck and licked voraciously around the second.

Everything burned. Even the ground underneath the car, where Wendy had been only moments ago, was ablaze. A floor of fire burned under the vehicle, reaching up and forming walls around the Humvees. The soldiers ran back to their own Hummer and quickly gunned the engine, racing out of sight.

The rear Hummer exploded, followed by the first. Wendy felt the force of the explosion, the heat drying her eyes. She smelled acrid, burning rubber as parts rained down upon the road and ditch. Tires, doors, metal rebar. Nowhere was safe from the flaming debris.

Nowhere, except the drainage pipe where she lay shivering, but protected. When she was about to crawl out, she heard police sirens and rescue vehicles arrive.

Terrified of being caught and questioned by the police, Wendy stayed in her small prison, and tried to fight back the waves of unconsciousness and exhaustion. But then she lost.

-33-

PETER'S FIST CONNECTED WITH the wall with a loud thud. His knuckles hurt, but the pain mirrored the crushing ache in his heart. She was gone.

Jax had gone after her, and now they were both gone. His tracker in the brace was destroyed, which could only mean one thing. He was dead, since he hadn't contacted him. And since Jax was the strongest of them, Peter could only assume she was too.

That, or she'd been taken.

Peter turned toward the mirror and lifted up his blue t-shirt. He grimaced at the slice on his upper rib. He'd been able to save the girl on the bike, but not without incident. It was a deep cut and now it was crusted over. The dark bruises that had formed were more worrying to him. It hurt to breathe and lift his arms.

He took a warm washcloth and cleaned the gash, but it started to bleed again. Too quickly, the rag turned red. Using his teeth, he opened a tear-off packet of ointment and globbed it over the wound before bandaging it with gauze and medical tape. He didn't want to have any of the boys treat him.

It was better if they thought he was invincible.

Oh, if they knew the truth about him, they'd realize he was more a liability than a leader. Peter ran his hands under the hot water and washed the blood away with a bar of soap. If only his feelings and problems could wash away as easily as the blood on his hands.

He needed Dr. Barrie. He couldn't do this alone. There was so much he didn't understand about what was happening. Neverland's monsters were getting stronger. Their attacks more frequent. He knew the lost boys couldn't keep going like they had been.

The boys would have to take the fight to Neverland if they could find their base, and he was scared. Scared that they'd lose boys, that he'd lose Tink, just like he lost Wendy.

Peter reached for a clean shirt and pulled it over his head before heading down the hall. He didn't know where he was going, but he found himself outside Wendy's empty room. "I'm so sorry," Peter mumbled softly.

Tink opened her door, grabbed his arm, and yanked him into her pigsty of a room.

"Look at this," she said excitedly, spinning her laptop on the desk to face him. He didn't know what he was looking at—just a news report showing a massive car wreck ablaze. Fire trucks were working to contain the fire.

Tink couldn't stop fidgeting, so there had to be something in the telecast he was missing. It was dark out and hard to make out the models of the cars, but then he noticed a familiar grill.

"It's the Red Skulls," Tink spoke up, practically bouncing in her chair. "That is what's left of their Hummers." She paused the screen and rewound the footage to play it again. Something moved—just the slightest shift—in the background.

"Is that a—" He wasn't sure what he was seeing, since shadows didn't always appear on recordings, but you'd get a faint hint of them sometimes.

"Shadow," Tink finished for him. "Didn't even need the goggles to see that. And this has been playing for the last hour. There's no reason for a shadow to still be in the vicinity unless..." She trailed off and glanced out her open door to Wendy's empty room.

"Wendy's gone, Tink. We don't know that a presence of a shadow means she's there, and I'm not sure that I can risk losing you, too."

"Relax, I'll wait till morning, when everything's chill and quiet, and I'll go snoop around."

"No!" Peter cried out in anguish. "I forbid you to leave."

He stormed out of her room and went to check on the boy they had recovered earlier. He was crying out in his sleep, and he didn't look good. Sweat covered his brow.

Peter knew the signs. They were going to lose him if he didn't turn the corner soon. Slightly was keeping an eye on the newcomer, and there was nothing Peter could do but wait. He sat by the boy's bed for most of the night, releasing Slightly for a few hours. It was almost morning before he did the final round of the night by heading to the control room.

Peter looked over his shoulder even though he knew no one was in the room with him. He pulled up the same newscast Tink had previously shown him and watched the screen for signs...and there it was...again. A shadow. And it was hanging around in the background, quite a distance from the wreckage.

Maybe Tink was right.

He pulled up the screen and watched for a dead zone to pop up. Sure enough, there was one in the vicinity of the wreck, just moving in circles. What shadow moved in circles? Could it be her? What were the chances? He was about to go investigate it himself when a green dot popped up in the area.

"Tink!" Peter growled.

-34-

SIRENS CAME AND WENT. The fire trucks spent hours putting out the flames. The tow trucks removed what remained of the cars. The fire and explosion had taken care of most of the pieces.

Wendy lay partially unconscious through all of it. No one saw the drainage pipe. And if they did, no one looked inside.

And Wendy dreamed. This time she caught more glimpses of memories—white walls, labs filled with beakers. A woman in heels. The ocean.

A beeping noise drew close, and Wendy felt something prod her in the shoulder. The insistent noise annoyed her, and the prodding kept on.

"Stop it!" Wendy grumbled and swatted at the offending thing.

"Oh darn. You're still alive," a feminine voice said sarcastically.

Sure enough, Tink's blonde head and her goggles filled the opening of the drainpipe.

"Oh, maybe you are dead, because it really reeks in there."

"Tink, is it really you?"

"No, it's the tooth fairy. Of course it's me, you knuck-lehead."

"You didn't cuss."

"Yeah, I'm working on enlarging my vocabulary."

Wendy crawled out of the drainpipe. Tink wrapped an arm around her and helped her out of the ditch. The road had been cleared of debris. All that was left were the small scrap pieces, glass, and the scorched roadway. The light hurt her eyes.

Wendy figured it had to be mid-morning.

"You found me. How did you find me, Tink?"

"With my dork-o-meter." She gestured to her black remote and antenna. This close, Wendy could see that the box was decorated with Hello Kitty stickers. Tink clicked off her device and stowed it back into her side bag, which she then stored in the back of her scooter.

Tink eyed Wendy's soiled clothes, and her little nose wrinkled in disdain. "Oh, hey. Do you mind jumping in the river?"

"What?"

"You are really, really dirty, and you reek of gas and smoke. Why do you smell like gas?"

"'Cause I was under a car when it was about to be lit on fire."

"That's so cool."

Wendy shot Tink a nasty glare, but then decided to take her advice to clean up. Wendy crossed the road and stepped into the tall grass shrubs. Her feet sank into the sand, and her first few steps were wobbly as she tried to regain her balance. Then she found the rhythm. One step at a time, she told herself.

The river seemed impossibly far off, and she was so thirsty it actually made her cracked lips ache for a sip. Wendy licked her lips and tasted salt, plus the foul taint of gas. She tried to spit the taste out, but every inch of her smelled of it.

She made it to the water's edge and collapsed to her knees, let the current rush over her knees and feet. The cold made her body numb.

Numb was good. She didn't want to feel.

Something rattled close by, and it took a moment for her to realize her teeth were chattering. She started to wash her hands and arms. The water felt good against her face and the airbag rash on her cheek. Wendy pushed herself to her feet and stepped farther into the river, hip-deep.

Trembling, she couldn't bring herself to go any farther. Memories and fear were suddenly overwhelming.

Wendy saw something beneath the water, a dark shape moving toward her. It came up out of the water—the shadow. She glanced behind at Tink, but the girl's goggles were on her forehead, and she didn't have her box out.

Tink couldn't see the shadow. The shadow dipped below the water, and Wendy felt a tug. Before she could say anything, it resurfaced and hovered inches from her face. She could almost feel its impatience with her. It reached out and touched Wendy's wrist. It felt as if a bolt of lightning shot through her brain, and mixed images began to appear.

A girl screamed and writhed on a cot somewhere in a white room. This vision was hazy, like watching the static snow on an old TV screen.

A large bloody gash on her arm eked black ooze, like a wound from the morphling. A doctor took the injector gun and inserted a gold vial. Then he pressed it into her arm. She had no idea whether what she was seeing was in the future or the past. The girl stopped screaming, her eyes opened and she sighed.

"There... there. You're safe now." The doctor spoke.

Whatever it was, it terrified her. She tried to pull away from the shadow's embrace to stop what she was seeing, and it finally let go, only to disappear into the water's inky blackness. Wendy tumbled backward into the water. Her feet found purchase on the sand, and she pushed herself upward. As soon as her head crested above the water she gasped. Her wet hair covered her eyes and face.

She coughed and fought her way back to the shoreline. Glancing at her wrist she saw the remnant of a shadow mark slowly fade back into her skin. Is that how it was communicating with her?

Tink was there next to Wendy, grabbing her under her arms and pulling her toward the riverbank.

"What happened?"

"I saw something—," she coughed.

"It must have been an angel."

"Why do you say that?" Wendy asked as she fell to the river's edge and collapsed. She rolled over to look at a white-faced Tink.

"One minute you were there, the next you were gone."

-35-

"WHAT?"

"No really, you actually disappeared. I watched you reappear right in front of me."

"That's not possible, Tink." Wendy trudged up the beach until she found a large piece of driftwood. She sat and took off her shirt, leaving her in just her tank top. She began to wring out the water. "I was here the whole time." Or at least she thought she was.

"Trust me, there's a lot of weird stuff that isn't possible, but this is. And you are becoming number one on my list of weird people." Tink plopped down on the driftwood next to Wendy and stared off into the water.

"Thanks for the vote of confidence," Wendy said sarcastically. "Nice to know I'm number one on one of my friend's lists."

"Whoa." Tink shot Wendy a disbelieving look. "We're not friends. I don't have friends. I have people I tolerate."

"Well then, it's nice to know I'm tolerable."

Tink nodded and hit her softly in the arm. "Now you get it."

Wendy offered a half-smile and her voice softened. "Except for Peter."

Tink looked away absently, rubbing her arms. "Yeah, he was the only one who was ever more than tolerable." She shot Wendy a heat-filled look before standing up and marching up the beach to her scooter.

Wendy followed her and felt the girl's pain radiating off her in waves. "Tink, I'm so sorry about Jax and Peter. I didn't me—"

Tink spun toward Wendy, her finger jabbing her angrily in the chest. "Don't. Don't you dare tell me you're sorry." Tears started to pour out of her eyes. "You have no idea what you've done." She snapped her green glitter helmet on and scooted forward on the scooter and started it up. She revved the engine and glanced back. Wendy was still dripping wet, but Tink just curled her lip. "Get on. I don't want to waste any more time because of you."

Wendy sat behind Tink and tried to give the girl as much room as she could. She didn't know where to place her hands on the spunky girl, so she rested them on her shoulders. She really hoped Tink wouldn't take any sharp turns, because she probably would slide off and die.

But maybe, with the mood Tink was in, that had been her plan all along.

On the ride back into town, Wendy finally cried in silence, grieving the loss of Peter. There was no way he could have survived being thrown from a Hummer at that speed. It was all her fault. Her heart ached, and she couldn't believe how empty it felt after only knowing him for such a short time. But that time together, felt like an eternity.

Peter showed her so much kindness—he cared so much he died for her.

The wind dried each and every tear.

And she wished that the wind could dry up her heart just as quickly, so she'd never hurt again.

The Neverwood Academy wouldn't be the same without Peter.

Wendy walked up to the old, abandoned house alone while Tink tucked her scooter into a hidden shed. The same homeless man who'd been sitting near the garbage before started to rustle around. He pulled a bottle up to his lips and took a drink. There was a distinct click of a camera sound and Wendy spun on him, ready to either attack or sprint away. When he continued to drink for an impossible amount of time, she studied him a little closer.

Something was off about the proportions. The elbow seemed bent at a weird angle; the knit hat was pulled a little low over his head. Then she saw the red blinking light and the camera lens hidden in the bottom of the bottle. She stepped closer, and the hand holding the bottle dropped. The homeless guy dropped his head to his chest, as if hiding from her.

Wendy bent down and ducked her head to look closer. His face looked waxy, and he was wearing way too many layers of clothes for how hot it was. She nudged his boot and it didn't move. She nudged it again and nothing happened. Feeling braver, Wendy leaned forward and gently shook the shoulder of the homeless man.

The whole head rolled forward and fell into his lap.

She bit back a scream and scrambled back as the recurring sound of a familiar chime blasted into her ear right behind her.

"Don't touch Homer!" Tink shrieked. "Stay there. Don't touch anything," she huffed.

"Homer?" Wendy looked back at the robotic head that had fallen from the robot sitting outside the warehouse.

"Heat Overseer Mechanical Emergency Robot. Homer. He's heat activated and monitors all activity. Usually we get lots of pictures of stray cats." Tink picked up Homer's head, sighed loudly at her creation, and pulled a screwdriver out of her tool belt. She went to work screwing his head back on. Then, reaching behind him, she flipped a switch off and on again until he rebooted. She carefully pulled his hat down over his head and readjusted his arm and camera.

"Did you make him?" Wendy asked in disbelief.

"Of course I did. He's our first warning signal." She ducked and peered into Homer's face. The bottle came up and Wendy heard the zoom of the camera.

"Hey, Tink," a male voice said through speaker.

"Fox, it's me, plus one."

"Gotcha. Proceed."

The front door unlocked this time, and they headed directly toward the fireplace. Wendy missed having Tootles greet them with the riddle.

"The first time you came, Homer was down. A few malfunctions, but I got it up working again." She entered the tunnel and the fireplace slowly closed after them. As soon as they passed into Neverwood, Tink gestured for Wendy to follow her toward the medical wing.

There was a twin bed in the middle of the room. On the bed was the young boy from yesterday. His leg was bandaged, and he looked like he was in a lot of pain.

"Is he…?"

"Alive? Yes," Slightly answered. "He's woken up a few times, but he's said nothing but gibberish. We think we might not have gotten him here in time. The morphling's poison was too strong. He's dying."

Wendy sat next to him, grabbing his hand. "Oh, Teddy," she whispered.

-36-

PETER'S BEST FRIEND HAD disobeyed a direct order. Her dot stayed in the area for a good fifteen minutes before it started to move in the direction of Neverwood. She must have found something, because she was speeding.

His heart went flying, and he kept cracking his knuckles. The anticipation was killing him, but he had plenty of time to think and question and doubt. Who was Wendy, really? Why were the shadows not taking her when she could obviously see them? Nothing made sense, and he was getting a huge headache.

His head snapped up. Tink's tracker showed she was in the building! Peter had been so lost in his thoughts, he didn't notice her arrival.

He launched himself from his chair and tried to calm himself as he headed downstairs. Voices entered and moved toward the medical wing. They were muffled, and he wasn't sure who it could be—but he hoped.

But when he got to the medical hall and saw her— battered, wet, but alive and next to the boy's bed.... Alive.

281

She reached out and touched the boy's hand, clasping it between hers. Peter's heart soared. He was so happy he could crow. He had to grab the doorframe to steady himself and to keep from running to her and whisking her far away.

"Oh, Teddy," Wendy whispered his name.

Footsteps sounded behind her.

"Who is he?" Peter asked suspiciously.

She turned and lost her train of thought when she saw his dark green eyes.

"You're alive? I thought you died!" She couldn't help herself. Tears of relief fell and Peter leaned in to wrap her in a hug.

"Takes more than that to kill me." Peter whispered. "But I'm asking you again. How do you know him? Who is he to you?"

"No one," Wendy answered. "I don't know him...just his name."

Slightly leaned against a far wall, his arms crossed. "She certainly raises more questions than answers lately."

Peter leaned back, and but kept his hands on her arms. "I need to ask you something?

"Anything.".

"Are you one of them?" She knew he meant the Red Skulls.

"No, I'm not."

"Then why were you there? Why did you show up right when another morphling attacked and the Red Skulls were on your heels?"

"I just knew he was going to be in trouble." She stopped, deciding no matter how she tried to explain it, they wouldn't believe it. It sounded sketchy even to her.

The boy cried out in his sleep, interrupting them. Peter moved over to the boy on the bed. He gently checked his pulse and pulled open his eyelids. His forehead was covered with a sweaty sheen, and his face looked pallid.

"What's wrong with him?"

"Morphling venom. It cut him deep."

"Isn't there a cure?" Wendy asked.

"If there is, we haven't found one yet."

Something nagged at the back of Wendy's mind. "Peter!" she said excitedly. "I think I know something that can help."

"Really." He clearly didn't believe her.

"I know what to do, and how to help."

"How?" Peter demanded.

"It's the..." She made a gun motion with her hand, and he gave her a blank look.

"We're not going to shoot the kid." Slightly sounded offended.

"No, it's...I...uh." She carefully sorted through what to tell him and what to leave out. "I think I know where to find a cure. Now I'm kicking myself for not bringing it, but I couldn't after..." She trailed off, unsure how to broach the subject of Jax's betrayal. "I'm sorry Peter, about Jax."

Peter looked away. "It happens. Sometimes we lose a lost boy. He was the best of us."

"Wait. What?" They really thought he was dead.

Tink quickly wiped at her eyes and sniffed. "Jax would want us to keep going, keep fighting," she said, trying to sound strong.

Wendy was about to correct them when the boy on the bed moaned, drawing everyone's attention to the current problem.

Slightly rushed forward. "Wendy, you said you could save him?"

Peter stood and came over to her. "Is it safe?"

"Safer than leaving him to die." She closed her eyes and tried to remember everything she had seen. Could she really believe what she saw? What if she was wrong and they were torturing that girl in her vision? No, her symptoms were very close to what she was seeing right here in the same room. "We need to hurry."

Peter looked into her eyes, and she silently pleaded with him to believe her. "Okay, Wendy. I trust you. Lead the way."

She ran out the door with Peter on her tail. Slightly ran after them and grabbed his leather jacket from a chair. He tossed Peter his keys and said, "Take my car."

"It'll be faster if we—" Peter started.

"It's broad daylight, Peter," Slightly gently reprimanded.

Wendy gave Slightly a confused look but he just smirked, "One day you'll understand."

"I still prefer my way of travel." Peter stared at the keys in his hands.

"Oh come on, Peter," Wendy pleaded. "We don't have time to take the bus. Just take the car."

The whole room erupted in laughter at Wendy's comment.

Peter just grabbed Wendy's hand and headed for the door. "You're so adorable."

Wendy took Peter back to the crash site and she immediately started searching the drainage ditch.

"Come on. I know it's here." She scoured the area and couldn't find any sign of the injector gun.

"What happened here, Wendy?" His voice was husky, filled with emotion. She turned to look at him. He wouldn't budge from the middle of the road.

"I was in one of the Hummers. Jax rammed the car and caused the accident, the driver died. Others came before I could escape, so I hid under the vehicle. They didn't want any evidence left behind so they torched everything." She went to him, and she reached up and touched his arm.

"About Jax. Peter, he—"

"Shhh." Peter interrupted. He touched her swollen eye. A jolt of static electricity raced through her body.

"Oh, Wendy, I'm sorry." She felt his breath catch. "This?"

"A gun slap," she whispered.

"And this?" he reached and touched the roughened scratches across her cheek.

"Airbag."

His hands felt glorious and warm as he caressed her wounds; all the pain faded under the feel of his touch. It was intoxicating. It was addicting. He leaned forward, and she inhaled as his hand brushed against the hollow of her neck.

She froze as his fingers trailed against her skin. It almost killed her to pull away from his touch, but she did. His hand reached for her but she let it slide away. Wendy went back to the ditch and continued to search.

Peter looked around at the pieces that remained—side mirror, part of a bumper. He had stopped in the center of the road, in the middle of the largest scorch mark.

The scent of burning rubber and tire still hung in the air like a cloak. Most of the grass was burned to a crisp, and the path of dead grass stopped only feet away from where Wendy had hidden. It was a miracle the smoke hadn't killed her. Or she was lucky she had passed out.

"What are we looking for?" Peter started looking through the grass and mud.

"An injector gun. About this big." She showed him the size with her hands.

She got down on her hands and knees and peered into the darkness of the drainage pipe. Her skin crawled. She didn't want to go back in there, but she couldn't find the gun out here. It had to be in there. She bit her lip and then Peter's hand stopped her.

"Let me." Without waiting for an affirmation, Peter crawled easily into the darkness. Moments later, he came out holding the silver injector gun. It was covered in mud, and Peter used his gray t-shirt to wipe it clean. "Is this what you were looking for?" He handed the metal gun to her, and she looked at it closer in the daylight.

Etched along the side, one word.

NEVERLAND

"This is it."

Peter's jaw twitched in anger. "No. I don't trust anything from them. And how is this going to save Teddy?"

"Not the gun, Peter." She continued to scan around the drainage pipe until she found the small silver case. She opened the case and showed Peter the row of medical vials. She held up a small gold vial, the same color she saw injected into the girl in her vision.

"If Neverland is using or working with these Morphlings, they have to have their own preventative measure against their poison. We just have to duplicate it." She handed Peter the golden vial and he held it up in the air to read the label.

"How do you know about this, Wendy?"

"Because...the shadow showed me."

Wendy gripped her head and tried to remember, but the pounding started again. "The shadows are showing me glimpses of the past and future."

"Why would they do that?"

"I don't know, but I can tell you I think they've been trying to communicate with me for a long time. It's only lately I've been able to make sense of it."

Peter sighed. "As much as I want to believe..." his voice drifted off and softened. "I can't help but wonder why? Who are you really? It's like you ring true to every part of my body and soul, and I'm afraid you're a trap. I have to protect the lost boys." He turned his back on her and looked out across the water.

A soft breeze blew against her neck and Wendy looked up to see a shadow floating just across the road. She beckoned to the shadow and it came almost eagerly. "Show me? Help me explain to him that I want to help."

Peter turned around just as the shadow pushed into Wendy and her head dropped back, her mouth went slack.

"No Wendy, don't!"

She was back in that place. Somewhere in the past or the future. Another lab, this one had a trapped morphling inside a glass room surrounded by light. The shadow spoke through images and she knew what she had to do.

The shadow left and she whispered a soft thanks, as Peter watched it fly away stunned.

"What just happened, Wendy?"

Wendy stormed up to Peter and ripped the injector gun out of his hands and opened the case.

He would never believe her unless she proved to him that she was right. "The gold one is the cure for the morphling's poison and I'm pretty sure this black one here..." She loaded the vial filled with purplish black liquid into the gun and handed it to Peter. "Is concentrated Morphling venom."

"How can we be sure? What if this is a trick?" He sounded so skeptical.

She pulled her hair to her side and looked up at him, her eyes rimmed with unshed tears. She took a deep breath. "Maybe I'm wrong. Maybe it's nothing, but I'm willing to take that chance to prove to you I'm not lying. To prove to you that this is the cure."

"Wendy, I'm not asking you to do this," Peter said disgustedly.

She grabbed the gun and pushed it against her neck. "If I don't, you'll never save Teddy."

"But if you're wrong and that other vial isn't the cure, you'll die." Now it was Peter's eyes that filled.

"If it proves to you that I'm not lying, then it's worth it. Some things are worth dying for. But I'll never be regret meeting... you, Peter." She closed her eyes and waited for the prick of the injector gun.

She felt it pull away, before warm lips crushed against hers. Peter was kissing her. It was warm, desperate, aggressive. But there was something off about the kiss. It wasn't a kiss of passion.

It was a kiss of regret. *He wasn't going to do it.*

She opened her eyes just as Peter lowered the gun to the ground.

"NO!" she twisted the gun out of his hand. Before he could recover she pressed it against her own neck and felt the cold compression of the injector needle.

"What did you do?" he gasped.

"I had...to. Peter?" Wendy grabbed onto his shirt and started to fall forward into his arms. Her body seized up, cold invaded her blood and everything started to go dark.

"No!" Peter yelled.

Peter watched Wendy seize up in front of him. Her eyes closed, her skin went cold. She had forced his hand—he had to try the cure. His hands shook as he loaded the other vial.

"Please let this work." He pressed it to her neck and pulled the trigger....

Nothing happened. He began to count in his head, wondering how long it would take to see results. He pulled her onto his lap and buried his face into her neck. "Please work," he mumbled into her hair. If he could use every wish on every star, he would use it now, to save her.

He felt her intake of breath, then the breathing steadied and he saw improvement. Still, she hadn't regained consciousness.

He drove like a madman to get Wendy to the medical wing at Neverwood. Now it was a waiting game. And he was never fond of waiting. He watched as Tink took a blood sample from Wendy, who lay on the bed. She never moved, even after the prick.

"I thought you didn't like her." Peter said.

Tink rolled her eyes. "I don't necessarily like the girl. I'll know more *if* we find the genetic marker." Tink withdrew the needle and put a Spiderman band-aid on Wendy's arm. She held up the vial of Wendy's blood. "But I'll tell you what I think: I think she's a lost girl."

"That can't be." He paled. "None made it off the island. The Red Skulls killed them all, and Jax burned Neverland to the ground."

"We know one girl escaped, Peter," she said softly. "One made it to the boat."

"No! She couldn't have survived," his voice trailed off. "It was impossible."

"Well, what if *that* girl did, Peter? What if that girl survived, the same way you did?"

Peter rubbed the scar on his chest and his eyes started to wander the room. "That would explain her lack of memories, but not how she ended up here." He went and sat on Wendy's bed, his hip touching hers.

"Check Peter," Tink encouraged. "I'm pretty sure she has one."

Peter was too afraid to look. "I would have noticed if she did."

Tink snorted. "Uh, I doubt you were looking that closely at her neck. Besides, it would have faded over time."

He never even thought to check for the marker on her, because she was a girl. Sometimes they'd find another lost boy, one that had chosen to not come to Neverwood, but never a girl. He started to hope. Peter let his gaze trace her features, tried to imagine the young freckle-faced girl.

How would she look grown up?

Like Wendy.

The resemblance was uncanny. Her hair had gotten lighter, turned a beautiful strawberry blonde, and her freckles had all but disappeared. If he had just opened his eyes and looked, he would have recognized it sooner.

His hand brushed against the side of her jacket and gently pulled on the collar. His breathing faltered, and he felt as if the bed, floor, and building were spinning.

It was her.

She was alive.

-37-

"SO HOW LONG IS she going to sleep for?" Tootles bounced on the mattress, making Wendy's head bob in the same rhythm against her pillow.

"We don't know," Slightly answered.

"Ay-yi-yi...I'm way-way-wake," Wendy answered.

Tootles stopped bouncing. "Yay, now it's time for you to take your medicine." He ran over to a table and picked up a yellow coffee mug with a grumpy cat face on it.

Wendy sat up, smoothing the blanket down beside her. Her neck itched, and she couldn't help but scratch at the still fresh injection site. Tootles was carefully walking, one foot in front of the other, trying not to spill the coffee. Next to him, Slightly was looking over her medical charts.

"Here's your medicine, Wendy."

"No, no medicine," she answered politely. "Unless it's coffee."

"It is coffee." Tootles smiled, showing off his adult teeth, which his little face hadn't yet grown into.

"Well then, pass that medicine over. Your patient is in dire straits."

Tootles laughed and handed her the cup, spilling just a bit on the blanket.

Wendy took a deep breath of the heavenly aroma before she took a sip. It was cold. She grimaced and was about to spit it out, but Tootles was watching her expectantly. She did her best and swallowed it without making another face. Poor Tootles had probably been waiting to serve her coffee for a long time.

Wait.

She knew who Tootles was? She was alive. "I still remember you. You're Tootles."

"'Course I'm Tootles. And you're Wendy girl."

"No, just Wendy is fine," she said.

"Well, you're the first girl brought here besides Tink, so I can't call you a lost boy. You're not a boy." He scrunched up his face in concentration, and Wendy laughed.

"Wait, what about Teddy. Is he …?"

"Naw, Teddy is just fine," Slightly answered, standing in the open door. "You can go look in on him if you want. He woke up an hour before you, feeling mighty jiffy. He's in the main room."

Wendy stared at the skinny kid in front of her and tried to put it together. "So the cure worked?"

"Well, Peter gave me the injector with the vial and told me what to do with it. I've administered it, and I'm also running some tests on it through our mass spec to see if I can duplicate the contents." Slightly's limp seemed a little worse today.

"Peter also told me what you did. Pretty bold move to inject yourself. You know, you could have just brought both back to me and I'd have tested it on Ditto."

"You would not have," Tootles laughed.

"No, I would have used *you* as my lab rat." Slightly teased. He winked at Wendy. "No really, we have rats."

Wendy flung the blankets off her lap and stood up. Her cheeks flushed red in embarrassment. Why didn't she even think of that?

"Ooh look," Tootles spoke in awe. "Her face is on fire."

Wendy threw open the door and went down the stairs into the main floor of the hideout. Ditto, twinning, sat on opposite ends of the couch, and Tink was sitting next to Teddy, who was awake and seemed to be adjusting quite easily.

"Where's Peter?" Wendy asked. "I want to speak to Peter."

"Not here, obviously." the twins said in unison.

"Hi, um, Wendy right?" Teddy stood up and offered his hand. "I've been told you're the one I need to thank for the medicine that helped me get better." He looked better, healthier, with a splash of freckles across his nose. "I'm...Teddy." He looked embarrassed, and Tink gave Wendy a searching stare. His cheeks flushed and he added meekly, "Miss Tink says you saved my life."

"Did not," Tink muttered indignantly. "She helped...sorta."

Wendy felt overcome with so many emotions— embarrassment, relief, thankfulness—that she didn't know how to process any of them. "It was...nothing. I'm glad it worked."

Rather than talk, she went in search of Peter for answers.

In the boys' hall, she found an open room with a crow on the door and stepped inside. She wasn't sure how she knew it was his, but she just knew. A queen bed with a simple blue duvet, a closed trunk at the foot of the bed, and on top of it stacks of fables and fairytales. There were no other personal items in the room.

"Wendy." Peter's voice surprised her. She turned, and he was standing in the doorway leaning against the frame, his hands in his pockets.

"Look, I'm sorry. I shouldn't have done that. I should have trusted you to find a less dramatic answer for the cure."

Something about his posture screamed vulnerability. All of his doubts and strain were wearing on him. "No, I understand your urgency. If it wasn't for your initiative, and forcing my hand, we might not have saved Teddy in time."

"Are you angry with me?" she asked.

He stayed frozen against the door. "No, but you'll probably be angry with me when I tell you what we did."

He wouldn't look at her. His eyes kept glancing to the floor and to the wall. His avoidance was making her stomach drop. "What did you do?"

He brought her hand up to his lips and gently kissed it. "I'll tell you in a second, but first, tell me about your family."

"What happened? Did something happen to my family? Are they okay?"

"No! No! They're fine. I just...I want one more moment where can talk, share things...before you hate me."

"I won't hate you, Peter."

"I hope not."

She blushed and stared at where his lips kissed her hand, savoring the moment, wishing he had kissed her on her lips. She moved and sat on his bed. "What's to tell? I've got a great family. My dad works at the local bank as a loan officer—on the weekend he's an assistant soccer coach for my brother, John's, team. My mom is a retired elementary teacher who's obsessed with crafting and baking. This time of the year our house smells like pumpkin and cinnamon because she's baking pies for the booster fundraisers."

Her shoulders slumped as she realized how much she missed them. She tried to hide the catch in her voice, but Peter probably heard it. "And the cookies. Man, we'd make so many cookies, and my fingers would be dyed orange from the gel food coloring. It was my job to frost the hundreds of pumpkin-shaped cookies, and John...Oh, he'd help, but really he'd eat more cookies than he'd decorate, and we'd usually have to chase him out of the kitchen." Wendy started to laugh but she couldn't stop the tears that came with the laughter. "My brother is my best friend. For as long as I could remember, we've been partners in crime."

"You miss them?" Peter, playing with her fingers, reached out to caress the back of her hand.

Wendy sniffed. "Desperately. What I wouldn't give to be able to go home."

"But they're *not* your family, are they?" Peter asked.

"They *are* my family," she argued.

He blushed. Swallowed. "No, I mean...you're adopted, aren't you?"

"How did you know?"

"If I had a guess, I'd say you've been with them for only about seven years, give or take a few depending on the foster system. And you don't have many memories from before those years. I'd also guess, when your new memories started, that they had to do with water, or they took place near water."

Wendy leaned back, jerking her hand from Peter's grip. "What's going on? Is this some kind of sick joke?" She felt like she was going to throw up. When Peter reached for her, she held up her hands and stood.

"Peter, you're scaring me."

"Here," he held out something to her. She glanced down, picked up the small metal piece—a thimble. When she realized what it was, she dropped it and retreated. Why was she terrified of the Monopoly piece?

"You don't remember, do you?"

She shook her head.

"Do you remember me telling you I knew one other person who could see shadows, but that she had died a long time ago when I was a kid?"

"Yeah?"

"I'm pretty sure that girl was you, Wendy."

Her breath caught in her throat "No, I'm not her."

"You also have a kiss." He pointed to her neck. "Just like the girl."

"A what?"

"It's what we called them as kids. A small mark on your neck, just above your collar bone."

Wendy's hand flew to her neck, and she blushed as she felt the spot that always itched. It was a white scar. It didn't mean he was right. He could have seen that anytime and just be making up the story.

"But it's really a brand. So small and overlapped that it looks like a birthmark. It's Neverland's mark." He stepped close to her again, reached for her fingers. "The Red Skull saw it and knew what it was. You're subject number 1-04. I'm subject 1-00. I was the first."

"How would you know my number? I've never been to Neverland." She pushed away from him. "That can't be. You're lying." It was hard to think with the pain building in her temples.

"It makes sense. Think about it. Why else would the shadows react to you, but not be desperate to take you there? It's because you've already been kissed. You already belong. You're one of us."

"No, I'm not." She shook her head. "I'm not one of them. Don't you think I'd know? I'd remember."

"Wendy, listen to me. It's true. All of it." Peter begged her, his voice pleading with her to understand. "When you were out cold, Tink took a blood sample and had it analyzed.

"What...how could you?" Seething, she turned, ready to storm out of the room.

"You have the PX-1 gene," he said, stopping her in her tracks. "The gene that stemmed from the PX-1 treatments."

"No, I don't," she denied. Shock had her reeling. This couldn't be right.

He shook his head and sighed. "Yes…you do, and that proves you were on the island the same time I was. You're a first generation lost girl."

Wendy started pacing, but Peter caught up and grabbed her wrist.

"Then why don't I remember?" Her head hurt terribly. "Why don't I remember you?"

"It was years ago. We were on a boat escaping Neverland—under attack. You started to fall overboard, and I grabbed you, but I got shot." He pulled his shirt down to reveal the scar on his chest, dangerously near his heart. "I couldn't hold onto you." His eyes turned glassy from unshed tears. "I tried. Oh, Wendy I tried to save you, but you slipped from my hands and fell into the ocean."

His words burned into her soul, and she felt herself slowly slide to the floor as she tried to wrap her mind around what had happened. "I don't believe you. I'd remember," she whispered.

"No, you wouldn't. In that way, you and I are a lot alike." Peter kneeled next to her and brought his face close to hers. He whispered, "You were my best friend. I died the day I lost you, Wendy."

She looked up at him with tears in her eyes, as his words forced disjointed and strange memories to come flooding back.

Everything she wanted to forget.

"No. Stop." She covered her ears with her hands and started to rock back and forth.

He pushed on. "I died that night in Tink's arms on the boat, but...a few hours later, I started breathing again, and I woke up with no memories. Tink calls it panning— for once a helpful side effect of Neverland's experiments on me. None of the others have ever come back. It took weeks of therapy with Dr. Mee to help me remember anything."

"Stop, Peter. Please. I don't want to hear anymore." Wendy sniffed, wiping her tears on the sleeve of her jacket. "I don't remember because it didn't happen." But the barrage of memories at his words told her that wasn't true. Lab coats, tubes and tables. Whirring air compressors. Injections. A rooftop. A fire. The forest. Water.

"The reason you don't remember any of this, Wendy...the reason you don't remember me or Neverland— it's because you also died that night."

-38-

THE ROOM STARTED TO close around Wendy, and things started to flicker in and out of focus. She was going to be sick.

Peter wrapped his arms around her. "Shh, it's okay. I've had a lot of time to think about it, and I think that's the reason you and I can see the shadows without the specs and no one else can. I think you died and came back to life early on during your first treatment at Neverland, but no one noticed. And you started to see the shadows. And then you drowned—or uh...panned. I didn't start to see them until after I panned."

"But you remember?"

"Well, like I said, I had lots of help from a counselor who's no longer with us, Dr. Mee. You didn't have anyone to help you like I did."

"So does that mean I can't die?"

"We'll all die someday. Who knows? Maybe we have a certain number of lives, like a video game. One day we just won't come back." He shrugged and smiled sadly.

"I...I think I believe you, because I see some things. And it makes a weird sort of sense. But there are just so many questions. It's a lot to take in, you know?"

"I get that. Hey, how about I take you to the beginning?" He raised his eyebrows. "Let you meet the man who created our haven."

"I'm not sure."

Peter smiled. "I think it will help you." He grabbed his jacket from a coat hanger and beckoned for her to follow him.

Wendy started to follow but slowed. "I thought you didn't know where he was. Which is why you're running Neverwood."

"I've always known where he was, Wendy," Peter answered.

They took the bus, and Wendy was quiet the whole ride, watching Peter out of the corner of her eye. He was distracted, worried. And she could tell from the glances he kept shooting her way, she was the reason behind his confusion.

She was even more confused when they got off and walked to Bernard Books.

"Peter, why are we here?"

He smiled sadly at her. "You can't have believed I would have left you alone for all that time unless you were with someone I trusted...even if he can't exactly remember either." Peter straightened his jacket and knocked softly on Mr. Bernard's office door.

They heard mumbling and then a chair scraping across the wood floor. "Come in, come in. Nana, move, you lazy girl. I can't get around you."

Peter opened the door and walked into Mr. Bernard's office. "Hello, Dr. Barrie," he said softly.

The old bookstore owner patted his shirt pocket looking for his glasses. When he found them, he put them on and looked at the two of them standing in the doorway. "Barrie? Barrie, yes...yes...that's right. I'm Barrie." A bright smile lit up his face and he started to chuckle. "Oh, you must see, my boy, what I'm working on." He gestured wildly for them to look at the mess of papers on his desk.

Wendy leaned over Peter and saw the sketches and pictures that he'd drawn on any available writing surface. Once again, she noticed a resemblance to Peter in many of the sketches. There was a sketch of a pirate ship with a red Jolly Roger, a crocodile, and an island.

"It will be the greatest story ever written! I'll be famous. Children will be talking about this for ages," Barrie crowed.

Wendy and Peter listened quietly as he spun a yarn about Neverland—a magical island where children went to avoid growing old, and how there was an evil Captain who was always trying to capture the children and a young boy who could fly. Not once did he mention Neverwood or the PX-1. She finally understood Peter's problem. The one person who knew the most about Neverland now believed everything was simply a child's tale.

-39-

PETER OPENED THE DOOR to Neverwood and let Wendy enter first. It was interesting how fast the place was finally starting to feel like a real home—when Wendy was there with him. They waved to Tootles and Fox who lounged in the main gathering room.

Teddy sat in a chair staring at them, his face unreadable, his eyes never leaving Wendy. How had no one else noticed that the boy couldn't look away from her? Smitten probably.

Peter took Wendy's hand and led her down a hallway to the stairwell. They climbed up to the roof. The sun had set, so it was chilly. Peter took off his jacket and put it around Wendy's shoulders. They looked out across the water and they could see boats floating down the river. For once, Peter was happy. He felt like he had done something right in the world.

"I'm so sorry. I didn't know about Mr. Barrie," Wendy spoke softly and nuzzled his jacket.

"Don't be sorry. It's what happened to all the adults when they left Neverland." He looked across the water and wished he'd never set foot on that hateful island. He despised the Red Skulls and the corporation and all the ill they created. "It was…a safeguard, if you will. Every one of the adults who helped us escape have slowly slipped into an early form of dementia."

"How is that possible?"

"They were given a different injection early on, at the beginning of the program. I think it was Neverland's way of getting revenge on anyone who left the island for a long period of time without taking an antidote. If they left, their mind would revert to a child-like state, and they'd forget everything they had done. They had to protect those heavily guarded secrets at all costs."

"Did he know, did *they* know what would happen to them if they left?" Wendy asked.

"Yeah, I think Dr. Barrie suspected as much, which is why he snuck his daughter Isabelle on his boat. You've met her too."

"Wait. What? Tink is really Isabelle?"

Peter chuckled. "Don't let her hear you call her that name. She despises any form of Isabelle—no Belle or Bella even. She was a genius like her father and loved to tinker around with computers—hence her nickname. Dr. Barrie taught her everything he knew about Neverland, and she's read up on all of the files he was able to sneak off the island with him. She was never infected like the rest of the adults, since he hid her on the boat.

"That's so sad."

Peter grasped Wendy's hand and gave it a great big squeeze. "Yes, it is, but we'll win one day, Wendy. We'll beat Captain Hook and his Red Skulls. And I think we're getting closer to it too, thanks to you. I really believe that this stuff you brought us will help us beat the morphlings."

"You really believe that?"

"I do. I really believe you hold a lot of the answers. Do you believe in me?"

"Of course," she answered wholeheartedly. And she did now. She was determined to find answers—from others and within her own memories.

Peter moved away from her and stepped over to the edge of the roof. Her face paled at seeing him balancing on the edge.

She raised her hands. "Don't, Peter. Stop." Wendy breathed out in a panic

"I'll be fine." Peter smiled at her.

"N-no. No you won't." Wendy said. She gasped, eyes widening. "I remember. You...you fell?"

Peter stood on the edge of the roof and grinned, thrilled that she was starting to remember. "I didn't fall, Wendy."

"Yes, I saw you." Her teeth were chattering as she tried to get her nerves under control.

"I stood on a roof like this once before, and I offered you my hand." He held his hand out, palm up.

She stepped closer to him, her feet sliding along the roof top very slowly, as if she was scared any sudden movement would send her flying off. "I remember now. You offered to take me away, you promised to save me."

"I'm here, Wendy, offering you the same chance. Take my hand."

She looked up at Peter as her feet came to the edge. She glanced down at the ground, stories below, and let out a squeal of fear. Peter laughed. She held her hand in his and stood toe-to-toe with him.

"I'm scared." She exhaled.

"Do you believe?"

"Yes."

He whispered, "I won't let you fall." Peter pulled her toward him possessively and leaned down.

Wendy rose up on tiptoes to meet him. Her lips tasted sweet and he could feel her fear recede. He lost himself to the kiss, never wanted it to end, never wanted to be without her again. Peter's hands tightened around her waist, as he ascended into the night sky.

She pulled away from the kiss. Her cheeks flushed, her eyes sparkled until she looked down. There was a moment of fear, which escalated into happiness.

"We're flying!" she laughed in excitement. "No, not we. You. You're flying. You can fly."

Peter's head fell back and he chuckled. He wanted to share this moment with her forever.

A door slammed and someone came onto the roof. Peter groaned and he slowly brought them back down until their feet touched the roof. They turned to see Teddy standing there, out of breath, a look of utter brokenness written across his face.

"I hate you," he bawled.

"Teddy, what's going on?" Peter pulled away from Wendy, who looked adorably flustered. Her cheeks were red from their intense kiss.

"You left me, abandoned me." His lips trembled and his hand reached into his coat pocket.

"What are you talking about?" Peter stepped away from the edge and moved toward the distraught boy. The boy seemed at the end of his rope, shaking now. Peter needed to act as a barrier between him and Wendy until he could diffuse the situation.

"Shortly after we arrived, you pretended you didn't even know me. How could you? You were supposed to protect me, stand up for me." He screamed in fury, his face turned red. "I carried your gift with me everywhere in the hopes that you'd acknowledge me...but you were too good for me. Showing off for your friends, ignoring me."

"I'm sorry if I disappointed you, Teddy. I never meant to leave you behind. Neverland lied to everyone...even you. But we can help you, Teddy." Peter took another step toward the boy.

More tears fell down Teddy's cheeks "No, not you. I don't know you. I just know she chose you over me, day after day. She forgot about me." He turned and pointed at Wendy. "Her...how could you forget about me? Your baby brother?"

Peter glanced at Wendy.

Her face was white with shock. He didn't know she had a brother, and if she had panned her first few days at Neverland, like he suspected, then she wouldn't have known she had one either. The boy should have said something to her, tried to help her remember.

"Teddy, I..." she looked like she was searching for an answer. Her mouth fell open.

"My name's not Teddy," he yelled angrily. "It's M—"

"Michael," Wendy interrupted him. "Yes, I remember now." She started to step forward, but Peter grabbed her arm and held her back. The boy was unstable. And if he'd survived Neverland, where had he been all these years? What had Neverland done to him? Was he a plant? Was this a lie to put him in their midst?

"I didn't know. I couldn't remember you. I swear." Wendy pleaded, but the boy just shook his head. "Michael, they did something to me."

"Yeah, well they did things to me too. Only I didn't escape it like you. Years I endured their torture. Years I waited for you to come back and rescue me. I told them you'd come back for us, but you never came."

"Wait, are you saying that there are others?" Peter felt like a fist punched him in the chest. "Other kids still alive?" Dr. Barrie had sacrificed so much for them, and yet others still suffered?

Maybe Dr. Barrie didn't know. Peter surely didn't, but that didn't make the guilt go away. He should've known somehow.

Michael ignored him. "I don't know who or what I am anymore." He gripped his head as if it was in pain. Tears flowed down his cheeks. "But you, Peter. You're weak. You're predictable. He said you'd take me to your base, if we made it look real enough. Granted, I wasn't supposed to get hurt."

"Who?" Peter asked, his mind whirling with possibilities.

"A traitor in your own midst." Michael laughed. "And you didn't even know it."

"Who are you talking about?" Peter yelled, his fists clenching as he tried to control his emotions.

"Jax," Wendy whispered. "It's Jax. He's still alive and he's working with the Red Skulls."

"I don't believe you." Peter shook his head.

Wendy touched his arm and he looked into her blue eyes and saw the truth.

A shadow flew behind Michael, and Peter watched it fly in circles—in what looked like agitation. He tried to ignore the shadow, but it dove past him and straight into Wendy's body. *What?*

Michael couldn't see the shadow.

Her head fell backward, and she convulsed for a second. Then the shadow moved through her and out the other side.

"You hurt me, Wendy. Real bad. But I know it wasn't your fault. It's his."

Wendy's eyes flew open and she screamed, lunging for Peter. He couldn't take his eyes off her, didn't understand what was happening. He just wanted her to be well.

Suddenly, Wendy shoved him in the chest just as gunfire exploded in the air. Peter spun and saw the smoking gun in Michael's hand. The young boy let it clatter to the ground, his face white at missing his target.

A feeling of dread overcame him. Peter turned.

Wendy stood in the exact spot he'd been moments ago. Her face was ashen, her right hand covering her chest, blood seeping between her fingers. She looked to him and tried to say his name, but blood bubbled up out of her lips.

"NOOOO!" Peter wailed.

Wendy stumbled, and fell backward off the roof.

-40-

S HE WAS WEIGHTLESS, and the sky seemed so bright as she fell. She heard Peter scream, and then he caught her midair.

They were flying. The cold wind rushed against her cheeks as he flew down to the path on the other side of Neverwood and gently set her down on the ground. The shock of the flight wore off, and…it hurt to breathe.

"Pe—ter?" Wendy gasped out. Blood pooled in her mouth.

"Oh, Wendy, I'm so sorry. I failed you again."

"I-I-I'm…" She started to choke as tears poured from her eyes. "I'm scared, Peter."

He wrapped his arms around her. "Shh, it will be okay. I promise. It will be over soon, and you'll be right as rain again." He was dying inside knowing he was losing her. She had already panned twice. He prayed she'd have one more in her.

"I don't want to die. I'll forget everything…I'll forget you." She was whining, and every word was like a dagger slowly twisting in him.

Her death was only seconds away...and his helpless-ness infuriated him. It was all his fault. He was the one who kept doing this to her, and he realized he couldn't continue to hurt those he loved. He wanted to protect Wendy, even if it meant protecting her from himself.

"Peter, I'll forget that...I love you." Her tears soaked his shirt, mingling with the blood. She coughed again, struggled for breath. "I...don't want to forget you...ever."

Peter gritted his teeth as tears burned in his eyes. "I love you, Wendy. I have since we were children...and this time I promise to take you home."

"To Neverwood?" she asked. Her chest rattled in the throes of death.

Tears blurred his vision. Her voice sounded dis-tant...weak.

"Wendy, forget everything. Forget Neverwood. Forget me."

He leaned down and gently pressed a kiss on her fore-head as Wendy died in his arms.

Wendy felt something wet hit her cheek. She was just waking up when she heard someone whisper her name. She groaned and opened her eyes but no one was there.

The only movement came from a gently moving curtain next to the bedroom window.

It was early morning. Sunlight was streaming in.

It took a few moments to focus on what she was seeing. She was lying on a bed with a white and pink duvet. It was someone's bedroom. Whose? She moved her arm but her whole body was sore, stiff.

It was a struggle to sit up in the bed—littered with way too many throw pillows. Who on earth had this many stupid throw pillows? There was an especially ugly one, with a stitched peacock on it, placed right in the middle, like a place of honor. Wendy let her feet touch the floor, and she noticed the grass stains on her pants...and the condition of the rest of her clothes.

Her shirt was ripped and stained with something dark—blood?—across the front. No way she could save it. She was going to have to get a new one. Wendy stood up and grabbed onto the white dresser for support—her right leg almost gave out on her. Her arm felt stiff, and her chest hurt when she tried to breathe. She looked in the mirror and poked her finger through the hole in her shirt.

"What?" Wendy couldn't believe the red scar on her chest. How? When? It looked fresh, but that wasn't possible. She must have hit her head harder than she thought, since that was the only explanation for what she imagined.

She looked down at the dresser and saw a hairbrush, curling iron, and lipstick. A handmade collage of photos were pinned on a corkboard on the wall next to the dresser. Wendy shuffled over and stared at the photos. A happy

315

teenage girl wearing a cheer uniform stared back at her. The same girl had her arms wrapped around another girl. There was one of her in a prom dress. She recognized the face, because she had just seen it seconds ago in the mirror. Her own face stared back at her.

This was her house. Her room.

That was her prom.

Wendy heard a dog bark and she looked out the open window to see a long shadow fly across the yard. She looked up but didn't see anything. Just a morning jogger. She didn't recognize the blue Prius parked out front or the white Nissan. She didn't even recognize the house across the street.

She changed shirts, tossing her ripped one in the trash.

She limped toward the bedroom door. With each step, she felt like she was getting stronger, gaining more control of her weakened limbs. She opened the door and peered out into the strange hallway before stepping out and walking down onto the landing.

A family portrait hung on the wall. All she could do was stare.

A gentleman with a five o'clock shadow rested his hand on the woman's shoulder. She had a very warm smile. Standing in back was a teenage boy who resembled the man, and Wendy herself smiled serenely in the front. She swallowed, feeling ill. Apparently, these strangers were her family.

The teenage boy threw the door open, his mouth filled with white foam and a toothbrush dangling precariously from his lips. "You're back?" White paste sputtered everywhere. He ducked back into the bathroom to spit and rinse. The kid rushed back into the hall, his lower lip quivering. The boy's eyes became glassy, and he wrapped his arms around Wendy and started to cry.

"I'm so glad you're safe."

"John, honey, time to eat." A woman's voice—a familiar one—called from downstairs.

John. His name was John. Wendy felt like one huge hurdle had been overcome. Now how many more before she could put the pieces of her shattered soul together?

At the smell of breakfast, her mouth began to water. Bacon. And she suddenly craved ice cream.

John let go of her and motioned for her to go downstairs ahead of him. Each step was slow, but somehow she knew how to get to the kitchen.

A woman bustled around the kitchen. Her red polka dot apron fit snugly around her thin waist as she stepped around the table with a pan of eggs, scooping them onto each plate. On the table, Wendy counted place settings for three people—not four.

On the counter were boxes and boxes of missing person posters. A map hung on the wall in the dining room with push pins all over it.

She called out softly, "Mom?"

Her mom turned, wooden spoon in hand, and her face drained of color. "Wendy?"

The pan of eggs clattered to the floor.

317

FIND OUT WHAT HAPPENS NEXT IN

LOST BOY

Neverwood Chronicles
Book 2

(COMING 2017)

Chanda Hahn is a NYT & USA Today Bestselling author of Reign and Forever. She uses her experience as a children's pastor, children's librarian and bookseller to write compelling and popular fiction for teens.

She was born in Seattle, Washington, grew up in Nebraska, and currently resides in Portland, Oregon with her husband and their twin children.

Visit Chanda Hahn's website to learn more about her other forthcoming books. www.chandahahn.com